ANTON CHEKHOV

Short Stories

COMPILED BY
PATRICIA MOORE

MG BOOKS
NEW DELHI (INDIA)

ANTON CHEKHOV

Published by

An Imprint of

MAANU GRAPHICS

(PUBLISHERS OF GENERAL BOOKS)

5FF, Ganpati Bhawan, 21 Ansari Road,
Darya Ganj, New Delhi-110002
Ph: 65285220, 64138266
E-mail : maanugraphics@yahoo.com
mgbooks.maanu@yahoo.com

Printed at
NEW Z. A. Printers, Delhi

CONTENTS

A GENTLEMAN FRIEND

THE charming Vanda, or, as she was described in her passport, the "Honourable Citizen Nastasya Kanavkin," found herself, on leaving the hospital, in a position she had never been in before: without a home to go to or a farthing in her pocket. What was she to do?

The first thing she did was to visit a pawn-broker's and pawn her turquoise ring, her one piece of jewellery. They gave her a rouble for the ring . . . but what can you get for a rouble? You can't buy for that sum a fashionable short jacket, nor a big hat, nor a pair of bronze shoes, and without those things she had a feeling of being, as it were, undressed. She felt as though the very horses and dogs were staring and laughing at the plainness of her dress. And clothes were all she thought about: the question what she should eat and where she should sleep did not trouble her in the least.

"If only I could meet a gentleman friend," she thought to herself, "I could get some money. . . . There isn't one who would refuse me, I know. . ."

But no gentleman she knew came her way. It would be easy enough to meet them in the evening at the "Renaissance," but they wouldn't let her in at the "Renaissance "in that shabby dress and with no hat. What was she to do?

After long hesitation, when she was sick of walking and sitting and thinking, Vanda made up her mind to fall back on her last resource: to go straight to the lodgings of some gentleman friend and ask for money.

She pondered which to go to. "Misha is out of the question; he's a married man. . . . The old chap with the red hair will be at his office at this time. . ."

Vanda remembered a dentist, called Finkel, a converted Jew, who six months ago had given her a bracelet, and on whose head she had once emptied a glass of beer at the supper at the German Club. She was awfully pleased at the thought of Finkel.

"He'll be sure to give it me, if only I find him at home," she thought, as she walked in his direction. "If he doesn't, I'll smash all the lamps in the house."

Before she reached the dentist's door she thought out her plan of action: she would run laughing up the stairs, dash into the dentist's room and demand twenty-five roubles. But as she touched the bell, this plan seemed to vanish from her mind of itself. Vanda began suddenly feeling frightened and nervous, which was not at all her way. She was bold and saucy enough at drinking parties, but now, dressed in everyday clothes, feeling herself in the position of an ordinary person asking a favour, who might be refused admittance, she felt suddenly timid and humiliated. She was ashamed and frightened.

"Perhaps he has forgotten me by now," she thought, hardly daring to pull the bell. "And how can I go up to him in such a dress, looking like a beggar or some working girl?"

And she rang the bell irresolutely.

She heard steps coming: it was the porter.

"Is the doctor at home?" she asked.

She would have been glad now if the porter had said "No," but the latter, instead of answering ushered her into the hall, and helped her off with her coat. The staircase impressed her as luxurious, and magnificent, but of all its splendours what caught her eye most was an immense looking-glass, in which she saw a ragged figure without a fashionable jacket, without a big hat, and without bronze shoes. And it seemed strange to Vanda that, now that she was humbly dressed and looked like a laundress or sewing girl, she felt ashamed, and no trace of her usual boldness and sauciness remained, and in her own mind she no longer thought of herself as Vanda, but as the Nastasya Kanavkin she used to be in the old days. . . .

"Walk in, please," said a maidservant, showing her into the consulting-room. "The doctor will be here in a minute. Sit down."

Vanda sank into a soft arm-chair.

"I'll ask him to lend it me," she thought; "that will be quite proper, for, after all, I do know him. If only that servant would go. I don't like to ask before her. What does she want to stand there for?"

Five minutes later the door opened and Finkel came in. He was a tall, dark Jew, with fat cheeks and bulging eyes. His cheeks, his eyes, his chest, his body, all of him was so well fed, so loathsome and repellent! At the "Renaissance" and the German Club he had usually been rather tipsy, and would spend his money freely on women, and be very long-suffering and patient with their pranks (when Vanda, for instance, poured the beer over his head, he simply smiled and shook his finger at her): now he had a cross, sleepy expression and looked solemn and frigid like a police captain, and he kept chewing something.

"What can I do for you?" he asked, without looking at Vanda.

Vanda looked at the serious countenance of the maid and the smug figure of Finkel, who apparently did not recognize her, and she turned red.

"What can I do for you?" repeated the dentist a little irritably.

"I've got toothache," murmured Vanda.

"Aha! . . . Which is the tooth? Where?"

Vanda remembered she had a hole in one of her teeth.

"At the bottom . . . on the right . . ." she said.

"Hm! . . . Open your mouth."

Finkel frowned and, holding his breath, began examining the tooth.

"Does it hurt?" he asked, digging into it with a steel instrument.

"Yes," Vanda replied, untruthfully.

"Shall I remind him?" she was wondering. "He would be sure to remember me. But that servant! Why will she stand there?"

Finkel suddenly snorted like a steam-engine right into her mouth, and said:

"I don't advise you to have it stopped. That tooth will never be worth keeping anyhow."

After probing the tooth a little more and soiling Vanda's lips and gums with his tobacco-stained fingers, he held his breath again, and put something cold into her mouth. Vanda suddenly felt a sharp pain, cried out, and clutched at Finkel's hand.

"It's all right, it's all right," he muttered; "don't you be frightened! That tooth would have been no use to you, anyway . . . you must be brave. . ."

And his tobacco-stained fingers, smeared with blood, held up the tooth to her eyes, while the maid approached and put a basin to her mouth.

"You wash out your mouth with cold water when you get home, and that will stop the bleeding," said Finkel.

He stood before her with the air of a man expecting her to go, waiting to be left in peace.

"Good-day," she said, turning towards the door.

"Hm! . . . and how about my fee?" enquired Finkel, in a jesting tone.

"Oh, yes!" Vanda remembered, blushing, and she handed the Jew the rouble that had been given her for her ring.

When she got out into the street she felt more overwhelmed with shame than before, but now it was not her poverty she was ashamed of. She was unconscious now of not having a big hat and a fashionable jacket. She walked along the street, spitting blood, and brooding on her life, her ugly, wretched life, and the insults she had endured, and would have to endure to-morrow, and next week, and all her life, up to the very day of her death.

"Oh! how awful it is! My God, how fearful!"

Next day, however, she was back at the "Renaissance," and dancing there. She had on an enormous new red hat, a new fashionable jacket, and bronze shoes. And she was taken out to supper by a young merchant up from Kazan.

ROTHSCHILD'S FIDDLE

THE town was a little one, worse than a village, and it was inhabited by scarcely any but old people who died with an infrequency that was really annoying. In the hospital and in the prison fortress very few coffins were needed. In fact business was bad. If Yakov Ivanov had been an undertaker in the chief town of the province he would certainly have had a house of his own, and people would have addressed him as Yakov Matveyitch; here in this wretched little town people called him simply Yakov; his nickname in the street was for some reason Bronze, and he lived in a poor way like a humble peasant, in a little old hut in which there was only one room, and in this room he and Marfa, the stove, a double bed, the coffins, his bench, and all their belongings were crowded together.

Yakov made good, solid coffins. For peasants and working people he made them to fit himself, and this was never unsuccessful, for there were none taller and stronger than he, even in the prison, though he was seventy. For gentry and for women he made them to measure, and used an iron foot-rule for the purpose. He was very unwilling to take orders for children's coffins, and made them straight off without measurements, contemptuously, and when he was paid for the work he always said:

"I must confess I don't like trumpery jobs."

Apart from his trade, playing the fiddle brought him in a small income.

The Jews' orchestra conducted by Moisey Ilyitch Shahkes, the tinsmith, who took more than half their receipts for himself, played as a rule at weddings in the town. As Yakov played very well on the fiddle, especially Russian songs, Shahkes sometimes invited him to join the orchestra at a fee of half a rouble a day, in addition to tips from the visitors. When Bronze sat in the orchestra first of all his face became crimson and perspiring; it was hot, there was a suffocating smell of garlic, the fiddle squeaked, the double bass wheezed close to his right ear, while the flute wailed at his left, played by a gaunt, red-haired Jew who had a perfect network of red and blue veins all over his face, and who bore the name of the famous millionaire Rothschild. And this accursed Jew contrived to play even the liveliest things plaintively. For no apparent reason Yakov little by little became possessed by hatred and contempt for the Jews, and especially for Rothschild; he began to pick quarrels with him, rail at him in unseemly language and once even tried to strike him, and Rothschild was offended and said, looking at him ferociously:

"If it were not that I respect you for your talent, I would have sent you flying out of the window."

Then he began to weep. And because of this Yakov was not often asked to play in the orchestra; he was only sent for in case of extreme necessity in the absence of one of the Jews.

Yakov was never in a good temper, as he was continually having to put up with terrible losses. For instance, it was a sin to work on Sundays or Saints' days, and Monday was an unlucky day, so that in the course of the year there were some two hundred days on which, whether he liked it or not, he had to sit with his hands folded. And only think, what a loss that meant. If anyone in the town had a wedding without music, or if Shahkes did not send for Yakov, that was a loss, too. The superintendent of the prison was ill for two years and was wasting away, and Yakov was impatiently waiting for him to die, but the superintendent went away to the chief town of the province to be doctored, and there took and died. There's a loss for you, ten roubles at least, as there would have been an expensive coffin to make, lined with brocade. The thought of his losses haunted Yakov, especially at night; he laid his fiddle on the bed beside him, and when all sorts of nonsensical ideas came into his mind he touched a string; the fiddle gave out a sound in the darkness, and he felt better.

On the sixth of May of the previous year Marfa had suddenly been taken ill. The old woman's breathing was laboured, she drank a great deal of water, and she staggered as she walked, yet she lighted the stove in the morning and even went herself to get water. Towards evening she lay down. Yakov played his fiddle all day; when it was quite dark he took the book in which he used every day to put down his losses, and, feeling dull, he began adding up the total for the year. It came to more than a thousand roubles. This so agitated him that he flung the reckoning beads down, and trampled them under his feet. Then he picked up the reckoning beads, and again spent a long time clicking with them and heaving deep, strained sighs. His face was crimson and wet with perspiration. He thought that if he had put that lost thousand roubles in the bank, the interest for a year would have been at least forty roubles, so that forty roubles was a loss too. In fact, wherever one turned there were losses and nothing else.

"Yakov!" Marfa called unexpectedly. "I am dying."

He looked round at his wife. Her face was rosy with fever, unusually bright and joyful-looking. Bronze, accustomed to seeing her face always pale, timid, and unhappy-looking, was bewildered. It looked as if she really were dying and were glad that she was going away for ever from that hut, from the coffins, and from Yakov. . . . And she gazed at the ceiling and moved her lips, and her expression was one of happiness, as though she saw death as her deliverer and were whispering with him.

It was daybreak; from the windows one could see the flush of dawn. Looking at the old woman, Yakov for some reason reflected that he had not once in his life been affectionate to her, had had no feeling for her, had never once thought to buy her a kerchief, or to bring her home some dainty from a wedding, but had done nothing but shout at her, scold her for his losses, shake his fists at her; it is true he had never actually beaten her, but he had frightened her, and at such times she had always been numb with terror. Why, he had forbidden her to drink tea because they spent too much without that, and she drank only hot water. And he understood why she had such a strange, joyful face now, and he was overcome with dread.

As soon as it was morning he borrowed a horse from a neighbour and took Marfa to the hospital. There were not many patients there, and so he had not long to wait, only three hours. To his great satisfaction the patients were not being received by the doctor, who was himself ill, but by the assistant, Maxim Nikolaitch, an old man of whom everyone in the town used to say that, though he drank and was quarrelsome, he knew more than the doctor.

"I wish you good-day," said Yakov, leading his old woman into the consulting room. "You must excuse us, Maxim Nikolaitch, we are always troubling you with our trumpery affairs. Here you see my better half is ailing, the partner of my life, as they say, excuse the expression. . . ."

Knitting his grizzled brows and stroking his whiskers the assistant began to examine the old woman, and she sat on a stool, a wasted, bent figure with a sharp nose and open mouth, looking like a bird that wants to drink.

"H———m . . . Ah! . . ." the assistant said slowly, and he heaved a sigh. "Influenza and possibly fever. There's typhus in the town now. Well, the old woman has lived her life, thank God. . . . How old is she?"

"She'll be seventy in another year, Maxim Nikolaitch."

"Well, the old woman has lived her life, it's time to say good-bye."

"You are quite right in what you say, of course, Maxim Nikolaitch," said Yakov, smiling from politeness, "and we thank you feelingly for your kindness, but allow me to say every insect wants to live."

"To be sure," said the assistant, in a tone which suggested that it depended upon him whether the woman lived or died. "Well, then, my good fellow, put a cold compress on her head, and give her these powders twice a day, and so good-bye. Bonjour."

From the expression of his face Yakov saw that it was a bad case, and that no sort of powders would be any help; it was clear to him that Marfa would die very soon, if not to-day, to-morrow. He nudged the assistant's elbow, winked at him, and said in a low voice:

"If you would just cup her, Maxim Nikolaitch."

"I have no time, I have no time, my good fellow. Take your old woman and go in God's name. Goodbye."

"Be so gracious," Yakov besought him. "You know yourself that if, let us say, it were her stomach or her inside that were bad, then powders or drops, but you see she had got a chill! In a chill the first thing is to let blood, Maxim Nikolaitch."

But the assistant had already sent for the next patient, and a peasant woman came into the consulting room with a boy.

"Go along! go along," he said to Yakov, frowning. "It's no use to –"

"In that case put on leeches, anyway! Make us pray for you for ever."

The assistant flew into a rage and shouted:

"You speak to me again! You blockhead. . . ."

Yakov flew into a rage too, and he turned crimson all over, but he did not utter a word. He took Marfa on his arm and led her out of the room. Only when they were sitting in the cart he looked morosely and ironically at the hospital, and said:

"A nice set of artists they have settled here! No fear, but he would have cupped a rich man, but even a leech he grudges to the poor. The Herods!"

When they got home and went into the hut, Marfa stood for ten minutes holding on to the stove. It seemed to her that if she were to lie down Yakov would talk to her about his losses, and scold her for lying down and not wanting to work. Yakov looked at her drearily and thought that to-morrow was St. John the Divine's, and next day St. Nikolay the Wonder-worker's, and the day after that was Sunday, and then Monday, an unlucky day. For four days he would not be able to work, and most likely Marfa would die on one of those days; so he would have to make the coffin to-day. He picked up his iron rule, went up to the old woman and took her measure. Then she lay down, and he crossed himself and began making the coffin.

When the coffin was finished Bronze put on his spectacles and wrote in his book: "Marfa Ivanov's coffin, two roubles, forty kopecks."

And he heaved a sigh. The old woman lay all the time silent with her eyes closed. But in the evening, when it got dark, she suddenly called the old man.

"Do you remember, Yakov," she asked, looking at him joyfully. "Do you remember fifty years ago God gave us a little baby with flaxen hair? We used always to be sitting by the river then, singing songs . . . under the willows," and laughing bitterly, she added: "The baby girl died."

Yakov racked his memory, but could not remember the baby or the willows.

"It's your fancy," he said.

The priest arrived; he administered the sacrament and extreme unction. Then Marfa began muttering something unintelligible, and towards morning she died. Old women, neighbours, washed her, dressed her, and laid her in the coffin. To avoid paying the sacristan, Yakov read the psalms over the body himself, and they got nothing out of him for the grave, as the grave-digger was a crony of his. Four peasants carried the coffin to the graveyard, not for money, but from respect. The coffin was followed by old women, beggars, and a couple of crazy saints, and the people who met it crossed themselves piously. . . . And Yakov was very much pleased that it was so creditable, so decorous, and so cheap, and no offence to anyone. As he took his last leave of Marfa he touched the coffin and thought: "A good piece of work!"

But as he was going back from the cemetery he was overcome by acute depression. He didn't feel quite well: his breathing was laboured and feverish, his legs felt weak, and he had a craving for drink. And thoughts of all sorts forced themselves on his mind. He remembered again that all his life he had never felt for Marfa, had never been affectionate to her. The fifty-two years they had lived in the same hut had dragged on a long, long time, but it had somehow happened that in all that time he had never once thought of her, had paid no attention to her, as though she had been a cat or a dog. And yet, every day, she had lighted the stove had cooked and baked, had gone for the water, had chopped the wood, had slept with him in the same bed, and when he came home drunk from the weddings always reverently hung his fiddle on the wall and put him to bed, and all this in silence, with a timid, anxious expression.

Rothschild, smiling and bowing, came to meet Yakov.

"I was looking for you, uncle," he said. "Moisey Ilyitch sends you his greetings and bids you come to him at once."

Yakov felt in no mood for this. He wanted to cry.

"Leave me alone," he said, and walked on.

"How can you," Rothschild said, fluttered, running on in front. "Moisey Ilyitch will be offended! He bade you come at once!"

Yakov was revolted at the Jew's gasping for breath and blinking, and having so many red freckles on his face. And it was disgusting to look at his green coat with black patches on it, and all his fragile, refined figure.

"Why are you pestering me, garlic?" shouted Yakov. "Don't persist!"

The Jew got angry and shouted too:

"Not so noisy, please, or I'll send you flying over the fence!"

"Get out of my sight!" roared Yakov, and rushed at him with his fists. "One can't live for you scabby Jews!"

Rothschild, half dead with terror, crouched down and waved his hands over his head, as though to ward off a blow; then he leapt up and ran away as fast as his legs could carry him: as he ran he gave little skips and kept clasping his hands, and Yakov could see how his long thin spine wriggled. Some boys, delighted at the incident, ran after him shouting "Jew! Jew!" Some dogs joined in the chase barking. Someone burst into a roar of laughter, then gave a whistle; the dogs barked with even more noise and unanimity. Then a dog must have bitten Rothschild, as a desperate, sickly scream was heard.

Yakov went for a walk on the grazing ground, then wandered on at random in the outskirts of the town, while the street boys shouted:

"Here's Bronze! Here's Bronze!"

He came to the river, where the curlews floated in the air uttering shrill cries and the ducks quacked. The sun was blazing hot, and there was a glitter from the water, so that it hurt the eyes to look at it. Yakov walked by a path along the bank and saw a plump, rosy-cheeked lady come out of the bathing-shed, and thought about her: "Ugh! you otter!"

Not far from the bathing-shed boys were catching crayfish with bits of meat; seeing him, they began shouting spitefully, "Bronze! Bronze!" And then he saw an old spreading willow-tree with a big hollow in it, and a crow's nest on it. . . . And suddenly there rose up vividly in Yakov's memory a baby with flaxen hair, and the willow-tree Marfa had spoken of. Why, that is it, the same willow-tree – green, still, and sorrowful. . . . How old it has grown, poor thing!

He sat down under it and began to recall the past. On the other bank, where now there was the water meadow, in those days there stood a big birchwood, and yonder on the bare hillside that could be seen on the horizon an old, old pine forest used to be a bluish patch in the distance. Big boats used to sail on the river. But now it was all smooth and unruffled, and on the other bank there stood now only one birch-tree, youthful and slender like a young lady, and there was nothing on the river but ducks and geese, and it didn't look as though there had ever been boats on it. It seemed as though even the geese were fewer than of old. Yakov shut his eyes, and in his imagination huge flocks of white geese soared, meeting one another.

He wondered how it had happened that for the last forty or fifty years of his life he had never once been to the river, or if he had been by it he had not paid attention to it. Why, it was a decent sized river, not a trumpery one; he might have gone in for fishing and sold the fish to merchants, officials, and the bar-keeper at the station, and then have put money in the bank; he might have sailed in a boat from one house to another, playing the fiddle, and people of all classes would have paid to hear him; he might have tried getting big boats afloat again – that would be better than making coffins; he might have bred geese, killed them and sent them in the winter to Moscow Why, the feathers alone would very likely mount up to ten roubles in the year. But he had wasted his time, he had done nothing of this. What losses! Ah! What losses! And if he had gone in for all those things at once – catching fish and playing the fiddle, and running boats and killing geese – what a fortune he would have made! But nothing of this had happened, even in his dreams; life had passed uselessly without any pleasure, had been wasted for nothing, not even a pinch of snuff; there was nothing left in front, and if one looked back — there was nothing there but losses, and such terrible ones, it made one cold all over. And why was it a man could not live so as to avoid these losses and misfortunes? One wondered why they had cut down the birch copse and the pine forest. Why was he walking with no reason on the grazing ground? Why do people always do what isn't needful? Why had Yakov all his life scolded, bellowed, shaken his fists, ill-treated his wife, and, one might ask, what necessity was there for him to frighten and insult the Jew that day? Why did people in general hinder each other from living? What losses were due to it! what terrible losses! If it were not for hatred and malice people would get immense benefit from one another.

In the evening and the night he had visions of the baby, of the willow, of fish, of slaughtered geese, and Marfa looking in profile like a bird that wants to drink, and the pale, pitiful face of Rothschild, and faces moved down from all sides and muttered of losses. He tossed from side to side, and got out of bed five times to play the fiddle.

In the morning he got up with an effort and went to the hospital. The same Maxim Nikolaitch told him to put a cold compress on his head, and gave him some powders, and from his tone and expression of face Yakov realized that it was a bad case and that no powders would be any use. As he went home afterwards, he reflected that death would be nothing but a benefit; he would not have to eat or drink, or pay taxes or offend people, and, as a man lies in his grave not for one year but for hundreds and thousands, if one reckoned it up the gain would be enormous. A man's life meant loss: death meant gain. This reflection was, of course, a just one, but yet it was bitter and mortifying; why was the order of the world so strange, that life, which is given to man only once, passes away without benefit?

He was not sorry to die, but at home, as soon as he saw his fiddle, it sent a pang to his heart and he felt sorry. He could not take the fiddle with him to the grave, and now it would be left forlorn, and the same thing would happen to it as to the birch copse and the pine forest. Everything in this world was wasted and would be wasted! Yakov went out of the hut and sat in the doorway, pressing the fiddle to his bosom. Thinking of his wasted, profitless life, he began to play, he did not know what, but it was plaintive and touching, and tears trickled down his cheeks. And the harder he thought, the more mournfully the fiddle wailed.

The latch clicked once and again, and Rothschild appeared at the gate. He walked across half the yard boldly, but seeing Yakov he stopped short, and seemed to shrink together, and probably from terror, began making signs with his hands as though he wanted to show on his fingers what o'clock it was.

"Come along, it's all right," said Yakov in a friendly tone, and he beckoned him to come up. "Come along!"

Looking at him mistrustfully and apprehensively, Rothschild began to advance, and stopped seven feet off.

"Be so good as not to beat me," he said, ducking. "Moisey Ilyitch has sent me again. 'Don't be afraid,' he said; 'go to Yakov again and tell him,' he said, 'we can't get on without him.' There is a wedding on Wednesday. . . . Ye—es! Mr. Shapovalov is marrying his daughter to a good man. . . . And it will be a grand wedding, oo-oo!" added the Jew, screwing up one eye.

"I can't come," said Yakov, breathing hard. "I'm ill, brother."

And he began playing again, and the tears gushed from his eyes on to the fiddle. Rothschild listened attentively, standing sideways to him and folding his arms on his chest. The scared and perplexed expression on his face, little by little, changed to a look of woe and suffering; he rolled his eyes as though he were experiencing an agonizing ecstasy, and articulated, "Vachhh!" and tears slowly ran down his cheeks and trickled on his greenish coat.

And Yakov lay in bed all the rest of the day grieving. In the evening, when the priest confessing him asked, Did he remember any special sin he had committed? straining his failing memory he thought again of Marfa's unhappy face, and the despairing shriek of the Jew when the dog bit him, and said, hardly audibly, "Give the fiddle to Rothschild."

"Very well," answered the priest.

And now everyone in the town asks where Rothschild got such a fine fiddle. Did he buy it or steal it? Or perhaps it had come to him as a pledge. He gave up the flute long ago, and now plays nothing but the fiddle. As plaintive sounds flow now from his bow, as came once from his flute, but when he tries to repeat what Yakov played, sitting in the doorway, the effect is something so sad and sorrowful that his audience weep, and he himself rolls his eyes and articulates "Vachhh! . . ." And this new air was so much liked in the town that the merchants and officials used to be continually sending for Rothschild and making him play it over and over again a dozen times.

⊕⊕

IVAN MATVEYITCH

BETWEEN five and six in the evening. A fairly well-known man of learning – we will call him simply the man of learning – is sitting in his study nervously biting his nails.

"It's positively revolting," he says, continually looking at his watch. "It shows the utmost disrespect for another man's time and work. In England such a person would not earn a farthing, he would die of hunger. You wait a minute, when you do come . . . ."

And feeling a craving to vent his wrath and impatience upon someone, the man of learning goes to the door leading to his wife's room and knocks.

"Listen, Katya," he says in an indignant voice. "If you see Pyotr Danilitch, tell him that decent people don't do such things. It's abominable! He recommends a secretary, and does not know the sort of man he is recommending! The wretched boy is two or three hours late with unfailing regularity every day. Do you call that a secretary? Those two or three hours are more precious to me than two or three years to other people. When he does come I will swear at him like a dog, and won't pay him and will kick him out. It's no use standing on ceremony with people like that!"

"You say that every day, and yet he goes on coming and coming."

"But to-day I have made up my mind. I have lost enough through him. You must excuse me, but I shall swear at him like a cabman."

At last a ring is heard. The man of learning makes a grave face; drawing himself up, and, throwing back his head, he goes into the entry. There his amanuensis Ivan Matveyitch, a young man of eighteen, with a face oval as an egg and no moustache, wearing a shabby, mangy overcoat and no goloshes, is already standing by the hatstand. He is in breathless haste, and scrupulously wipes his huge clumsy boots on the doormat, trying as he does so to conceal from the maidservant a hole in his boot through which a white sock is peeping. Seeing the man of learning he smiles with that broad, prolonged, somewhat foolish smile which is seen only on the faces of children or very good-natured people.

"Ah, good evening!" he says, holding out a big wet hand. "Has your sore throat gone?"

"Ivan Matveyitch," says the man of learning in a shaking voice, stepping back and clasping his hands together. "Ivan Matveyitch."

Then he dashes up to the amanuensis, clutches him by the shoulders, and begins feebly shaking him.

"What a way to treat me!" he says with despair in his voice. "You dreadful, horrid fellow, what a way to treat me! Are you laughing at me, are you jeering at me? Eh?"

Judging from the smile which still lingered on his face Ivan Matveyitch had expected a very different reception, and so, seeing the man of learning's countenance eloquent of indignation, his oval face grows longer than ever, and he opens his mouth in amazement.

"What is . . . what is it?" he asks.

"And you ask that?" the man of learning clasps his hands. "You know how precious time is to me, and you are so late. You are two hours late! . . . Have you no fear of God?"

"I haven't come straight from home," mutters Ivan Matveyitch, untying his scarf irresolutely. "I have been at my aunt's name-day party, and my aunt lives five miles away. . . . If I had come straight from home, then it would have been a different thing."

"Come, reflect, Ivan Matveyitch, is there any logic in your conduct? Here you have work to do, work at a fixed time, and you go flying off after name-day parties and aunts! But do make haste and undo your wretched scarf! It's beyond endurance, really!"

The man of learning dashes up to the amanuensis again and helps him to disentangle his scarf.

"You are done up like a peasant woman, . . . Come along, . . . Please make haste!"

Blowing his nose in a dirty, crumpled-up handkerchief and pulling down his grey reefer jacket, Ivan Matveyitch goes through the hall and the drawing-room to the study. There a place and paper and even cigarettes had been put ready for him long ago.

"Sit down, sit down," the man of learning urges him on, rubbing his hands impatiently. "You are an unsufferable person. . . . You know the work has to be finished by a certain time, and then you are so late. One is forced to scold you. Come, write, . . . Where did we stop?"

Ivan Matveyitch smooths his bristling cropped hair and takes up his pen. The man of learning walks up and down the room, concentrates himself, and begins to dictate:

"The fact is . . . comma . . . that so to speak fundamental forms . . . have you written it? . . . forms are conditioned entirely by the essential nature of those principles . . . comma . . . which find in them their expression and can only be embodied in them. . . . New line, . . . There's a stop there, of course. . . . More independence is found . . . is found . . . by the forms which have not so much a political . . . comma . . . as a social character . ."

"The high-school boys have a different uniform now . . . a grey one," said Ivan Matveyitch, "when I was at school it was better: they used to wear regular uniforms."

"Oh dear, write please!" says the man of learning wrathfully. "Character . . . have you written it? Speaking of the forms relating to the organization . . . of administrative functions, and not to the regulation of the life of the people . . . comma . . . it cannot be said that they are marked by the nationalism of their forms . . . the last three words in inverted commas. . . . Aie, aie . . . tut, tut . . . so what did you want to say about the high school?"

"That they used to wear a different uniform in my time."

"Aha! . . . indeed, . . . Is it long since you left the high school?"

"But I told you that yesterday. It is three years since I left school. . . . I left in the fourth class."

"And why did you give up high school?" asks the man of learning, looking at Ivan Matveyitch's writing.

"Oh, through family circumstances."

"Must I speak to you again, Ivan Matveyitch? When will you get over your habit of dragging out the lines? There ought not to be less than forty letters in a line."

"What, do you suppose I do it on purpose?" says Ivan Matveyitch, offended. "There are more than forty letters in some of the other lines. . . . You count them. And if you think I don't put enough in the line, you can take something off my pay."

"Oh dear, that's not the point. You have no delicacy, really. . . . At the least thing you drag in money. The great thing is to be exact, Ivan Matveyitch, to be exact is the great thing. You ought to train yourself to be exact."

The maidservant brings in a tray with two glasses of tea on it, and a basket of rusks. . . . Ivan Matveyitch takes his glass awkwardly with both hands, and at once begins drinking it. The tea is too hot. To avoid burning his mouth Ivan Matveyitch tries to take a tiny sip. He eats one rusk, then a second, then a third, and, looking sideways, with embarrassment, at the man of learning, timidly stretches after a fourth. . . . The noise he makes in swallowing, the relish with which he smacks his lips, and the expression of hungry greed in his raised eyebrows irritate the man of learning.

"Make haste and finish, time is precious."

"You dictate, I can drink and write at the same time. . . . I must confess I was hungry."

"I should think so after your walk!"

"Yes, and what wretched weather! In our parts there is a scent of spring by now. . . . There are puddles everywhere; the snow is melting."

"You are a southerner, I suppose?"

"From the Don region. . . . It's quite spring with us by March. Here it is frosty, everyone's in a fur coat, . . . but there you can see the grass . . . it's dry everywhere, and one can even catch tarantulas."

"And what do you catch tarantulas for?"

"Oh! . . . to pass the time . . ." says Ivan Matveyitch, and he sighs. "It's fun catching them. You fix a bit of pitch on a thread, let it down into their hole and begin hitting the tarantula on the back with the pitch, and the brute gets cross, catches hold of the pitch with his claws, and gets stuck. . . . And what we used to do with them! We used to put a basinful of them together and drop a bihorka in with them."

"What is a bihorka?"

"That's another spider, very much the same as a tarantula. In a fight one of them can kill a hundred tarantulas."

"H'm! . . . But we must write, . . . Where did we stop?"

The man of learning dictates another twenty lines, then sits plunged in meditation.

Ivan Matveyitch, waiting while the other cogitates, sits and, craning his neck, puts the collar of his shirt to rights. His tie will not set properly, the stud has come out, and the collar keeps coming apart.

"H'm! . . ." says the man of learning. "Well, haven't you found a job yet, Ivan Matveyitch?"

"No. And how is one to find one? I am thinking, you know, of volunteering for the army. But my father advises my going into a chemist's."

"H'm! . . . But it would be better for you to go into the university. The examination is difficult, but with patience and hard work you could get through. Study, read more. . . . Do you read much?"

"Not much, I must own . . ." says Ivan Matveyitch, lighting a cigarette.

"Have you read Turgenev?"

"N-no. . . ."

"And Gogol?"

"Gogol. H'm! . . . Gogol. . . . No, I haven't read him!"

"Ivan Matveyitch! Aren't you ashamed? Aie! aie! You are such a nice fellow, so much that is original in you . ... you haven't even read Gogol! You must read him! I will give you his works! It's essential to read him! We shall quarrel if you don't!"

Again a silence follows. The man of learning meditates, half reclining on a soft lounge, and Ivan Matveyitch, leaving his collar in peace, concentrates his whole attention on his boots. He has not till then noticed that two big puddles have been made by the snow melting off his boots on the floor. He is ashamed.

"I can't get on to-day . . ." mutters the man of learning. "I suppose you are fond of catching birds, too, Ivan Matveyitch?"

"That's in autumn, . . . I don't catch them here, but there at home I always did."

"To be sure . . . very good. But we must write, though."

The man of learning gets up resolutely and begins dictating, but after ten lines sits down on the lounge again.

"No. . . . Perhaps we had better put it off till to-morrow morning," he says. "Come to-morrow morning, only come early, at nine o'clock. God preserve you from being late!"

Ivan Matveyitch lays down his pen, gets up from the table and sits in another chair. Five minutes pass in silence, and he begins to feel it is time for him to go, that he is in the way; but in the man of learning's study it is so snug and light and warm, and the impression of the nice rusks and sweet tea is still so fresh that there is a pang at his heart at the mere thought of home. At home there is poverty, hunger, cold, his grumbling father, scoldings, and here it is so quiet and unruffled, and interest even is taken in his tarantulas and birds.

The man of learning looks at his watch and takes up a book.

"So you will give me Gogol?' says Ivan Matveyitch, getting up.

"Yes, yes! But why are you in such a hurry, my dear boy? Sit down and tell me something . . ."

Ivan Matveyitch sits down and smiles broadly. Almost every evening he sits in this study and always feels something extraordinarily soft, attracting him, as it were akin, in the voice and the glance of the man of learning. There are moments when he even fancies that the man of learning is becoming attached to him, used to him, and that if he scolds him for being late, it's simply because he misses his chatter about tarantulas and how they catch goldfinches on the Don.

ZINOTCHKA

THE party of sportsmen spent the night in a peasant's hut on some newly mown hay. The moon peeped in at the window; from the street came the mournful wheezing of a concertina; from the hay came a sickly sweet, faintly troubling scent. The sportsmen talked about dogs, about women, about first love, and about snipe. After all the ladies of their acquaintance had been picked to pieces, and hundreds of stories had been told, the stoutest of the sportsmen, who looked in the darkness like a haycock, and who talked in the mellow bass of a staff officer, gave a loud yawn and said:

"It is nothing much to be loved; the ladies are created for the purpose of loving us men. But, tell me, has any one of you fellows been hated – passionately, furiously hated? Has any one of you watched the ecstasies of hatred? Eh?"

No answer followed.

"Has no one, gentlemen?" asked the staff officer's bass voice. "But I, now, have been hated, hated by a pretty girl, and have been able to study the symptoms of first hatred directed against myself. It was the first, because it was something exactly the converse of first love. What I am going to tell, however, happened when I knew nothing about love or hate. I was eight at the time, but that made no difference; in this case it was not *he* but *she* that mattered. Well, I beg your attention. One fine summer evening, just before sunset, I was sitting in the nursery, doing my lesson with my governess, Zinotchka, a very charming and poetical creature who had left boarding school not long before. Zinotchka looked absent-mindedly towards the window and said:

" 'Yes. We breathe in oxygen; now tell me, Petya, what do we breathe out?'

" 'Carbonic acid gas,' I answered, looking towards the same window.

" 'Right,' assented Zinotchka. 'Plants, on the contrary, breathe in carbonic acid gas, and breathe out oxygen. Carbonic acid gas is contained in seltzer water, and in the fumes from the samovar. . . . It is a very noxious gas. Near Naples there is the so-called Cave of Dogs, which contains carbonic acid gas; a dog dropped into it is suffocated and dies.'

"This luckless Cave of Dogs near Naples is a chemical marvel beyond which no governess ventures to go. Zinotchka always hotly maintained the usefulness of natural science, but I doubt if she knew any chemistry beyond this Cave.

"Well, she told me to repeat it. I repeated it. She asked me what was meant by the horizon. I answered. And meantime, while we were ruminating over the horizon and the Cave, in the yard below, my father was just getting ready to go shooting. The dogs yapped, the trace horses shifted from one leg to another impatiently and coquetted with the coachman, the footman packed the waggonette with parcels and all sorts of things. Beside the waggonette stood a brake in which my mother and sisters were sitting to drive to a name-day party at the Ivanetskys'. No one was left in the house but Zinotchka, me, and my eldest brother, a student, who had toothache. You can imagine my envy and my boredom.

" 'Well, what do we breathe in?' asked Zinotchka, looking at the window.

" 'Oxygen. . .'

" 'Yes. And the horizon is the name given to the place where it seems to us as though the earth meets the sky.'

"Then the waggonette drove off, and after it the brake. . . . I saw Zinotchka take a note out of her pocket, crumple it up convulsively and press it to her temple, then she flushed crimson and looked at her watch.

" 'So, remember,' she said, 'that near Naples is the so-called Cave of Dogs. . . .' She glanced at her watch again and went on: 'where the sky seems to us to meet the earth. . . .'

"The poor girl in violent agitation walked about the room, and once more glanced at her watch. There was another half-hour before the end of our lesson.

" 'Now arithmetic,' she said, breathing hard and turning over the pages of the sum-book with a trembling hand. 'Come, you work out problem 325 and I . . . will be back directly.'

"She went out. I heard her scurry down the stairs, and then I saw her dart across the yard in her blue dress and vanish through the garden gate. The rapidity of her movements, the flush on her cheeks and her excitement, aroused my curiosity. Where had she run, and what for? Being intelligent beyond my years I soon put two and two together, and understood it all: she had run into the garden, taking advantage of the absence of my stern parents, to steal in among the raspberry bushes, or to pick herself some cherries. If that were so, dash it all, I would go and have some cherries too. I threw aside the sum-book and ran into the garden. I ran to the cherry orchard, but she was not there. Passing by the raspberries, the gooseberries, and the watchman's shanty, she crossed the kitchen garden and reached the pond, pale, and starting at every sound. I stole after her, and what I saw, my friends, was this. At the edge of the pond, between the thick stumps of two old willows, stood my elder brother, Sasha; one could not see from his face that he had toothache. He looked towards Zinotchka as she approached him, and his whole figure was lighted up by an expression of happiness as though by sunshine. And Zinotchka, as though she were being driven into the Cave of Dogs, and were being forced to breathe carbonic acid gas, walked towards him, scarcely able to move one leg before the other, breathing hard, with her head thrown back. . . . To judge from appearances she was going to a rendezous for the first time in her life. But at last she reached him. . . . For half a minute they gazed at each other in silence, as though they could not believe their eyes. Thereupon some force seemed to shove Zinotchka; she laid her hands on Sasha's shoulders and let her head droop upon his waistcoat. Sasha laughed, muttered something incoherent, and with the clumsiness of a man head over ears in love, laid both hands on Zinotchka's face. And the weather, gentlemen, was exquisite. . . . The hill behind which the sun was setting, the two willows, the green bank, the sky — all together with Sasha and Zinotchka were reflected in the pond . . . perfect stillness . . . you can imagine it. Millions of butterflies with long whiskers gleamed golden above the reeds; beyond the garden they were driving the cattle. In fact, it was a perfect picture.

"Of all I had seen the only thing I understood was that Sasha was kissing Zinotchka. That was improper. If *maman* heard of it they would both catch it. Feeling for some reason ashamed I went back to the nursery, not waiting for the end of the rendezvous. There I sat over the sum-book, pondered and reflected. A triumphant smile strayed upon my countenance. On one side it was agreeable to be the possessor of another person's secret; on the other it was also very agreeable that such authorities as Sasha and Zinotchka might at any moment be convicted by me of ignorance of the social proprieties. Now they were in my power, and their peace was entirely dependent on my magnanimity. I'd let them know.

"When I went to bed, Zinotchka came into the nursery as usual to find out whether I had dropped asleep without undressing and whether I had said my prayers. I looked at her pretty, happy face and grinned. I was bursting with my secret and itching to let it out. I had to drop a hint and enjoy the effect.

" 'I know,' I said, grinning. 'Gy—y.'

" 'What do you know?'

" 'Gy—y! I saw you near the willows kissing Sasha. I followed you and saw it all.'

"Zinotchka started, flushed all over, and overwhelmed by 'my hint' she sank down on the chair, on which stood a glass of water and a candlestick.

" 'I saw you . . . kissing . . .' I repeated, sniggering and enjoying her confusion. 'Aha! I'll tell mamma!'

"Cowardly Zinotchka gazed at me intently, and convincing herself that I really did know all about it, clutched my hand in despair and muttered in a trembling whisper:

" 'Petya, it is low. . . . I beg of you, for God's sake. . . . Be a man . . . don't tell anyone. . . . Decent people don't spy. . . . It's low. . . . I entreat you.'

"The poor girl was terribly afraid of my mother, a stern and virtuous lady — that was one thing; and the second was that my grinning countenance could not but outrage her first love so pure and poetical, and you can imagine the state of her heart. Thanks to me, she did not sleep a wink all night, and in the morning she appeared at breakfast with blue rings round her eyes. When I met Sasha after breakfast I could not refrain from grinning and boasting:

" 'I know! I saw you yesterday kissing Mademoiselle Zina!'

"Sasha looked at me and said:

" 'You are a fool.'

"He was not so cowardly as Zinotchka, and so my effect did not come off. That provoked me to further efforts. If Sasha was not frightened it was evident that he did not believe that I had seen and knew all about it; wait a bit, I would show him.

"At our lessons before dinner Zinotchka did not look at me, and her voice faltered. Instead of trying to scare me she tried to propitiate me in every way, giving me full marks, and not complaining to my father of my naughtiness. Being intelligent beyond my years I exploited her secret: I did not learn my lessons, walked into the schoolroom on my head, and said all sorts of rude things. In fact, if I had remained in that vein till to-day I should have become a famous blackmailer. Well, a week passed. Another person's secret irritated and fretted me like a splinter in my soul. I longed at all costs to blurt it out and gloat over the effect. And one day at dinner, when we had a lot of visitors, I gave a stupid snigger, looked fiendishly at Zinotchka and said:

" 'I know. Gy—y! I saw! . . .'

" 'What do you know?' asked my mother.

"I looked still more fiendishly at Zinotchka and Sasha. You ought to have seen how the girl flushed up, and how furious Sasha's eyes were! I bit my tongue and did not go on. Zinotchka gradually turned pale, clenched her teeth, and ate no more dinner. At our evening lessons that day I noticed a striking change in Zinotchka's face. It looked sterner, colder, as it were, more like marble, while her eyes gazed strangely straight into my face, and I give you my word of honour I have never seen such terrible, annihilating eyes, even in hounds when they overtake the wolf. I understood their expression perfectly, when in the middle of a lesson she suddenly clenched her teeth and hissed through them:

" 'I hate you! Oh, you vile, loathsome creature, if you knew how I hate you, how I detest your cropped head, your vulgar, prominent ears!'

"But at once she took fright and said:

" 'I am not speaking to you, I am repeating a part out of a play....'

"Then, my friends, at night I saw her come to my bedside and gaze a long time into my face. She hated me passionately, and could not exist away from me. The contemplation of my hated pug of a face had become a necessity to her. I remember a lovely summer evening . . . with the scent of hay, perfect stillness, and so on. The moon was shining. I was walking up and down the avenue, thinking of cherry jam. Suddenly Zinotchka, looking pale and lovely, came up to me, she caught hold of my hand, and breathlessly began expressing herself:

" 'Oh, how I hate you! I wish no one harm as I do you! Let me tell you that! I want you to understand that!'

"You understand, moonlight, her pale face, breathless with passion, the stillness . . . little pig as I was I actually enjoyed it. I listened to her, looked at her eyes. . . . At first I liked it, and enjoyed the novelty. Then I was suddenly seized with terror, I gave a scream, and ran into the house at breakneck speed.

"I made up my mind that the best thing to do was to complain to *maman*. And I did complain, mentioning incidentally how Sasha had kissed Zinotchka. I was stupid, and did not know what would follow, or I should have kept the secret to myself. . . . After hearing my story *maman* flushed with indignation and said:

" 'It is not your business to speak about that, you are still very young. . . . But, what an example for children.'

"My *maman* was not only virtuous but diplomatic. To avoid a scandal she did not get rid of Zinotchka at once, but set to work gradually, systematically, to pave the way for her departure, as one does with well-bred but intolerable people. I remember that when Zinotchka did leave us the last glance she cast at the house was directed at the window at which I was sitting, and I assure you, I remember that glance to this day.

"Zinotchka soon afterwards became my brother's wife. She is the Zinaida Nikolaevna whom you know. The next time I met her I was already an ensign. In spite of all her efforts she could not recognize the hated Petya in the ensign with his moustache, but still she did not treat me quite like a relation. . . . And even now, in spite of my good-humoured baldness, meek corpulence, and unassuming air, she still looks askance at me, and feels put out when I go to see my brother. Hatred it seems can no more be forgotten than love. . . .

"Tchoo! I hear the cock crowing! Good-night. Milord! Lie down!"

A TRIVIAL INCIDENT

IT was a sunny August midday as, in company with a Russian prince who had come down in the world, I drove into the immense so-called Shabelsky pine-forest where we were intending to look for woodcocks. In virtue of the part he plays in this story my poor prince deserves a detailed description. He was a tall, dark man, still youngish, though already somewhat battered by life; with long moustaches like a police captain's; with prominent black eyes, and with the manners of a retired army man. He was a man of Oriental type, not very intelligent, but straightforward and honest, not a bully, not a fop, and not a rake – virtues which, in the eyes of the general public, are equivalent to a certificate of being a nonentity and a poor creature. People generally did not like him (he was never spoken of in the district, except as "the illustrious duffer"). I personally found the poor prince extremely nice with his misfortunes and failures, which made up indeed his whole life. First of all he was poor. He did not play cards, did not drink, had no occupation, did not poke his nose into anything, and maintained a perpetual silence but yet he had somehow succeeded in getting through thirty to forty thousand roubles left him at his father's death. God only knows what had become of the money. All that I can say is that owing to lack of supervision a great deal was stolen by stewards, bailiffs, and even footmen; a great deal went on lending money, giving bail, and standing security. There were few landowners in the district who did not owe him money. He gave to all who asked, and not so much from good nature or confidence in people as from exaggerated gentlemanliness as though he would say: "Take it and feel how *comme il faut* I am!" By the time I made his acquaintance he had got into debt himself, had learned what it was like to have a second mortgage on his land, and had sunk so deeply into difficulties that there was no chance of his ever getting out of them again. There were days when he had no dinner, and went about with an empty cigar-holder, but he was always seen clean and fashionably dressed, and always smelt strongly of ylang-ylang.

The prince's second misfortune was his absolute solitariness. He was not married, he had no friends nor relations. His silent and reserved character and his *comme il faut* deportment, which became the more conspicuous the more anxious he was to conceal his poverty, prevented him from becoming intimate with people. For love affairs he was too heavy, spiritless, and cold, and so rarely got on with women. . . .

When we reached the forest this prince and I got out of the chaise and walked along a narrow woodland path which was hidden among huge ferns. But before we had gone a hundred paces a tall, lank figure with a long oval face, wearing a shabby reefer jacket, a straw hat, and patent leather boots, rose up from behind a young fir-tree some three feet high, as though he had sprung out of the ground. The stranger held in one hand a basket of mushrooms, with the other he playfully fingered a cheap watch-chain on his waistcoat. On seeing us he was taken aback, smoothed his waistcoat, coughed politely, and gave an agreeable smile, as though he were delighted to see such nice people as us. Then, to our complete surprise, he came up to us, scraping with his long feet on the grass, bending his whole person, and, still smiling agreeably, lifted his hat and pronounced in a sugary voice with the intonations of a whining dog:

"Aie, aie . . . gentlemen, painful as it is, it is my duty to warn you that shooting is forbidden in this wood. Pardon me for venturing to disturb you, though unacquainted, but . . . allow me to present myself. I am Grontovsky, the head clerk on Madame Kandurin's estate."

"Pleased to make your acquaintance, but why can't we shoot?"

"Such is the wish of the owner of this forest!"

The prince and I exchanged glances. A moment passed in silence. The prince stood looking pensively at a big fly agaric at his feet, which he had crushed with his stick. Grontovsky went on smiling agreeably. His whole face was twitching, exuding honey, and even the watch-chain on his waistcoat seemed to be smiling and trying to impress us all with its refinement. A shade of embarrassment passed over us like an angel passing; all three of us felt awkward.

"Nonsense!" I said. "Only last week I was shooting here!"

"Very possible!" Grontovsky sniggered through his teeth. "As a matter of fact everyone shoots here regardless of the prohibition. But once I have met you, it is my duty . . . my sacred duty to warn you. I am a man in a dependent position. If the forest were mine, on the word of honour of a Grontovsky, I should not oppose your agreeable pleasure. But whose fault is it that I am in a dependent position?"

The lanky individual sighed and shrugged his shoulders. I began arguing, getting hot and protesting, but the more loudly and impressively I spoke the more mawkish and sugary Grontovsky's face became. Evidently the consciousness of a certain power over us afforded him the greatest gratification. He was enjoying his condescending tone, his politeness, his manners, and with peculiar relish pronounced his sonorous surname, of which he was probably very fond. Standing before us he felt more than at ease, but judging from the confused sideway glances he cast from time to time at his basket, only one thing was spoiling his satisfaction — the mushrooms, womanish, peasantish, prose, derogatory to his dignity.

"We can't go back!" I said. "We have come over ten miles!"

"What's to be done?" sighed Grontovsky. "If you had come not ten but a hundred thousand miles, if the king even had come from America or from some other distant land, even then I should think it my duty . . . sacred, so to say, obligation . . ."

"Does the forest belong to Nadyezhda Lvovna?" asked the prince.

"Yes, Nadyezhda Lvovna . . ."

"Is she at home now?"

"Yes . . . I tell you what, you go to her, it is not more than half a mile from here; if she gives you a note, then I. . . . I needn't say! Ha – ha . . . he – he – !"

"By all means," I agreed. "It's much nearer than to go back. . . . You go to her, Sergey Ivanitch," I said, addressing the prince. "You know her."

The prince, who had been gazing the whole time at the crushed agaric, raised his eyes to me, thought a minute, and said:

"I used to know her at one time, but . . . it's rather awkward for me to go to her. Besides, I am in shabby clothes. . . . You go, you don't know her. . . . It's more suitable for you to go."

I agreed. We got into our chaise and, followed by Grontovsky's smiles, drove along the edge of the forest to the manor house. I was not acquainted with Nadyezhda Lvovna Kandurin, née Shabelsky. I had never seen her at close quarters, and knew her only by hearsay. I knew that she was incredibly wealthy, richer than anyone else in the province. After the death of her father, Shabelsky, who was a landowner with no other children, she was left with several estates, a stud farm, and a lot of money. I had heard that, though she was only twenty-five or twenty-six, she was ugly, uninteresting, and as insignificant as anybody, and was only distinguished from the ordinary ladies of the district by her immense wealth.

It has always seemed to me that wealth is felt, and that the rich must have special feelings unknown to the poor. Often as I passed by Nadyezhda Lvovna's big fruit garden, in which stood the large, heavy house with its windows always curtained, I thought: "What is she thinking at this moment? Is there happiness behind those blinds?" and so on. Once I saw her from a distance in a fine light cabriolet, driving a handsome white horse, and, sinful man that I am, I not only envied her, but even thought that in her poses, in her movements, there was something special, not to be found in people who are not rich, just as persons of a servile nature succeed in discovering "good family" at the first glance in people of the most ordinary exterior, if they are a little more distinguished than themselves. Nadyezhda Lvovna's inner life was only known to me by scandal. It was said in the district that five or six years ago, before she was married, during her father's lifetime, she had been passionately in love with Prince Sergey Ivanitch, who was now beside me in the chaise. The prince had been fond of visiting her father, and used to spend whole days in his billiard room, where he played pyramids indefatigably till his arms and legs ached. Six months before the old man's death he had suddenly given up visiting the Shabelskys. The gossip of the district having no positive facts to go upon explained this abrupt change in their relations in various ways. Some said that the prince, having observed the plain daughter's feeling for him and being unable to reciprocate it, considered it the duty of a gentleman to cut short his visits. Others maintained that old Shabelsky had discovered why his daughter was pining away, and had proposed to the poverty-stricken prince that he should marry her; the prince, imagining in his narrow-minded way that they were trying to buy him together with his title, was indignant, said foolish things, and quarrelled with them. What was true and what was false in this nonsense was difficult to say. But that there was a portion of truth in it was evident, from the fact that the prince always avoided conversation about Nadyezhda Lvovna.

I knew that soon after her father's death Nadyezhda Lvovna had married one Kandurin, a bachelor of law, not wealthy, but adroit, who had come on a visit to the neighbourhood. She married him not from love, but because she was touched by the love of the legal gentleman who, so it was said, had cleverly played the love-sick swain. At the time I am describing, Kandurin was for some reason living in Cairo, and writing thence to his friend, the marshal of the district, "Notes of Travel," while she sat languishing behind lowered blinds, surrounded by idle parasites, and whiled away her dreary days in petty philanthropy.

On the way to the house the prince fell to talking.

"It's three days since I have been at home," he said in a half whisper, with a sidelong glance at the driver. "I am not a child, nor a silly woman, and I have no prejudices, but I can't stand the bailiffs. When I see a bailiff in my house I turn pale and tremble, and even have a twitching in the calves of my legs. Do you know Rogozhin refused to honour my note?"

The prince did not, as a rule, like to complain of his straitened circumstances; where poverty was concerned he was reserved and exceedingly proud and sensitive, and so this announcement surprised me. He stared a long time at the yellow clearing, warmed by the sun, watched a long string of cranes float in the azure sky, and turned facing me.

"And by the sixth of September I must have the money ready for the bank . . . the interest for my estate," he said aloud, by now regardless of the coachman. "And where am I to get it? Altogether, old man, I am in a tight fix! An awfully tight fix!"

The prince examined the cock of his gun, blew on it for some reason, and began looking for the cranes which by now were out of sight.

"Sergey Ivanitch," I asked, after a minute's silence, "imagine if they sell your Shatilovka, what will you do?"

"I? I don't know! Shatilovka can't be saved, that's clear as daylight, but I cannot imagine such a calamity. I can't imagine myself without my daily bread secure. What can I do? I have had hardly any education; I have not tried working yet; for government service it is late to begin, . . . Besides, where could I serve? Where could I be of use? Admitting that no great cleverness is needed for serving in our Zemstvo, for example, yet I suffer from . . . the devil knows what, a sort of faintheartedness, I haven't a ha'p'orth of pluck. If I went into the Service I should always feel I was not in my right place. I am not an idealist; I am not a Utopian; I haven't any special principles; but am simply, I suppose, stupid and thoroughly incompetent, a neurotic and a coward. Altogether not like other people. All other people are like other people, only I seem to be something . . . a poor thing. . . . I met Naryagin last Wednesday – you know him? – drunken, slovenly . . . doesn't pay his debts, stupid" (the prince frowned and tossed his head) . . . "a horrible person! He said to me, staggering: 'I'm being balloted for as a justice of the peace!' Of course, they won't elect him, but, you see, he believes he is fit to be a justice of the peace and considers that position within his capacity. He has boldness and self-confidence. I went to see our investigating magistrate too. The man gets two hundred and fifty roubles a month, and does scarcely anything. All he can do is to stride backwards and forwards for days together in nothing but his underclothes, but, ask him, he is convinced he is doing his work and honourably performing his duty. I couldn't go on like that! I should be ashamed to look the clerk in the face."

At that moment Grontovsky, on a chestnut horse, galloped by us with a flourish. On his left arm the basket bobbed up and down with the mushrooms dancing in it. As he passed us he grinned and waved his hand, as though we were old friends.

"Blockhead!" the prince filtered through his teeth, looking after him. "It's wonderful how disgusting it sometimes is to see satisfied faces. A stupid, animal feeling due to hunger, I expect. . . . What was I saying? Oh, yes, about going into the Service, . . . I should be ashamed to take the salary, and yet, to tell the truth, it is stupid. If one looks at it from a broader point of view, more seriously, I am eating what isn't mine now. Am I not? But why am I not ashamed of that. . . . It is a case of habit, I suppose . . . and not being able to realize one's true position. . . . But that position is most likely awful. . ."

I looked at him, wondering if the prince were showing off. But his face was mild and his eyes were mournfully following the movements of the chestnut horse racing away, as though his happiness were racing away with it.

Apparently he was in that mood of irritation and sadness when women weep quietly for no reason, and men feel a craving to complain of themselves, of life, of God. . . .

When I got out of the chaise at the gates of the house the prince said to me:

"A man once said, wanting to annoy me, that I have the face of a cardsharper. I have noticed that cardsharpers are usually dark. Do you know, it seems that if I really had been born a cardsharper I should have remained a decent person to the day of my death, for I should never have had the boldness to do wrong. I tell you frankly I have had the chance once in my life of getting rich if I had told a lie, a lie to myself and one woman . . . and one other person whom I know would have forgiven me for lying; I should have put into my pocket a million. But I could not. I hadn't the pluck!"

From the gates we had to go to the house through the copse by a long road, level as a ruler, and planted on each side with thick, lopped lilacs. The house looked somewhat heavy, tasteless, like a façade on the stage. It rose clumsily out of a mass of greenery, and caught the eye like a great stone thrown on the velvety turf. At the chief entrance I was met by a fat old footman in a green swallow-tail coat and big silver-rimmed spectacles; without making any announcement, only looking contemptuously at my dusty figure, he showed me in. As I mounted the soft carpeted stairs there was, for some reason, a strong smell of india-rubber. At the top I was enveloped in an atmosphere found only in museums, in signorial mansions and old-fashioned merchant houses; it seemed like the smell of something long past, which had once lived and died and had left its soul in the rooms. I passed through three or four rooms on my way from the entry to the drawing-room. I remember bright yellow, shining floors, lustres wrapped in stiff muslin, narrow, striped rugs which stretched not straight from door to door, as they usually do, but along the walls, so that not venturing to touch the bright floor with my muddy boots I had to describe a rectangle in each room. In the drawing-room, where the footman left me, stood old-fashioned ancestral furniture in white covers, shrouded in twilight. It looked surly and elderly, and, as though out of respect for its repose, not a sound was audible.

Even the clock was silent . . . it seemed as though the Princess Tarakanov had fallen asleep in the golden frame, and the water and the rats were still and motionless through magic. The daylight, afraid of disturbing the universal tranquillity, scarcely pierced through the lowered blinds, and lay on the soft rugs in pale, slumbering streaks.

Three minutes passed and a big, elderly woman in black, with her cheek bandaged up, walked noiselessly into the drawing-room. She bowed to me and pulled up the blinds. At once, enveloped in the bright sunlight, the rats and water in the picture came to life and movement, Princess Tarakanov was awakened, and the old chairs frowned gloomily.

"Her honour will be here in a minute, sir . . ." sighed the old lady, frowning too.

A few more minutes of waiting and I saw Nadyezhda Lvovna. What struck me first of all was that she certainly was ugly, short, scraggy, and round-shouldered. Her thick, chestnut hair was magnificent; her face, pure and with a look of culture in it, was aglow with youth; there was a clear and intelligent expression in her eyes; but the whole charm of her head was lost through the thickness of her lips and the over-acute facial angle.

I mentioned my name, and announced the object of my visit.

"I really don't know what I am to say!" she said, in hesitation, dropping her eyes and smiling. "I don't like to refuse, and at the same time. . . ."

"Do, please," I begged.

Nadyezhda Lvovna looked at me and laughed. I laughed too. She was probably amused by what Grontovsky had so enjoyed – that is, the right of giving or withholding permission; my visit suddenly struck me as queer and strange.

"I don't like to break the long-established rules," said Madame Kandurin. "Shooting has been forbidden on our estate for the last six years. No!" she shook her head resolutely. "Excuse me, I must refuse you. If I allow you I must allow others. I don't like unfairness. Either let all or no one."

"I am sorry!" I sighed. "It's all the sadder because we have come more than ten miles. I am not alone," I added, "Prince Sergey Ivanitch is with me."

I uttered the prince's name with no *arrière pensée,* not prompted by any special motive or aim; I simply blurted it out without thinking, in the simplicity of my heart. Hearing the familiar name Madame Kandurin started, and bent a prolonged gaze upon me. I noticed her nose turn pale.

"That makes no difference . . ." she said, dropping her eyes.

As I talked to her I stood at the window that looked out on the shrubbery. I could see the whole shrubbery with the avenues and the ponds and the road by which I had come. At the end of the road, beyond the gates, the back of our chaise made a dark patch. Near the gate, with his back to the house, the prince was standing with his legs apart, talking to the lanky Grontovsky.

Madame Kandurin had been standing all the time at the other window. She looked from time to time towards the shrubbery, and from the moment I mentioned the prince's name she did not turn away from the window.

"Excuse me," she said, screwing up her eyes as she looked towards the road and the gate, "but it would be unfair to allow you only to shoot. . . . And, besides, what pleasure is there in shooting birds? What's it for? Are they in your way?"

A solitary life, immured within four walls, with its indoor twilight and heavy smell of decaying furniture, disposes people to sentimentality. Madame Kandurin's idea did her credit, but I could not resist saying:

"If one takes that line one ought to go barefoot. Boots are made out of the leather of slaughtered animals."

"One must distinguish between a necessity and a caprice," Madame Kandurin answered in a toneless voice.

She had by now recognized the prince, and did not take her eyes off his figure. It is hard to describe the delight and the suffering with which her ugly face was radiant! Her eyes were smiling and shining, her lips were quivering and laughing, while her face craned closer to the panes. Keeping hold of a flower-pot with both hands, with bated breath and with one foot slightly lifted, she reminded me of a dog pointing and waiting with passionate impatience for "Fetch it!"

I looked at her and at the prince who could not tell a lie once in his life, and I felt angry and bitter against truth and falsehood, which play such an elemental part in the personal happiness of men.

The prince started suddenly, took aim and fired. A hawk, flying over him, fluttered its wings and flew like an arrow far away.

"He aimed too high!" I said. "And so, Nadyezhda Lvovna," I sighed, moving away from the window, "you will not permit . . ." — Madame Kandurin was silent.

"I have the honour to take my leave," I said, "and I beg you to forgive my disturbing you. . ."

Madame Kandurin would have turned facing me, and had already moved through a quarter of the angle, when she suddenly hid her face behind the hangings, as though she felt tears in her eyes that she wanted to conceal.

"Good-bye. . . . Forgive me . . ." she said softly.

I bowed to her back, and strode away across the bright yellow floors, no longer keeping to the carpet. I was glad to get away from this little domain of gilded boredom and sadness, and I hastened as though anxious to shake off a heavy, fantastic dream with its twilight, its enchanted princess, its lustres. . . .

At the front door a maidservant overtook me and thrust a note into my hand: "Shooting is permitted on showing this. N. K.," I read.

A DOCTOR'S VISIT

THE Professor received a telegram from the Lyalikovs' factory; he was asked to come as quickly as possible. The daughter of some Madame Lyalikov, apparently the owner of the factory, was ill, and that was all that one could make out of the long, incoherent telegram. And the Professor did not go himself, but sent instead his assistant, Korolyov.

It was two stations from Moscow, and there was a drive of three miles from the station. A carriage with three horses had been sent to the station to meet Korolyov; the coachman wore a hat with a peacock's feather on it, and answered every question in a loud voice like a soldier: "No, sir!" "Certainly, sir!"

It was Saturday evening; the sun was setting, the workpeople were coming in crowds from the factory to the station, and they bowed to the carriage in which Korolyov was driving. And he was charmed with the evening, the farmhouses and villas on the road, and the birch-trees, and the quiet atmosphere all around, when the fields and woods and the sun seemed preparing, like the workpeople now on the eve of the holiday, to rest, and perhaps to pray. . . .

He was born and had grown up in Moscow; he did not know the country, and he had never taken any interest in factories, or been inside one, but he had happened to read about factories, and had been in the houses of manufacturers and had talked to them; and whenever he saw a factory far or near, he always thought how quiet and peaceable it was outside, but within there was always sure to be impenetrable ignorance and dull egoism on the side of the owners, wearisome, unhealthy toil on the side of the workpeople, squabbling, vermin, vodka. And now when the workpeople timidly and respectfully made way for the carriage, in their faces, their caps, their walk, he read physical impurity, drunkenness, nervous exhaustion, bewilderment.

They drove in at the factory gates. On each side he caught glimpses of the little houses of workpeople, of the faces of women, of quilts and linen on the railings. "Look out!" shouted the coachman, not pulling up the horses. It was a wide courtyard without grass, with five immense blocks of buildings with tall chimneys a little distance one from another, warehouses and barracks, and over everything a sort of grey powder as though from dust. Here and there, like oases in the desert, there were pitiful gardens, and the green and red roofs of the houses in which the managers and clerks lived. The coachman suddenly pulled up the horses, and the carriage stopped at the house, which had been newly painted grey; here was a flower garden, with a lilac bush covered with dust, and on the yellow steps at the front door there was a strong smell of paint.

"Please come in, doctor," said women's voices in the passage and the entry, and at the same time he heard sighs and whisperings. "Pray walk in. . . . We've been expecting you so long. . . we're in real trouble. Here, this way."

Madame Lyalikov — a stout elderly lady wearing a black silk dress with fashionable sleeves, but, judging from her face, a simple uneducated woman — looked at the doctor in a flutter, and could not bring herself to hold out her hand to him; she did not dare. Beside her stood a personage with short hair and a pince-nez; she was wearing a blouse of many colours, and was very thin and no longer young. The servants called her Christina Dmitryevna, and Korolyov guessed that this was the governess. Probably, as the person of most education in the house, she had been charged to meet and receive the doctor, for she began immediately, in great haste, stating the causes of the illness, giving trivial and tiresome details, but without saying who was ill or what was the matter.

The doctor and the governess were sitting talking while the lady of the house stood motionless at the door, waiting. From the conversation Korolyov learned that the patient was Madame Lyalikov's only daughter and heiress, a girl of twenty, called Liza; she had been ill for a long time, and had consulted various doctors, and the previous night she had suffered till morning from such violent palpitations of the heart, that no one in the house had slept, and they had been afraid she might die.

"She has been, one may say, ailing from a child," said Christina Dmitryevna in a sing-song voice, continually wiping her lips with her hand. "The doctors say it is nerves; when she was a little girl she was scrofulous, and the doctors drove it inwards, so I think it may be due to that."

They went to see the invalid. Fully grown up, big and tall, but ugly like her mother, with the same little eyes and disproportionate breadth of the lower part of the face, lying with her hair in disorder, muffled up to the chin, she made upon Korolyov at the first minute the impression of a poor, destitute creature, sheltered and cared for here out of charity, and he could hardly believe that this was the heiress of the five huge buildings.

"I am the doctor come to see you," said Korolyov. "Good evening."

He mentioned his name and pressed her hand, a large, cold, ugly hand; she sat up, and, evidently accustomed to doctors, let herself be sounded, without showing the least concern that her shoulders and chest were uncovered.

"I have palpitations of the heart," she said, "It was so awful all night. . . . I almost died of fright! Do give me something."

"I will, I will; don't worry yourself."

Korolyov examined her and shrugged his shoulders.

"The heart is all right," he said; "it's all going on satisfactorily; everything is in good order. Your nerves must have been playing pranks a little, but that's so common. The attack is over by now, one must suppose; lie down and go to sleep."

At that moment a lamp was brought into the bed-room. The patient screwed up her eyes at the light, then suddenly put her hands to her head and broke into sobs. And the impression of a destitute, ugly creature vanished, and Korolyov no longer noticed the little eyes or the heavy development of the lower part of the face. He saw a soft, suffering expression which was intelligent and touching: she seemed to him altogether graceful, feminine, and simple; and he longed to soothe her, not with drugs, not with advice, but with simple, kindly words. Her mother put her arms round her head and hugged her. What despair, what grief was in the old woman's face! She, her mother, had reared her and brought her up, spared nothing, and devoted her whole life to having her daughter taught French, dancing, music: had engaged a dozen teachers for her; had consulted the best doctors, kept a governess. And now she could not make out the reason of these tears, why there was all this misery, she could not understand, and was bewildered; and she had a guilty, agitated, despairing expression, as though she had omitted something very important, had left something undone, had neglected to call in somebody – and whom, she did not know.

"Lizanka, you are crying again . . . again," she said, hugging her daughter to her. "My own, my darling, my child, tell me what it is! Have pity on me! Tell me."

Both wept bitterly. Korolyov sat down on the side of the bed and took Liza's hand.

"Come, give over; it's no use crying," he said kindly. "Why, there is nothing in the world that is worth those tears. Come, we won't cry; that's no good. . . ."

And inwardly he thought:

"It's high time she was married. . . ."

"Our doctor at the factory gave her kalibromati," said the

governess, "but I notice it only makes her worse. I should have thought that if she is given anything for the heart it ought to be drops. . . . I forget the name. . . . Convallaria, isn't it?"

And there followed all sorts of details. She interrupted the doctor, preventing his speaking, and there was a look of effort on her face, as though she supposed that, as the woman of most education in the house, she was duty bound to keep up a conversation with the doctor, and on no other subject but medicine.

Korolyov felt bored.

"I find nothing special the matter," he said, addressing the mother as he went out of the bedroom. "If your daughter is being attended by the factory doctor, let him go on attending her. The treatment so far has been perfectly correct, and I see no reason for changing your doctor. Why change? It's such an ordinary trouble; there's nothing seriously wrong."

He spoke deliberately as he put on his gloves, while Madame Lyalikov stood without moving, and looked at him with her tearful eyes.

"I have half an hour to catch the ten o'clock train," he said. "I hope I am not too late."

"And can't you stay?" she asked, and tears trickled down her cheeks again. "I am ashamed to trouble you, but if you would be so good. . . . For God's sake," she went on in an undertone, glancing towards the door, "do stay to-night with us! She is all I have . . . my only daughter. . . . She frightened me last night; I can't get over it. . . . Don't go away, for goodness' sake! . . ."

He wanted to tell her that he had a great deal of work in Moscow, that his family were expecting him home; it was disagreeable to him to spend the evening and the whole night in a strange house quite needlessly; but he looked at her face, heaved a sigh, and began taking off his gloves without a word.

All the lamps and candles were lighted in his honour in the drawing-room and the dining-room. He sat down at the piano and began turning over the music. Then he looked at the pictures on the walls, at the portraits. The pictures, oil-paintings in gold frames, were views of the Crimea – a stormy sea with a ship, a Catholic monk with a wineglass; they were all dull, smooth daubs, with no trace of talent in them. There was not a single good-looking face among the portraits, nothing but broad cheekbones and astonished-looking eyes. Lyalikov, Liza's father, had a low forehead and a self-satisfied expression; his uniform sat like a sack on his bulky plebeian figure; on his breast was a medal and a Red Cross Badge. There was little sign of culture, and the luxury was senseless and haphazard, and was as ill fitting as that uniform. The floors irritated him with their brilliant polish, the lustres on the chandelier irritated him, and he was reminded for some reason of the story of the merchant who used to go to the baths with a medal on his neck....

He heard a whispering in the entry; some one was softly snoring. And suddenly from outside came harsh, abrupt, metallic sounds, such as Korolyov had never heard before, and which he did not understand now; they roused strange, unpleasant echoes in his soul.

"I believe nothing would induce me to remain here to live . . ." he thought, and went back to the music-books again.

"Doctor, please come to supper!" the governess called him in a low voice.

He went into supper. The table was large and laid with a vast number of dishes and wines, but there were only two to supper: himself and Christina Dmitryevna. She drank Madeira, ate rapidly, and talked, looking at him through her pince-nez:

"Our workpeople are very contented. We have performances at the factory every winter; the workpeople act themselves. They have lectures with a magic lantern, a splendid tea-room, and everything they want. They are very much attached to us, and when they heard that Lizanka was worse they had a service sung for her. Though they have no education, they have their feelings, too."

"It looks as though you have no man in the house at all," said Korolyov.

"Not one. Pyotr Nikanoritch died a year and a half ago, and left us alone. And so there are the three of us. In the summer we live here, and in winter we live in Moscow, in Polianka. I have been living with them for eleven years — as one of the family."

At supper they served sterlet, chicken rissoles, and stewed fruit; the wines were expensive French wines.

"Please don't stand on ceremony, doctor," said Christina Dmitryevna, eating and wiping her mouth with her fist, and it was evident she found her life here exceedingly pleasant. "Please have some more."

After supper the doctor was shown to his room, where a bed had been made up for him, but he did not feel sleepy. The room was stuffy and it smelt of paint; he put on his coat and went out.

It was cool in the open air; there was already a glimmer of dawn, and all the five blocks of buildings, with their tall chimneys, barracks, and warehouses, were distinctly outlined against the damp air. As it was a holiday, they were not working, and the windows were dark, and in only one of the buildings was there a furnace burning; two windows were crimson, and fire mixed with smoke came from time to time from the chimney. Far away beyond the yard the frogs were croaking and the nightingales singing.

Looking at the factory buildings and the barracks, where the workpeople were asleep, he thought again what he always thought when he saw a factory. They may have performances for the workpeople, magic lanterns, factory doctors, and improvements of all sorts, but, all the same, the workpeople he had met that day on his way from the station did not look in any way different from those he had known long ago in his childhood, before there were factory performances and improvements. As a doctor accustomed to judging correctly of chronic complaints, the radical cause of which was incomprehensible and incurable, he looked upon factories as something baffling, the cause of which also was obscure and not removable, and all the improvements in the life of the factory hands he looked upon not as superfluous, but as comparable with the treatment of incurable illnesses.

"There is something baffling in it, of course . . ." he thought, looking at the crimson windows. "Fifteen hundred or two thousand workpeople are working without rest in unhealthy surroundings, making bad cotton goods, living on the verge of starvation, and only waking from this nightmare at rare intervals in the tavern; a hundred people act as overseers, and the whole life of that hundred is spent in imposing fines, in abuse, in injustice, and only two or three so-called owners enjoy the profits, though they don't work at all, and despise the wretched cotton. But what are the profits, and how do they enjoy them? Madame Lyalikov and her daughter are unhappy – it makes one wretched to look at them; the only one who enjoys her life is Christina Dmitryevna, a stupid, middle-aged maiden lady in pince-nez. And so it appears that all these five blocks of buildings are at work, and inferior cotton is sold in the Eastern markets, simply that Christina Dmitryevna may eat sterlet and drink Madeira."

Suddenly there came a strange noise, the same sound Korolyov had heard before supper. Some one was striking on a sheet of metal near one of the buildings; he struck a note, and then at once checked the vibrations, so that short, abrupt, discordant sounds were produced, rather like "Dair . . . dair . . . dair. . . ." Then there was half a minute of stillness, and from another building there came sounds equally abrupt and unpleasant, lower bass notes: "Drin . . . drin . . . drin. . ." Eleven times. Evidently it was the watchman striking the hour. Near the third building he heard: "Zhuk . . . zhuk . . . zhuk. . . ." And so near all the buildings, and then behind the barracks and beyond the gates. And in the stillness of the night it seemed as though these sounds were uttered by a monster with crimson eyes – the devil himself, who controlled the owners and the work-people alike, and was deceiving both.

Korolyov went out of the yard into the open country.

"Who goes there?" some one called to him at the gates in an abrupt voice.

"It's just like being in prison," he thought, and made no answer.

Here the nightingales and the frogs could be heard more distinctly, and one could feel it was a night in May. From the station came the noise of a train; somewhere in the distance drowsy cocks were crowing; but, all the same, the night was still, the world was sleeping tranquilly. In a field not far from the factory there could be seen the framework of a house and heaps of building material:

Korolyov sat down on the planks and went on thinking.

"The only person who feels happy here is the governess,

and the factory hands are working for her gratification. But that's only apparent: she is only the figurehead. The real person, for whom everything is being done, is the devil."

And he thought about the devil, in whom he did not believe, and he looked round at the two windows where the fires were gleaming. It seemed to him that out of those crimson eyes the devil himself was looking at him – that unknown force that had created the mutual relation of the strong and the weak, that coarse blunder which one could never correct. The strong must hinder the weak from living – such was the law of Nature; but only in a newspaper article or in a school book was that intelligible and easily accepted. In the hotchpotch which was everyday life, in the tangle of trivialities out of which human relations were woven, it was no longer a law, but a logical absurdity, when the strong and the weak were both equally victims of their mutual relations, unwillingly submitting to some directing force, unknown, standing outside life, apart from man.

So thought Korolyov, sitting on the planks, and little by little he was possessed by a feeling that this unknown and mysterious force was really close by and looking at him. Meanwhile the east was growing paler, time passed rapidly; when there was not a soul anywhere near, as though everything were dead, the five buildings and their chimneys against the grey background of the dawn had a peculiar look – not the same as by day; one forgot altogether that inside there were steam motors, electricity, telephones, and kept thinking of lake-dwellings, of the Stone Age, feeling the presence of a crude, unconscious force. . . .

And again there came the sound: "Dair . . . dair . . . dair . . . dair . . ." twelve times. Then there was stillness, stillness for half a minute, and at the other end of the yard there rang out.

"Drin . . . drin . . . drin. . . ."

"Horribly disagreeable," thought Korolyov.

"Zhuk . . . zhuk . . ." there resounded from a third place, abruptly, sharply, as though with annoyance – "Zhuk . . . zhuk. . . ."

And it took four minutes to strike twelve. Then there was a hush; and again it seemed as though everything were dead.

Korolyov sat a little longer, then went to the house, but sat up for a good while longer. In the adjoining rooms there was whispering, there was a sound of shuffling slippers and bare feet.

"Is she having another attack?" thought Korolyov.

He went out to have a look at the patient. By now it was quite light in the rooms, and a faint glimmer of sunlight, piercing through the morning mist, quivered on the floor and on the wall of the drawing-room. The door of Liza's room was open, and she was sitting in a low chair beside her bed, with her hair down, wearing a dressing-gown and wrapped in a shawl. The blinds were down on the windows.

"How do you feel?" asked Korolyov.

"Well, thank you."

He touched her pulse, then straightened her hair, that had fallen over her forehead.

"You are not asleep," he said. "It's beautiful weather outside. It's spring. The nightingales are singing, and you sit in the dark and think of something."

She listened and looked into his face; her eyes were sorrowful and intelligent, and it was evident she wanted to say something to him.

"Does this happen to you often?" he said.

She moved her lips, and answered:

"Often, I feel wretched almost every night."

At that moment the watchman in the yard began striking two o'clock. They heard: "Dair . . . dair . . ." and she shuddered.

"Do those knockings worry you?" he asked.

"I don't know. Everything here worries me," she answered, and pondered. "Everything worries me. I hear sympathy in your voice; it seemed to me as soon as I saw you that I could tell you all about it."

"Tell me, I beg you."

"I want to tell you of my opinion. It seems to me that I have no illness, but that I am weary and frightened, because it is bound to be so and cannot be otherwise. Even the healthiest person can't help being uneasy if, for instance, a robber is moving about under his window. I am constantly being doctored," she went on, looking at her knees, and she gave a shy smile. "I am very grateful, of course, and I do not deny that the treatment is a benefit; but I should like to talk, not with a doctor, but with some intimate friend who would understand me and would convince me that I was right or wrong."

"Have you no friends?" asked Korolyov.

"I am lonely. I have a mother; I love her, but, all the same, I am lonely. That's how it happens to be. . . . Lonely people read a great deal, but say little and hear little. Life for them is mysterious; they are mystics and often see the devil where he is not. Lermontov's Tamara was lonely and she saw the devil."

"Do you read a great deal?"

"Yes. You see, my whole time is free from morning till night. I read by day, and by night my head is empty; instead of thoughts there are shadows in it."

"Do you see anything at night?" asked Korolyov.

"No, but I feel. . . ."

She smiled again, raised her eyes to the doctor, and looked at him so sorrowfully, so intelligently; and it seemed to him that she trusted him, and that she wanted to speak frankly to him, and that she thought the same as he did. But she was silent, perhaps waiting for him to speak.

And he knew what to say to her. It was clear to him that she needed as quickly as possible to give up the five buildings and the million if she had it — to leave that devil that looked out at night; it was clear to him, too, that she thought so herself, and was only waiting for some one she trusted to confirm her.

But he did not know how to say it. How? One is shy of asking men under sentence what they have been sentenced for; and in the same way it is awkward to ask very rich people what they want so much money for, why they make such a poor use of their wealth, why they don't give it up, even when they see in it their unhappiness; and if they begin a conversation about it themselves, it is usually embarrassing, awkward, and long.

"How is one to say it?" Korolyov wondered. "And is it necessary to speak?"

And he said what he meant in a roundabout way:

"You in the position of a factory owner and a wealthy heiress are dissatisfied; you don't believe in your right to it; and here now you can't sleep. That, of course, is better than if you were satisfied, slept soundly, and thought everything was satisfactory. Your sleeplessness does you credit; in any case, it is a good sign. In reality, such a conversation as this between us now would have been unthinkable for our parents. At night they did not talk, but slept sound; we, our generation, sleep badly, are restless, but talk a great deal, and are always trying to settle whether we are right or not. For our children or grandchildren that question – whether they are right or not – will have been settled. Things will be clearer for them than for us. Life will be good in fifty years' time; it's only a pity we shall not last out till then. It would be interesting to have a peep at it."

"What will our children and grandchildren do?" asked Liza.

"I don't know. . . . I suppose they will throw it all up and go away."

"Go where?"

"Where? . . . Why, where they like," said Korolyov; and he laughed. "There are lots of places a good, intelligent person can go to."

He glanced at his watch.

"The sun has risen, though," he said. "It is time you were asleep. Undress and sleep soundly. Very glad to have made your acquaintance," he went on, pressing her hand. "You are a good, interesting woman. Good-night!"

He went to his room and went to bed.

In the morning when the carriage was brought round they all came out on to the steps to see him off. Liza, pale and exhausted, was in a white dress as though for a holiday, with a flower in her hair; she looked at him, as yesterday, sorrowfully and intelligently, smiled and talked, and all with an expression as though she wanted to tell him something special, important – him alone. They could hear the larks trilling and the church bells pealing. The windows in the factory buildings were sparkling gaily, and, driving across the yard and afterwards along the road to the station, Korolyov thought neither of the workpeople nor of lake dwellings, nor of the devil, but thought of the time, perhaps close at hand, when life would be as bright and joyous as that still Sunday morning; and he thought how pleasant it was on such a morning in the spring to drive with three horses in a good carriage, and to bask in the sunshine.

AN UPHEAVAL

MASHENKA PAVLETSKY, a young girl who had only just finished her studies at a boarding school, returning from a walk to the house of the Kushkins, with whom she was living as a governess, found the household in a terrible turmoil. Mihailo, the porter who opened the door to her, was excited and red as a crab.

Loud voices were heard from upstairs.

"Madame Kushkin is in a fit, most likely, or else she has quarrelled with her husband," thought Mashenka.

In the hall and in the corridor she met maid-servants. One of them was crying. Then Mashenka saw, running out of her room, the master of the house himself, Nikolay Sergeitch, a little man with a flabby face and a bald head, though he was not old. He was red in the face and twitching all over. He passed the governess without noticing her, and throwing up his arms, exclaimed:

"Oh, how horrible it is! How tactless! How stupid! How barbarous! Abominable!"

Mashenka went into her room, and then, for the first time in her life, it was her lot to experience in all its acuteness the feeling that is so familiar to persons in dependent positions, who eat the bread of the rich and powerful, and cannot speak their minds. There was a search going on in her room. The lady of the house, Fedosya Vassilyevna, a stout, broad-shouldered, uncouth woman with thick black eyebrows, a faintly perceptible moustache, and red hands, who was exactly like a plain, illiterate cook in face and manners, was standing, without her cap on, at the table, putting back into Mashenka's workbag balls of wool, scraps of materials, and bits of paper. . . . Evidently the governess's arrival took her by surprise, since, on looking round and seeing the girl's pale and astonished face, she was a little taken aback, and muttered:

"*Pardon.* I... I upset it accidentally.... My sleeve caught in it..."

And saying something more, Madame Kushkin rustled her long skirts and went out. Mashenka looked round her room with wondering eyes, and, unable to understand it, not knowing what to think, shrugged her shoulders, and turned cold with dismay. What had Fedosya Vassilyevna been looking for in her work-bag? If she really had, as she said, caught her sleeve in it and upset everything, why had Nikolay Sergeitch dashed out of her room so excited and red in the face? Why was one drawer of the table pulled out a little way? The money-box, in which the governess put away ten kopeck pieces and old stamps, was open. They had opened it, but did not know how to shut it, though they had scratched the lock all over. The whatnot with her books on it, the things on the table, the bed — all bore fresh traces of a search. Her linen-basket, too. The linen had been carefully folded, but it was not in the same order as Mashenka had left it when she went out. So the search had been thorough, most thorough. But what was it for? Why? What had happened? Mashenka remembered the excited porter, the general turmoil which was still going on, the weeping servant-girl; had it not all some connection with the search that had just been made in her room? Was not she mixed up in something dreadful? Mashenka turned pale, and feeling cold all over, sank on to her linen-basket.

A maid-servant came into the room.

"Liza, you don't know why they have been rummaging in my room?" the governess asked her.

"Mistress has lost a brooch worth two thousand," said Liza.

"Yes, but why have they been rummaging in my room?"

"They've been searching every one, miss. They've searched all my things, too. They stripped us all naked and searched us. . . . God knows, miss, I never went near her toilet-table, let alone touching the brooch. I shall say the same at the police-station."

"But . . . why have they been rummaging here?" the governess still wondered.

"A brooch has been stolen, I tell you. The mistress has been rummaging in everything with her own hands. She even searched Mihailo, the porter, herself. It's a perfect disgrace! Nikolay Sergeitch simply looks on and cackles like a hen. But you've no need to tremble like that, miss. They found nothing here. You've nothing to be afraid of if you didn't take the brooch."

"But, Liza, it's vile . . . it's insulting," said Mashenka, breathless with indignation. "It's so mean, so low! What right had she to suspect me and to rummage in my things?"

"You are living with strangers, miss," sighed Liza. "Though you are a young lady, still you are . . . as it were . . . a servant. . . . It's not like living with your papa and mamma."

Mashenka threw herself on the bed and sobbed bitterly. Never in her life had she been subjected to such an outrage, never had she been so deeply insulted. . . . She, well-educated, refined, the daughter of a teacher, was suspected of theft; she had been searched like a street-walker! She could not imagine a greater insult. And to this feeling of resentment was added an oppressive dread of what would come next. All sorts of absurd ideas came into her mind. If they could suspect her of theft, then they might arrest her, strip her naked, and search her, then lead her through the street with an escort of soldiers, cast her into a cold, dark cell with mice and woodlice, exactly like the dungeon in which Princess Tarakanov was imprisoned. Who would stand up for her? Her parents lived far away in the provinces; they had not the money to come to her. In the capital she was as solitary as in a desert, without friends or kindred. They could do what they liked with her.

"I will go to all the courts and all the lawyers," Mashenka thought, trembling. "I will explain to them, I will take an oath. . . . They will believe that I could not be a thief!"

Mashenka remembered that under the sheets in her basket she had some sweetmeats, which, following the habits of her schooldays, she had put in her pocket at dinner and carried off to her room. She felt hot all over, and was ashamed at the thought that her little secret was known to the lady of the house; and all this terror, shame, resentment, brought on an attack of palpitation of the heart, which set up a throbbing in her temples, in her heart, and deep down in her stomach.

"Dinner is ready," the servant summoned Mashenka.

"Shall I go, or not?"

Mashenka brushed her hair, wiped her face with a wet towel, and went into the dining-room. There they had already begun dinner. At one end of the table sat Fedosya Vassilyevna with a stupid, solemn, serious face; at the other end Nikolay Sergeitch. At the sides there were the visitors and the children. The dishes were handed by two footmen in swallowtails and white gloves. Every one knew that there was an upset in the house, that Madame Kushkin was in trouble, and every one was silent. Nothing was heard but the sound of munching and the rattle of spoons on the plates.

The lady of the house, herself, was the first to speak.

"What is the third course?" she asked the footman in a weary, injured voice.

"*Esturgeon à la russe,*" answered the footman.

"I ordered that, Fenya," Nikolay Sergeitch hastened to observe. "I wanted some fish. If you don't like it, *ma chère,* don't let them serve it. I just ordered it. . . ."

Fedosya Vassilyevna did not like dishes that she had not ordered herself, and now her eyes filled with tears.

Come, don't let us agitate ourselves," Mamikov, her household doctor, observed in a honeyed voice, just touching her arm, with a smile as honeyed. "We are nervous enough as it is. Let us forget the brooch! Health is worth more than two thousand roubles!"

"It's not the two thousand I regret," answered the lady, and a big tear rolled down her cheek. "It's the fact itself that revolts me! I cannot put up with thieves in my house. I don't regret it — I regret nothing; but to steal from me is such ingratitude! That's how they repay me for my kindness. . . ."

They all looked into their plates, but Mashenka fancied after the lady's words that every one was looking at her. A lump rose in her throat; she began crying and put her handkerchief to her lips.

"*Pardon,*" she muttered. "I can't help it. My head aches. I'll go away."

And she got up from the table, scraping her chair awkwardly, and went out quickly, still more overcome with confusion.

"It's beyond everything!" said Nikolay Sergeitch, frowning. "What need was there to search her room? How out of place it was!"

"I don't say she took the brooch," said Fedosya Vassilyevna, "but can you answer for her? To tell the truth, I haven't much confidence in these learned paupers."

"It really was unsuitable, Fenya. . . . Excuse me, Fenya, but you've no kind of legal right to make a search."

"I know nothing about your laws. All I know is that I've lost my brooch. And I will find the brooch!" She brought her fork down on the plate with a clatter, and her eyes flashed angrily. "And you eat your dinner, and don't interfere in what doesn't concern you!"

Nikolay Sergeitch dropped his eyes mildly and sighed. Meanwhile Mashenka, reaching her room, flung herself on her bed. She felt now neither alarm nor shame, but she felt an intense longing to go and slap the cheeks of this hard, arrogant, dull-witted, prosperous woman.

Lying on her bed she breathed into her pillow and dreamed of how nice it would be to go and buy the most expensive brooch and fling it into the face of this bullying woman. If only it were God's will that Fedosya Vassilyevna should come to ruin and wander about begging, and should taste all the horrors of poverty and dependence, and that Mashenka, whom she had insulted, might give her alms! Oh, if only she could come in for a big fortune, could buy a carriage, and could drive noisily past the windows so as to be envied by that woman!

But all these were only dreams, in reality there was only one thing left to do — to get away as quickly as possible, not to stay another hour in this place. It was true it was terrible to lose her place, to go back to her parents, who had nothing; but what could she do? Mashenka could not bear the sight of the lady of the house nor of her little room; she felt stifled and wretched here. She was so disgusted with Fedosya Vassilyevna, who was so obsessed by her illnesses and her supposed aristocratic rank, that everything in the world seemed to have become coarse and unattractive because this woman was living in it. Mashenka jumped up from the bed and began packing.

"May I come in?" asked Nikolay Sergeitch at the door; he had come up noiselessly to the door, and spoke in a soft, subdued voice. "May I?"

"Come in."

He came in and stood still near the door. His eyes looked dim and his red little nose was shiny. After dinner he used to drink beer, and the fact was perceptible in his walk, in his feeble, flabby hands.

"What's this?" he asked, pointing to the basket.

"I am packing. Forgive me, Nikolay Sergeitch, but I cannot remain in your house. I feel deeply insulted by this search!"

"I understand. . . . Only you are wrong to go. Why should you? They've searched your things, but you . . . what does it matter to you? You will be none the worse for it."

Mashenka was silent and went on packing. Nikolay Sergeitch pinched his moustache, as though wondering what he should say next, and went on in an ingratiating voice:

"I understand, of course, but you must make allowances. You know my wife is nervous, headstrong; you mustn't judge her too harshly."

Mashenka did not speak.

"If you are so offended," Nikolay Sergeitch went on, "well, if you like, I'm ready to apologise. I ask your pardon."

Mashenka made no answer, but only bent lower over her box. This exhausted, irresolute man was of absolutely no significance in the household. He stood in the pitiful position of a dependent and hanger-on, even with the servants, and his apology meant nothing either.

"H'm! . . . You say nothing! That's not enough for you. In that case, I will apologise for my wife. In my wife's name. . . . She behaved tactlessly, I admit it as a gentleman. . . ."

Nikolay Sergeitch walked about the room, heaved a sigh, and went on:

"Then you want me to have it rankling here, under my heart. . . . You want my conscience to torment me. . . ."

"I know it's not your fault, Nikolay Sergeitch," said Mashenka, looking him full in the face with her big tear-stained eyes. "Why should you worry yourself?"

"Of course, no. . . . But still, don't you. . . go away. I entreat you."

Mashenka shook her head. Nikolay Sergeitch stopped at the window and drummed on the pane with his finger-tips.

"Such misunderstandings are simply torture to me," he said. "Why, do you want me to go down on my knees to you, or what? Your pride is wounded, and here you've been crying and packing up to go; but I have pride, too, and you do not spare it! Or do you want me to tell you what I would not tell as Confession? Do you? Listen; you want me to tell you what I won't tell the priest on my deathbed?"

Mashenka made no answer.

"I took my wife's brooch," Nikolay Sergeitch said quickly. "Is that enough now? Are you satisfied? Yes, I . . . took it. . . . But, of course, I count on your discretion. . . . For God's sake, not a word, not half a hint to any one!"

Mashenka, amazed and frightened, went on packing; she snatched her things, crumpled them up, and thrust them anyhow into the box and the basket. Now, after this candid avowal on the part of Nikolay Sergeitch, she could not remain another minute, and could not understand how she could have gone on living in the house before.

"And it's nothing to wonder at," Nikolay Sergeitch went on after a pause. "It's an everyday story! I need money, and she . . . won't give it to me. It was my father's money that bought this house and everything, you know! It's all mine, and the brooch belonged to my mother, and . . . it's all mine! And she took it, took possession of everything. . . . I can't go to law with her, you'll admit. . . . I beg you most earnestly, overlook it . . . stay on. *Tout comprendre, tout pardonner.* Will you stay?"

"No!" said Mashenka resolutely, beginning to tremble. "Let me alone, I entreat you!"

"Well, God bless you!" sighed Nikolay Sergeitch, sitting down on the stool near the box. "I must own I like people who still can feel resentment, contempt, and so on. I could sit here forever and look at your indignant face. . . . So you won't stay, then? I understand. . . . It's bound to be so. . . Yes, of course. . . . It's all right for you, but for me – wo-o-o-o! . . . I can't stir a step out of this cellar. I'd go off to one of our estates, but in every one of them there are some of my wife's rascals. . . stewards, experts, damn them all! They mortgage and remortgage. . . . You mustn't catch fish, must keep off the grass, mustn't break the trees."

"Nikolay Sergeitch!" his wife's voice called from the drawing-room. "Agnia, call your master!"

"Then you won't stay?" asked Nikolay Sergeitch, getting up quickly and going towards the door. "You might as well stay, really. In the evenings I could come and have a talk with you. Eh? Stay! If you go, there won't be a human face left in the house. It's awful!"

Nikolay Sergeitch's pale, exhausted face besought her, but Mashenka shook her head, and with a wave of his hand he went out.

Half an hour later she was on her way.

THE HEAD OF THE FAMILY

IT is, as a rule, after losing heavily at cards or after a drinking-bout when an attack of dyspepsia is setting in that Stepan Stepanitch Zhilin wakes up in an exceptionally gloomy frame of mind. He looks sour, rumpled, and dishevelled; there is an expression of displeasure on his grey face, as though he were offended or disgusted by something. He dresses slowly, sips his Vichy water deliberately, and begins walking about the rooms.

"I should like to know what b-b-beast comes in here and does not shut the door!" he grumbles angrily, wrapping his dressing-gown about him and spitting loudly. "Take away that paper! Why is it lying about here? We keep twenty servants, and the place is more untidy than a pot-house. Who was that ringing? Who the devil is that?"

"That's Anfissa, the midwife who brought our Fedya into the world," answers his wife.

"Always hanging about . . . these cadging toadies!"

"There's no making you out, Stepan Stepanitch. You asked her yourself, and now you scold."

"I am not scolding; I am speaking. You might find something to do, my dear, instead of sitting with your hands in your lap trying to pick a quarrel. Upon my word, women are beyond my comprehension! Beyond my comprehension! How can they waste whole days doing nothing? A man works like an ox, like a b-beast, while his wife, the partner of his life, sits like a pretty doll, sits and does nothing but watch for an opportunity to quarrel with her husband by way of diversion. It's time to drop these schoolgirlish ways, my dear. You are not a schoolgirl, not a young lady; you are a wife and mother! You turn away? Aha! It's not agreeable to listen to the bitter truth!

"It's strange that you only speak the bitter truth when your liver is out of order."

"That's right; get up a scene."

"Have you been out late? Or playing cards?"

"What if I have? Is that anybody's business? Am I obliged to give an account of my doings to any one? It's my own money I lose, I suppose? What I spend as well as what is spent in this house belongs to me — me. Do you hear? To me!"

And so on, all in the same style. But at no other time is Stepan Stepanitch so reasonable, virtuous, stern or just as at dinner, when all his household are sitting about him. It usually begins with the soup. After swallowing the first spoonful Zhilin suddenly frowns and puts down his spoon.

"Damn it all!" he mutters; "I shall have to dine at a restaurant, I suppose."

"What's wrong?" asks his wife anxiously. "Isn't the soup good?"

"One must have the taste of a pig to eat hogwash like that! There's too much salt in it; it smells of dirty rags . . . more like bugs than onions. . . . It's simply revolting, Anfissa Ivanovna," he says, addressing the midwife. "Every day I give no end of money for housekeeping. . . . I deny myself everything, and this is what they provide for my dinner! I suppose they want me to give up the office and go into the kitchen to do the cooking myself."

"The soup is very good to-day," the governess ventures timidly.

"Oh, you think so?" says Zhilin, looking at her angrily from under his eyelids. "Every one to his taste, of course. It must be confessed our tastes are very different, Varvara Vassilyevna. You, for instance, are satisfied with the behaviour of this boy" (Zhilin with a tragic gesture points to his son Fedya); "you are delighted with him, while I . . . I am disgusted. Yes!"

Fedya, a boy of seven with a pale, sickly face, leaves off eating and drops his eyes. His face grows paler still.

"Yes, you are delighted, and I am disgusted. Which of us is right, I cannot say, but I venture to think as his father, I know my own son better than you do. Look how he is sitting! Is that the way decently brought up children sit? Sit properly."

Fedya tilts his chin up, cranes his neck, and fancies that he is holding himself better. Tears come into his eyes.

"Eat your dinner! Hold your spoon properly! You wait. I'll show you, you horrid boy! Don't dare to whimper! Look straight at me!"

Fedya tries to look straight at him, but his face is quivering and his eyes fill with tears.

"A-ah! . . . you cry? You are naughty and then you cry? Go and stand in the corner, you beast!"

"But . . . let him have his dinner first," his wife intervenes.

"No dinner for him! Such bla . . . such rascals don't deserve dinner!"

Fedya, wincing and quivering all over, creeps down from his chair and goes into the corner.

"You won't get off with that!" his parent persists. "If nobody else cares to look after your bringing up, so be it; I must begin. . . . I won't let you be naughty and cry at dinner, my lad! Idiot! You must do your duty! Do you understand? Do your duty! Your father works and you must work, too! No one must eat the bread of idleness! You must be a man! A m-man!"

"For God's sake, leave off," says his wife in French. "Don't nag at us before outsiders, at least. . . . The old woman is all ears; and now, thanks to her, all the town will hear of it."

I am not afraid of outsiders," answers Zhilin in Russian. "Anfissa Ivanovna sees that I am speaking the truth. Why, do you think I ought to be pleased with the boy? Do you know what he costs me? Do you know, you nasty boy, what you cost me? Or do you imagine that I coin money, that I get it for nothing? Don't howl! Hold your tongue! Do you hear what I say? Do you want me to whip you, you young ruffian?"

Fedya wails aloud and begins to sob.

"This is insufferable," says his mother, getting up from the table and flinging down her dinner-napkin. "You never let us have dinner in peace! Your bread sticks in my throat."

And putting her handkerchief to her eyes, she walks out of the dining-room.

"Now she is offended," grumbles Zhilin, with a forced smile. "She's been spoilt. . . . That's how it is, Anfissa Ivanovna; no one likes to hear the truth nowadays. . . . It's all my fault, it seems."

Several minutes of silence follow. Zhilin looks round at the plates, and noticing that no one has yet touched their soup, heaves a deep sigh, and stares at the flushed and uneasy face of the governess.

"Why don't you eat, Varvara Vassilyevna?" he asks. "Offended, I suppose? I see. . . . You don't like to be told the truth. You must forgive me, it's my nature; I can't be a hypocrite. . . . I always blurt out the plain truth" (a sigh). "But I notice that my presence is unwelcome. No one can eat or talk while I am here. . . . Well, you should have told me, and I would have gone away. . . . I will go."

Zhilin gets up and walks with dignity to the door. As he passes the weeping Fedya he stops.

"After all that has passed here, you are free," he says to Fedya, throwing back his head with dignity. "I won't meddle in your bringing up again. I wash my hands of it! I humbly apologise that as a father, from a sincere desire for your welfare, I have disturbed you and your mentors. At the same time, once for all I disclaim all responsibility for your future. . . ."

Fedya wails and sobs more loudly than ever. Zhilin turns with dignity to the door and departs to his bedroom.

When he wakes from his after-dinner nap he begins to feel the stings of conscience. He is ashamed to face his wife, his son, Anfissa Ivanovna, and even feels very wretched when he recalls the scene at dinner, but his amour-propre is too much for him; he has not the manliness to be frank, and he goes on sulking and grumbling.

Waking up next morning, he feels in excellent spirits, and whistles gaily as he washes. Going into the dining-room to breakfast, he finds there Fedya, who, at the sight of his father, gets up and looks at him helplessly.

"Well, young man?" Zhilin greets him good-humouredly, sitting down to the table. "What have you got to tell me, young man? Are you all right? Well, come, chubby; give your father a kiss."

With a pale, grave face Fedya goes up to his father and touches his cheek with his quivering lips, then walks away and sits down in his place without a word.

VOLODYA

AT five o'clock one Sunday afternoon in summer, Volodya, a plain, shy, sickly-looking lad of seventeen, was sitting in the arbour of the Shumihins' country villa, feeling dreary. His despondent thought flowed in three directions. In the first place, he had next day, Monday, an examination in mathematics; he knew that if he did not get through the written examination on the morrow, he would be expelled, for he had already been two years in the sixth form and had two and three-quarter marks for algebra in his annual report. In the second place, his presence at the villa of the Shumihins, a wealthy family with aristocratic pretensions, was a continual source of mortification to his amour-propre. It seemed to him that Madame Shumihin looked upon him and his *maman* as poor relations and dependents, that they laughed at his *maman* and did not respect her. He had on one occasion accidently overheard Madame Shumihin, in the verandah, telling her cousin Anna Fyodorovna that his *maman* still tried to look young and got herself up, that she never paid her losses at cards, and had a partiality for other people's shoes and tobacco. Every day Volodya besought his *maman* not to go to the Shumihins', and drew a picture of the humiliating part she played with these gentlefolk. He tried to persuade her, said rude things, but she – a frivolous, pampered woman, who had run through two fortunes, her own and her husband's, in her time, and always gravitated towards acquaintances of high rank – did not understand him, and twice a week Volodya had to accompany her to the villa he hated.

In the third place, the youth could not for one instant get rid of a strange, unpleasant feeling which was absolutely new to him. . . . It seemed to him that he was in love with Anna Fyodorovna, the Shumihins' cousin, who was staying with them. She was a vivacious, loud-voiced, laughter-loving, healthy, and vigorous lady of thirty, with rosy cheeks, plump shoulders, a plump round chin and a continual smile on her thin lips. She was neither young nor beautiful – Volodya knew that perfectly well; but for some reason he could not help thinking of her, looking at her while she shrugged her plump shoulders and moved her flat back as she played croquet, or after prolonged laughter and running up and down stairs, sank into a low chair, and, half closing her eyes and gasping for breath, pretended that she was stifling and could not breathe. She was married. Her husband, a staid and dignified architect, came once a week to the villa, slept soundly, and returned to town. Volodya's strange feeling had begun with his conceiving an unaccountable hatred for the architect, and feeling relieved every time he went back to town.

Now, sitting in the arbour, thinking of his examination next day, and of his *maman,* at whom they laughed, he felt an intense desire to see Nyuta (that was what the Shumihins called Anna Fyodorovna), to hear her laughter and the rustle of her dress. . . . This desire was not like the pure, poetic love of which he read in novels and about which he dreamed every night when he went to bed; it was strange, incomprehensible; he was ashamed of it, and afraid of it as of something very wrong and impure, something which it was disagreeable to confess even to himself.

"It's not love," he said to himself. "One can't fall in love with women of thirty who are married. It is only a little intrigue. . . . Yes, an intrigue. . . ."

Pondering on the "intrigue," he thought of his uncontrollable shyness, his lack of moustache, his freckles, his narrow eyes, and put himself in his imagination side by side with Nyuta, and the juxtaposition seemed to him impossible; then he made haste to imagine himself bold, handsome, witty, dressed in the latest fashion.

When his dreams were at their height, as he sat huddled together and looking at the ground in a dark corner of the arbour, he heard the sound of light footsteps. Some one was coming slowly along the avenue. Soon the steps stopped and something white gleamed in the entrance.

"Is there any one here?" asked a woman's voice.

Volodya recognised the voice, and raised his head in a fright.

"Who is here?" asked Nyuta, going into the arbour. "Ah, it is you, Volodya? What are you doing here? Thinking? And how can you go on thinking, thinking, thinking? . . . That's the way to go out of your mind!"

Volodya got up and looked in a dazed way at Nyuta. She had only just come back from bathing. Over her shoulder there was hanging a sheet and a rough towel, and from under the white silk kerchief on her head he could see the wet hair sticking to her forehead. There was the cool damp smell of the bath-house and of almond soap still hanging about her. She was out of breath from running quickly. The top button of her blouse was undone, so that the boy saw her throat and bosom.

"Why don't you say something?" said Nyuta, looking Volodya up and down. "It's not polite to be silent when a lady talks to you. What a clumsy seal you are though, Volodya! You always sit, saying nothing, thinking like some philosopher. There's not a spark of life or fire in you! You are really horrid! . . . At your age you ought to be living, skipping, and jumping, chattering, flirting, falling in love."

Volodya looked at the sheet that was held by a plump white hand, and thought. . . .

"He's mute," said Nyuta, with wonder; "it is strange, really. . . . Listen! Be a man! Come, you might smile at least! Phew, the horrid philosopher!" she laughed. "But do you know, Volodya, why you are such a clumsy seal? Because you don't devote yourself to the ladies. Why don't you? It's true there are no girls here, but there is nothing to prevent your flirting with the married ladies! Why don't you flirt with me, for instance?"

Volodya listened and scratched his forehead in acute and painful irresolution.

"It's only very proud people who are silent and love solitude," Nyuta went on, pulling his hand away from his forehead. "You are proud, Volodya. Why do you look at me like that from under your brows? Look me straight in the face, if you please! Yes, now then, clumsy seal!"

Volodya made up his mind to speak. Wanting to smile, he twitched his lower lip, blinked, and again put his hand to his forehead.

"I . . . I love you," he said.

Nyuta raised her eyebrows in surprise, and laughed.

"What do I hear?" she sang, as prima-donnas sing at the opera when they hear something awful. "What? What did you say? Say it again, say it again. . . ."

"I . . . I love you!" repeated Volodya.

And without his will's having any part in his action, without reflection or understanding, he took half a step towards Nyuta and clutched her by the arm. Everything was dark before his eyes, and tears came into them. The whole world was turned into one big, rough towel which smelt of the bathhouse.

"Bravo, bravo!" he heard a merry laugh. "Why don't you speak? I want you to speak! Well?"

Seeing that he was not prevented from holding her arm, Volodya glanced at Nyuta's laughing face, and clumsily, awkwardly, put both arms round her waist, his hands meeting behind her back. He held her round the waist with both arms, while, putting her hands up to her head, showing the dimples in her elbows, she set her hair straight under the kerchief and said in a calm voice:

"You must be tactful, polite, charming, and you can only become that under feminine influence. But what a wicked, angry face you have! You must talk, laugh. . . . Yes, Volodya, don't be surly; you are young and will have plenty of time for philosophising. Come, let go of me; I am going. Let go."

Without effort she released her waist, and, humming something, walked out of the arbour. Volodya was left alone. He smoothed his hair, smiled, and walked three times to and fro across the arbour, then he sat down on the bench and smiled again. He felt insufferably ashamed, so much so that he wondered that human shame could reach such a pitch of acuteness and intensity. Shame made him smile, gesticulate, and whisper some disconnected words.

He was ashamed that he had been treated like a small boy, ashamed of his shyness, and, most of all, that he had had the audacity to put his arms round the waist of a respectable married woman, though, as it seemed to him, he had neither through age nor by external quality, nor by social position any right to do so.

He jumped up, went out of the arbour, and, without looking round, walked into the recesses of the garden furthest from the house.

"Ah! only to get away from here as soon as possible," he thought, clutching his head. "My God! as soon as possible."

The train by which Volodya was to go back with his *maman* was at eight-forty. There were three hours before the train started, but he would with pleasure have gone to the station at once without waiting for his *maman*.

At eight o'clock he went to the house. His whole figure

was expressive of determination: what would be, would be! He made up his mind to go in boldly, to look them straight in the face, to speak in a loud voice, regardless of everything.

He crossed the terrace, the big hall and the drawing-room, and there stopped to take breath. He could hear them in the dining-room, drinking tea. Madame Shumihin, *maman,* and Nyuta were talking and laughing about something.

Volodya listened.

"I assure you!" said Nyuta. "I could not believe my eyes! When he began declaring his passion and — just imagine! — put his arms round my waist, I should not have recognised him. And you know he has a way with him! When he told me he was in love with me, there was something brutal in his face, like a Circassian."

"Really!" gasped *maman,* going off into a peal of laughter. "Really! How he does remind me of his father!"

Volodya ran back and dashed out into the open air.

"How could they talk of it aloud!" he wondered in agony, clasping his hands and looking up to the sky in horror. "They talk aloud in cold blood . . . and *maman* laughed! . . . *Maman!* My God, why didst Thou give me such a mother? Why?"

But he had to go to the house, come what might. He walked three times up and down the avenue, grew a little calmer, and went into the house.

"Why didn't you come in in time for tea?" Madame Shumihin asked sternly.

"I am sorry, it's . . . it's time for me to go," he muttered, not raising his eyes. "*Maman,* it's eight o'clock!"

"You go alone, my dear," said his *maman* languidly. "I am staying the night with Lili. Goodbye, my dear. . . . Let me make the sign of the cross over you."

She made the sign of the cross over her son, and said in French, turning to Nyuta:

"He's rather like Lermontov . . . isn't he?"

Saying good-bye after a fashion, without looking any one in the face, Volodya went out of the dining-room. Ten minutes later he was walking along the road to the station, and was glad of it. Now he felt neither frightened nor ashamed; he breathed freely and easily.

About half a mile from the station, he sat down on a stone by the side of the road, and gazed at the sun, which was half hidden behind a barrow. There were lights already here and there at the station, and one green light glimmered dimly, but the train was not yet in sight. It was pleasant to Volodya to sit still without moving, and to watch the evening coming little by little. The darkness of the arbour, the footsteps, the smell of the bath-house, the laughter, and the waist – all these rose with amazing vividness before his imagination, and all this was no longer so terrible and important as before.

"It's of no consequence. . . . She did not pull her hand away, and laughed when I held her by the waist," he thought. "So she must have liked it. If she had disliked it she would have been angry . . . ."

And now Volodya felt sorry that he had not had more boldness there in the arbour. He felt sorry that he was so stupidly going away, and he was by now persuaded that if the same thing happened again he would be bolder and look at it more simply.

And it would not be difficult for the opportunity to occur again. They used to stroll about for a long time after supper at the Shumihins'. If Volodya went for a walk with Nyuta in the dark garden, there would be an opportunity!

"I will go back," he thought, "and will go by the morning train to-morrow. . . . I will say I have missed the train."

And he turned back. . . . Madame Shumihin, *Maman,* Nyuta, and one of the nieces were sitting on the verandah, playing *vint.* When Volodya told them the lie that he had missed the train, they were uneasy that he might be late for the examination day, and advised him to get up early. All the while they were playing he sat on one side, greedily watching Nyuta and waiting. . . . He already had a plan prepared in his mind: he would go up to Nyuta in the dark, would take her by the hand, then would embrace her; there would be no need to say anything, as both of them would understand without words.

But after supper the ladies did not go for a walk in the garden, but went on playing cards. They played till one o'clock at night, and then broke up to go to bed.

"How stupid it all is!" Volodya thought with vexation as he got into bed. "But never mind; I'll wait till to-morrow . . . to-morrow in the arbour. It doesn't matter. . . ."

He did not attempt to go to sleep, but sat in bed, hugging his knees and thinking. All thought of the examination was hateful to him. He had already made up his mind that they would expel him, and that there was nothing terrible about his being expelled. On the contrary, it was a good thing – a very good thing, in fact. Next day he would be as free as a bird; he would put on ordinary clothes instead of his school uniform, would smoke openly, come out here, and make love to Nyuta when he liked; and he would not be a schoolboy but "a young man." And as for the rest of it, what is called a career, a future, that was clear; Volodya would go into the army or the telegraph service, or he would go into a chemist's shop and work his way up till he was a dispenser. . . . There were lots of callings. An hour or two passed, and he was still sitting and thinking. . . .

Towards three o'clock, when it was beginning to get light, the door creaked cautiously and his *maman* came into the room.

"Aren't you asleep?" she asked, yawning. "Go to sleep; I have only come in for a minute. . . . I am only fetching the drops. . . ."

"What for?"

"Poor Lili has got spasms again. Go to sleep, my child, your examination's to-morrow. . . ."

She took a bottle of something out of the cupboard, went to the window, read the label, and went away.

"Marya Leontyevna, those are not the drops!" Volodya heard a woman's voice, a minute later. "That's convallaria, and Lili wants morphine. Is your son asleep? Ask him to look for it. . . ."

It was Nyuta's voice. Volodya turned cold. He hurriedly put on his trousers, flung his coat over his shoulders, and went to the door.

"Do you understand? Morphine," Nyuta explained in a whisper. "There must be a label in Latin. Wake Volodya; he will find it."

Maman opened the door and Volodya caught sight of

Nyuta. She was wearing the same loose wrapper in which she had gone to bathe. Her hair hung loose and disordered on her shoulders, her face looked sleepy and dark in the half-light. . . .

"Why, Volodya is not asleep," she said. "Volodya, look in the cupboard for the morphine, there's a dear! What a nuisance Lili is! She has always something the matter."

Maman muttered something, yawned, and went away.

"Look for it," said Nyuta. "Why are you standing still?"

Volodya went to the cupboard, knelt down, and began looking through the bottles and boxes of medicine. His hands were trembling, and he had a feeling in his chest and stomach as though cold waves were running all over his inside. He felt suffocated and giddy from the smell of ether, carbolic acid, and various drugs, which he quite unnecessarily snatched up with his trembling fingers and spilled in so doing.

"I believe *maman* has gone," he thought. "That's a good thing . . . a good thing. . . ."

"Will you be quick?" said Nyuta, drawling.

"In a minute. . . . Here, I believe this is morphine," said Volodya, reading on one of the labels the word "morph . . ." "Here it is!"

Nyuta was standing in the doorway in such a way that one foot was in his room and one was in the passage. She was tidying her hair, which was difficult to put in order because it was so thick and long, and looked absent-mindedly at Volodya. In her loose wrap, with her sleepy face and her hair down, in the dim light that came into the white sky not yet lit by the sun, she seemed to Volodya captivating, magnificent. . . . Fascinated, trembling all over, and remembering with relish how he had held that exquisite body in his arms in the arbour, he handed her the bottle and said:

"How wonderful you are!"

"What?"

She came into the room.

"What?" she asked, smiling.

He was silent and looked at her, then, just as in the arbour, he took her hand, and she looked at him with a smile and waited for what would happen next.

"I love you," he whispered.

She left off smiling, thought a minute, and said:

"Wait a little; I think somebody is coming. Oh, these schoolboys!" she said in an undertone, going to the door and peeping out into the passage. "No, there is no one to be seen. . . ."

She came back.

Then it seemed to Volodya that the room, Nyuta, the sunrise and himself – all melted together in one sensation of acute, extraordinary, incredible bliss, for which one might give up one's whole life and face eternal torments. . . . But half a minute passed and all that vanished. Volodya saw only a fat, plain face, distorted by an expression of repulsion, and he himself suddenly felt a loathing for what had happened.

"I must go away, though," said Nyuta, looking at Volodya with disgust. "What a wretched, ugly . . . fie, ugly duckling!"

How unseemly her long hair, her loose wrap, her steps, her voice seemed to Volodya now! . . .

" 'Ugly duckling' . . ." he thought after she had gone away. "I really am ugly . . . everything is ugly."

The sun was rising, the birds were singing loudly; he could hear the gardener walking in the garden and the creaking of his wheelbarrow . . . and soon afterwards he heard the lowing of the cows and the sounds of the shepherd's pipe. The sunlight and the sounds told him that somewhere in this world there is a pure, refined, poetical life. But where was it? Volodya had never heard a word of it from his *maman* or any of the people round about him.

When the footman came to wake him for the morning train, he pretended to be asleep. . . .

"Bother it! Damn it all!" he thought.

He got up between ten and eleven.

Combing his hair before the looking-glass, and looking at his ugly face, pale from his sleepless night, he thought:

"It's perfectly true . . . an ugly duckling!"

When *maman* saw him and was horrified that he was not at his examination, Volodya said:

"I overslept myself, *maman*. . . . But don't worry, I will get a medical certificate."

Madame Shumihin and Nyuta waked up at one o'clock. Volodya heard Madame Shumihin open her window with a bang, heard Nyuta go off into a peal of laughter in reply to her coarse voice. He saw the door open and a string of nieces and other toadies (among the latter was his *maman*) file into lunch, caught a glimpse of Nyuta's freshly washed laughing face, and, beside her, the black brows and beard of her husband the architect, who had just arrived.

Nyuta was wearing a Little Russian dress which did not suit her at all, and made her look clumsy; the architect was making dull and vulgar jokes. The rissoles served at lunch had too much onion in them – so it seemed to Volodya. It also seemed to him that Nyuta laughed loudly on purpose, and kept glancing in his direction to give him to understand that the memory of the night did not trouble her in the least, and that she was not aware of the presence at table of the "ugly duckling."

At four o'clock Volodya drove to the station with his *maman*. Foul memories, the sleepless night, the prospect of expulsion from school, the stings of conscience – all roused in him now an oppressive, gloomy anger. He looked at *maman*'s sharp profile, at her little nose, and at the raincoat which was a present from Nyuta, and muttered:

"Why do you powder? It's not becoming at your age! You make yourself up, don't pay your debts at cards, smoke other people's tobacco. . . . It's hateful! I don't love you . . . I don't love you!"

He was insulting her, and she moved her little eyes about in alarm, flung up her hands, and whispered in horror:

"What are you saying, my dear! Good gracious! the coachman will hear! Be quiet or the coachman will hear! He can overhear everything."

"I don't love you . . . I don't love you!" he went on breathlessly. "You've no soul and no morals. . . . Don't dare to wear that raincoat! Do you hear? Or else I will tear it into rags. . . ."

"Control yourself, my child," *maman* wept; "the coachman can hear!"

"And where is my father's fortune? Where is your money? You have wasted it all. I am not ashamed of being poor, but I am ashamed of having such a mother. . . . When my schoolfellows ask questions about you, I always blush."

In the train they had to pass two stations before they reached the town. Volodya spent all the time on the little platform between two carriages and shivered all over. He did not want to go into the compartment because there the mother he hated was sitting. He hated himself, hated the ticket collectors, the smoke from the engine, the cold to which he attributed his shivering. And the heavier the weight on his heart, the more strongly he felt that somewhere in the world, among some people, there was a pure, honourable, warm, refined life, full of love, affection, gaiety, and serenity. . . . He felt this and was so intensely miserable that one of the passengers, after looking in his face attentively, actually asked:

"You have the toothache, I suppose?"

In the town *maman* and Volodya lived with Marya Petrovna, a lady of noble rank, who had a large flat and let rooms to boarders. *maman* had two rooms, one with windows and two pictures in gold frames hanging on the walls, in which her bed stood and in which she lived, and a little dark room opening out of it in which Volodya lived. Here there was a sofa on which he slept, and, except that sofa, there was no other furniture; the rest of the room was entirely filled up with wicker baskets full of clothes, cardboard hat-boxes, and all sorts of rubbish, which *maman* preserved for some reason or other. Volodya prepared his lessons either in his mother's room or in the "general room," as the large room in which the boarders assembled at dinner-time and in the evening was called.

On reaching home he lay down on his sofa and put the quilt over him to stop his shivering. The cardboard hat-boxes, the wicker baskets, and the other rubbish, reminded him that he had not a room of his own, that he had no refuge in which he could get away from his mother, from her visitors, and from the voices that were floating up from the "general room." The satchel and the books lying about in the corners reminded him of the examination he had missed. . . . For some reason there came into his mind, quite inappropriately, Mentone, where he had lived with his father when he was seven years old; he thought of Biarritz and two little English girls with whom he ran about on the sand. . . . He tried to recall to his memory the colour of the sky, the sea, the height of the waves, and his mood at the time, but he could not succeed. The English girls flitted before his imagination as though they were living; all the rest was a medley of images that floated away in confusion. . . .

"No; it's cold here," thought Volodya. He got up, put on his overcoat, and went into the "general room."

There they were drinking tea. There were three people at the samovar: *maman;* an old lady with tortoiseshell pince-nez, who gave music lessons; and Avgustin Mihalitch, an elderly and very stout Frenchman, who was employed at a perfumery factory.

"I have had no dinner to-day," said *maman.* "I ought to send the maid to buy some bread."

"Dunyasha!" shouted the Frenchman.

It appeared that the maid had been sent out somewhere by the lady of the house.

"Oh, that's of no consequence," said the Frenchman, with a broad smile. "I will go for some bread myself at once. Oh, it's nothing."

He laid his strong, pungent cigar in a conspicuous place, put on his hat and went out. After he had gone away *maman* began telling the music teacher how she had been staying at the Shumihins', and how warmly they welcomed her.

"Lili Shumihin is a relation of mine, you know," she said. "Her late husband, General Shumihin, was a cousin of my husband. And she was a Baroness Kolb by birth. . . ."

"*Maman,* that's false!" said Volodya irritably. "Why tell lies?"

He knew perfectly well that what his mother said was true; in what she was saying about General Shumihin and about Baroness Kolb there was not a word of lying, but nevertheless he felt that she was lying. There was a suggestion of falsehood in her manner of speaking, in the expression of her face, in her eyes, in everything.

"You are lying," repeated Volodya; and he brought his fist down on the table with such force that all the crockery shook and *maman*'s tea was spilt over. "Why do you talk about generals and baronesses? It's all lies!"

The music teacher was disconcerted, and coughed into her handkerchief, affecting to sneeze, and *maman* began to cry.

"Where can I go?" thought Volodya.

He had been in the street already; he was ashamed to go to his schoolfellows. Again, quite incongruously, he remembered the two little English girls. . . . He paced up and down the "general room," and went into Avgustin Mihalitch's room. Here there was a strong smell of ethereal oils and glycerine soap. On the table, in the window, and even on the chairs, there were a number of bottles, glasses, and wineglasses containing fluids of various colours. Volodya took up from the table a newspaper, opened it and read the title *Figaro*. . . There was a strong and pleasant scent about the paper. Then he took a revolver from the table. . . .

"There, there! Don't take any notice of it." The music teacher was comforting *maman* in the next room. "He is young! Young people of his age never restrain themselves. One must resign oneself to that."

"No, Yevgenya Andreyevna; he's too spoilt," said *maman* in a singsong voice. "He has no one in authority over him, and I am weak and can do nothing. Oh, I am unhappy!"

Volodya put the muzzle of the revolver to his mouth, felt something like a trigger or spring, and pressed it with his finger. . . . Then felt something else projecting, and once more pressed it. Taking the muzzle out of his mouth, he wiped it with the lapel of his coat, looked at the lock. He had never in his life taken a weapon in his hand before. . . .

"I believe one ought to raise this . . ." he reflected. "Yes, it seems so."

Avgustin Mihalitch went into the "general room," and with a laugh began telling them about something. Volodya put the muzzle in his mouth again, pressed it with his teeth, and pressed something with his fingers. There was a sound of a shot. . . . Something hit Volodya in the back of his head with terrible violence, and he fell on the table with his face downwards among the bottles and glasses. Then he saw his father, as in Mentone, in a top-hat with a wide black band on it, wearing mourning for some lady, suddenly seize him by both hands, and they fell headlong into a very deep, dark pit.

Then everything was blurred and vanished.

THE HUSBAND

IN the course of the maneuvres the N— — cavalry regiment halted for a night at the district town of K— —. Such an event as the visit of officers always has the most exciting and inspiring effect on the inhabitants of provincial towns.

The shopkeepers dream of getting rid of the rusty sausages and "best brand" sardines that have been lying for ten years on their shelves; the inns and restaurants keep open all night; the Military Commandant, his secretary, and the local garrison put on their best uniforms; the police flit to and fro like mad, while the effect on the ladies is beyond all description.

The ladies of K— —, hearing the regiment approaching, forsook their pans of boiling jam and ran into the street. Forgetting their morning *deshabille* and general untidiness, they rushed breathless with excitement to meet the regiment, and listened greedily to the band playing the march.

Looking at their pale, ecstatic faces, one might have thought those strains came from some heavenly choir rather than from a military brass band.

"The regiment!" they cried joyfully. "The regiment is coming!"

What could this unknown regiment that came by chance to-day and would depart at dawn to-morrow mean to them?

Afterwards, when the officers were standing in the middle of the square, and, with their hands behind them, discussing the question of billets, all the ladies were gathered together at the examining magistrate's and vying with one another in their criticisms of the regiment. They already knew, goodness knows how, that the colonel was married, but not living with his wife; that the senior officer's wife had a baby born dead every year; that the adjutant was hopelessly in love with some countess, and had even once attempted suicide. They knew everything. When a pock-marked soldier in a red shirt darted past the windows, they knew for certain that it was Lieutenant Rymzov's orderly running about the town, trying to get some English bitter ale on tick for his master. They had only caught a passing glimpse of the officers' backs, but had already decided that there was not one handsome or interesting man among them. . . . Having talked to their hearts' content, they sent for the Military Commandant and the committee of the club, and instructed them at all costs to make arrangements for a dance.

Their wishes were carried out. At nine o'clock in the evening the military band was playing in the street before the club, while in the club itself the officers were dancing with the ladies of K— —. The ladies felt as though they were on wings. Intoxicated by the dancing, the music, and the clank of spurs, they threw themselves heart and soul into making the acquaintance of their new partners, and quite forgot their old civilian friends. Their fathers and husbands, forced temporarily into the background, crowded round the meagre refreshment table in the entrance hall. All these government cashiers, secretaries, clerks, and superintendents — stale, sickly-looking, clumsy figures — were perfectly well aware of their inferiority. They did not even enter the ball-room, but contented themselves with watching their wives and daughters in the distance dancing with the accomplished and graceful officers.

Among the husbands was Shalikov, the tax-collector — a narrow, spiteful soul, given to drink, with a big, closely cropped head, and thick, protruding lips. He had had a university education; there had been a time when he used to read progressive literature and sing students' songs, but now, as he said of himself, he was a tax-collector and nothing more.

He stood leaning against the doorpost, his eyes fixed on his wife, Anna Pavlovna, a little brunette of thirty, with a long nose and a pointed chin. Tightly laced, with her face carefully powdered, she danced without pausing for breath — danced till she was ready to drop exhausted. But though she was exhausted in body, her spirit was inexhaustible. . . .

One could see as she danced that her thoughts were with the past, that faraway past when she used to dance at the "College for Young Ladies," dreaming of a life of luxury and gaiety, and never doubting that her husband was to be a prince or, at the worst, a baron.

The tax-collector watched, scowling with spite. . . .

It was not jealousy he was feeling. He was ill-humoured – first, because the room was taken up with dancing and there was nowhere he could play a game of cards; secondly, because he could not endure the sound of wind instruments; and, thirdly, because he fancied the officers treated the civilians somewhat too casually and disdainfully. But what above everything revolted him and moved him to indignation was the expression of happiness on his wife's face.

"It makes me sick to look at her!" he muttered. "Going on for forty, and nothing to boast of at any time, and she must powder her face and lace herself up! And frizzing her hair! Flirting and making faces, and fancying she's doing the thing in style! Ugh! you're a pretty figure, upon my soul!"

Anna Pavlovna was so lost in the dance that she did not once glance at her husband.

"Of course not! Where do we poor country bumpkins come in!" sneered the tax-collector.

"We are at a discount now. . . . We're clumsy seals, unpolished provincial bears, and she's the queen of the ball! She has kept enough of her looks to please even officers. . . They'd not object to making love to her, I dare say!"

During the mazurka the tax-collector's face twitched with spite. A black-haired officer with prominent eyes and Tartar cheekbones danced the mazurka with Anna Pavlovna. Assuming a stern expression, he worked his legs with gravity and feeling, and so crooked his knees that he looked like a jack-a-dandy pulled by strings, while Anna Pavlovna, pale and thrilled, bending her figure languidly and turning her eyes up, tried to look as though she scarcely touched the floor, and evidently felt herself that she was not on earth, not at the local club, but somewhere far, far away – in the clouds. Not only her face but her whole figure was expressive of beatitude. . . . The tax-collector could endure it no longer; he felt a desire to jeer at that beatitude, to make Anna Pavlovna feel that she had forgotten herself, that life was by no means so delightful as she fancied now in her excitement. . . .

"You wait; I'll teach you to smile so blissfully," he muttered. "You are not a boarding-school miss, you are not a girl. An old fright ought to realise she is a fright!"

Petty feelings of envy, vexation, wounded vanity, of that small, provincial misanthropy engendered in petty officials by vodka and a sedentary life, swarmed in his heart like mice. Waiting for the end of the mazurka, he went into the hall and walked up to his wife. Anna Pavlovna was sitting with her partner, and, flirting her fan and coquettishly dropping her eyelids, was describing how she used to dance in Petersburg (her lips were pursed up like a rosebud, and she pronounced "at home in Pütürsburg").

"Anyuta, let us go home," croaked the tax-collector.

Seeing her husband standing before her, Anna Pavlovna started as though recalling the fact that she had a husband; then she flushed all over: she felt ashamed that she had such a sickly-looking, ill-humoured, ordinary husband.

"Let us go home," repeated the tax-collector.

"Why? It's quite early!"

"I beg you to come home!" said the tax-collector deliberately, with a spiteful expression.

"Why? Has anything happened?" Anna Pavlovna asked in a flutter.

"Nothing has happened, but I wish you to go home at once. . . . I wish it; that's enough, and without further talk, please."

Anna Pavlovna was not afraid of her husband, but she felt ashamed on account of her partner, who was looking at her husband with surprise and amusement. She got up and moved a little apart with her husband.

"What notion is this?" she began. "Why go home? Why, it's not eleven o'clock."

"I wish it, and that's enough. Come along, and that's all about it."

"Don't be silly! Go home alone if you want to."

"All right; then I shall make a scene."

The tax-collector saw the look of beatitude gradually vanish from his wife's face, saw how ashamed and miserable she was — and he felt a little happier.

"Why do you want me at once?" asked his wife.

"I don't want you, but I wish you to be at home. I wish it, that's all."

At first Anna Pavlovna refused to hear of it, then she began entreating her husband to let her stay just another half-hour; then, without knowing why, she began to apologise, to protest — and all in a whisper, with a smile, that the spectators might not suspect that she was having a tiff with her husband. She began assuring him she would not stay long, only another ten minutes, only five minutes; but the tax-collector stuck obstinately to his point.

"Stay if you like," he said, "but I'll make a scene if you do."

And as she talked to her husband Anna Pavlovna looked thinner, older, plainer. Pale, biting her lips, and almost crying, she went out to the entry and began putting on her things.

"You are not going?" asked the ladies in surprise. "Anna Pavlovna, you are not going, dear?"

"Her head aches," said the tax-collector for his wife.

Coming out of the club, the husband and wife walked all the way home in silence. The tax-collector walked behind his wife, and watching her downcast, sorrowful, humiliated little figure, he recalled the look of beatitude which had so irritated him at the club, and the consciousness that the beatitude was gone filled his soul with triumph. He was pleased and satisfied, and at the same time he felt the lack of something; he would have liked to go back to the club and make every one feel dreary and miserable, so that all might know how stale and worthless life is when you walk along the streets in the dark and hear the slush of the mud under your feet, and when you know that you will wake up next morning with nothing to look forward to but vodka and cards. Oh, how awful it is!

And Anna Pavlovna could scarcely walk. . . . She was still under the influence of the dancing, the music, the talk, the lights, and the noise; she asked herself as she walked along why God had thus afflicted her. She felt miserable, insulted, and choking with hate as she listened to her husband's heavy footsteps. She was silent, trying to think of the most offensive, biting, and venomous word she could hurl at her husband, and at the same time she was fully aware that no word could penetrate her tax-collector's hide. What did he care for words? Her bitterest enemy could not have contrived for her a more helpless position.

And meanwhile the band was playing and the darkness was full of the most rousing, intoxicating dance-tunes.

TERROR

My Friend's Story

DMITRI PETROVITCH SILIN had taken his degree and entered the government service in Petersburg, but at thirty he gave up his post and went in for agriculture. His farming was fairly successful, and yet it always seemed to me that he was not in his proper place, and that he would do well to go back to Petersburg. When sunburnt, grey with dust, exhausted with toil, he met me near the gates or at the entrance, and then at supper struggled with sleepiness and his wife took him off to bed as though he were a baby; or when, overcoming his sleepiness, he began in his soft, cordial, almost imploring voice, to talk about his really excellent ideas, I saw him not as a farmer nor an agriculturist, but only as a worried and exhausted man, and it was clear to me that he did not really care for farming, but that all he wanted was for the day to be over and "Thank God for it."

I liked to be with him, and I used to stay on his farm for two or three days at a time. I liked his house, and his park, and his big fruit garden, and the river – and his philosophy, which was clear, though rather spiritless and rhetorical. I suppose I was fond of him on his own account, though I can't say that for certain, as I have not up to now succeeded in analysing my feelings at that time. He was an intelligent, kind-hearted, genuine man, and not a bore, but I remember that when he confided to me his most treasured secrets and spoke of our relation to each other as friendship, it disturbed me unpleasantly, and I was conscious of awkwardness. In his affection for me there was something inappropriate, tiresome, and I should have greatly preferred commonplace friendly relations.

The fact is that I was extremely attracted by his wife, Marya Sergeyevna. I was not in love with her, but I was attracted by her face, her eyes, her voice, her walk. I missed her when I did not see her for a long time, and my imagination pictured no one at that time so eagerly as that young, beautiful, elegant woman. I had no definite designs in regard to her, and did not dream of anything of the sort, yet for some reason, whenever we were left alone, I remembered that her husband looked upon me as his friend, and I felt awkward. When she played my favourite pieces on the piano or told me something interesting, I listened with pleasure, and yet at the same time for some reason the reflection that she loved her husband, that he was my friend, and that she herself looked upon me as his friend, obtruded themselves upon me, my spirits flagged, and I became listless, awkward, and dull. She noticed this change and would usually say:

"You are dull without your friend. We must send out to the fields for him."

And when Dmitri Petrovitch came in, she would say:

"Well, here is your friend now. Rejoice."

So passed a year and a half.

It somehow happened one July Sunday that Dmitri Petrovitch and I, having nothing to do, drove to the big village of Klushino to buy things for supper. While we were going from one shop to another the sun set and the evening came on – the evening which I shall probably never forget in my life. After buying cheese that smelt like soap, and petrified sausages that smelt of tar, we went to the tavern to ask whether they had any beer. Our coachman went off to the blacksmith to get our horses shod, and we told him we would wait for him near the church. We walked, talked, laughed over our purchases, while a man who was known in the district by a very strange nickname, "Forty Martyrs," followed us all the while in silence with a mysterious air like a detective. This Forty Martyrs was no other than Gavril Syeverov, or more simply Gavryushka, who had been for a short time in my service as a footman and had been dismissed by me for drunkenness. He had been in Dmitri Petrovitch's service, too, and by him had been dismissed for the same vice. He was an inveterate drunkard, and indeed his whole life was as drunk and disorderly as himself. His father had been a priest and his mother of noble rank, so by birth he belonged to the privileged class; but however carefully I scrutinized his exhausted, respectful, and always perspiring face, his red beard now turning grey, his pitifully torn reefer jacket and his red shirt, I could not discover in him the faintest trace of anything we associate with privilege. He spoke of himself as a man of education, and used to say that he had been in a clerical school, but had not finished his studies there, as he had been expelled for smoking; then he had sung in the bishop's choir and lived for two years in a monastery, from which he was also expelled, but this time not for smoking but for "his weakness." He had walked all over two provinces, had presented petitions to the Consistory, and to various government offices, and had been four times on his trial. At last, being stranded in our district, he had served as a footman, as a forester, as a kennelman, as a sexton, had married a cook who was a widow and rather a loose character, and had so hopelessly sunk into a menial position, and had grown so used to filth and dirt, that he even spoke of his privileged origin with a certain scepticism, as of some myth. At the time I am describing, he was hanging about without a job, calling himself a carrier and a huntsman, and his wife had disappeared and made no sign.

From the tavern we went to the church and sat in the porch, waiting for the coachman. Forty Martyrs stood a little way off and put his hand before his mouth in order to cough in it respectfully if need be. By now it was dark; there was a strong smell of evening dampness, and the moon was on the point of rising. There were only two clouds in the clear starry sky exactly over our heads: one big one and one smaller; alone in the sky they were racing after one another like mother and child, in the direction where the sunset was glowing.

"What a glorious day!" said Dmitri Petrovitch.

"In the extreme . . ." Forty Martyrs assented, and he

coughed respectfully into his hand. "How was it, Dmitri Petrovitch, you thought to visit these parts?" he asked in an ingratiating voice, evidently anxious to get up a conversation.

Dmitri Petrovitch made no answer. Forty Martyrs heaved a deep sigh and said softly, not looking at us:

"I suffer solely through a cause to which I must answer to Almighty God. No doubt about it, I am a hopeless and incompetent man; but believe me, on my conscience, I am without a crust of bread and worse off than a dog. . . . Forgive me, Dmitri Petrovitch."

Silin was not listening, but sat musing with his head propped on his fists. The church stood at the end of the street on the high river-bank, and through the trellis gate of the enclosure we could see the river, the water-meadows on the near side of it, and the crimson glare of a camp fire about which black figures of men and horses were moving. And beyond the fire, further away, there were other lights, where there was a little village. They were singing there. On the river, and here and there on the meadows, a mist was rising. High narrow coils of mist, thick and white as milk, were trailing over the river, hiding the reflection of the stars and hovering over the willows. Every minute they changed their form, and it seemed as though some were embracing, others were bowing, others lifting up their arms to heaven with wide sleeves like priests, as though they were praying. . . . Probably they reminded Dmitri Petrovitch of ghosts and of the dead, for he turned facing me and asked with a mournful smile:

"Tell me, my dear fellow, why is it that when we want to tell some terrible, mysterious, and fantastic story, we draw our material, not from life, but invariably from the world of ghosts and of the shadows beyond the grave."

"We are frightened of what we don't understand."

"And do you understand life? Tell me: do you understand life better than the world beyond the grave?"

Dmitri Petrovitch was sitting quite close to me, so that I felt his breath upon my cheek. In the evening twilight his pale, lean face seemed paler than ever and his dark beard was black as soot. His eyes were sad, truthful, and a little frightened, as though he were about to tell me something horrible. He looked into my eyes and went on in his habitual imploring voice:

"Our life and the life beyond the grave are equally incomprehensible and horrible. If any one is afraid of ghosts he ought to be afraid, too, of me, and of those lights and of the sky, seeing that, if you come to reflect, all that is no less fantastic and beyond our grasp than apparitions from the other world. Prince Hamlet did not kill himself because he was afraid of the visions that might haunt his dreams after death. I like that famous soliloquy of his, but, to be candid, it never touched my soul. I will confess to you as a friend that in moments of depression I have sometimes pictured to myself the hour of my death. My fancy invented thousands of the gloomiest visions, and I have succeeded in working myself up to an agonizing exaltation, to a state of nightmare, and I assure you that that did not seem to me more terrible than reality. What I mean is, apparitions are terrible, but life is terrible, too. I don't understand life and I am afraid of it, my dear boy; I don't know. Perhaps I am a morbid person, unhinged. It seems to a sound, healthy man that he understands everything he sees and hears, but that 'seeming' is lost to me, and from day to day I am poisoning myself with terror. There is a disease, the fear of open spaces, but my disease is the fear of life. When I lie on the grass and watch a little beetle which was born yesterday and understands nothing, it seems to me that its life consists of nothing else but fear, and in it I see myself."

"What is it exactly you are frightened of?" I asked.

"I am afraid of everything. I am not by nature a profound thinker, and I take little interest in such questions as the life beyond the grave, the destiny of humanity, and, in fact, I am rarely carried away to the heights. What chiefly frightens me is the common routine of life from which none of us can escape. I am incapable of distinguishing what is true and what is false in my actions, and they worry me. I recognize that education and the conditions of life have imprisoned me in a narrow circle of falsity, that my whole life is nothing else than a daily effort to deceive myself and other people, and to avoid noticing it; and I am frightened at the thought that to the day of my death I shall not escape from this falsity. To-day I do something and to-morrow I do not understand why I did it. I entered the service in Petersburg and took fright; I came here to work on the land, and here, too, I am frightened. . . . I see that we know very little and so make mistakes every day. We are unjust, we slander one another and spoil each other's lives, we waste all our powers on trash which we do not need and which hinders us from living; and that frightens me, because I don't understand why and for whom it is necessary. I don't understand men, my dear fellow, and I am afraid of them. It frightens me to look at the peasants, and I don't know for what higher objects they are suffering and what they are living for. If life is an enjoyment, then they are unnecessary, superfluous people; if the object and meaning of life is to be found in poverty and unending, hopeless ignorance, I can't understand for whom and what this torture is necessary. I understand no one and nothing. Kindly try to understand this specimen, for instance," said Dmitri Petrovitch, pointing to Forty Martyrs. "Think of him!"

Noticing that we were looking at him, Forty Martyrs coughed deferentially into his fist and said:

"I was always a faithful servant with good masters, but the great trouble has been spirituous liquor. If a poor fellow like me were shown consideration and given a place, I would kiss the ikon. My word's my bond."

The sexton walked by, looked at us in amazement, and began pulling the rope. The bell, abruptly breaking upon the stillness of the evening, struck ten with a slow and prolonged note.

"It's ten o'clock, though," said Dmitri Petrovitch. "It's time we were going. Yes, my dear fellow," he sighed, "if only you knew how afraid I am of my ordinary everyday thoughts, in which one would have thought there should be nothing dreadful. To prevent myself thinking I distract my mind with work and try to tire myself out that I may sleep sound at night. Children, a wife — all that seems ordinary with other people; but how that weighs upon me, my dear fellow!"

He rubbed his face with his hands, cleared his throat, and laughed.

"If I could only tell you how I have played the fool in my life! " he said. "They all tell me that I have a sweet wife, charming children, and that I am a good husband and father.

They think I am very happy and envy me. But since it has come to that, I will tell you in secret: my happy family life is only a grievous misunderstanding, and I am afraid of it." His pale face was distorted by a wry smile. He put his arm round my waist and went on in an undertone:

"You are my true friend; I believe in you and have a deep respect for you. Heaven gave us friendship that we may open our hearts and escape from the secrets that weigh upon us. Let me take advantage of your friendly feeling for me and tell you the whole truth. My home life, which seems to you so enchanting, is my chief misery and my chief terror. I got married in a strange and stupid way. I must tell you that I was madly in love with Masha before I married her, and was courting her for two years. I asked her to marry me five times, and she refused me because she did not care for me in the least. The sixth, when burning with passion I crawled on my knees before her and implored her to take a beggar and marry me, she consented. . . . What she said to me was: 'I don't love you, but I will be true to you. . . .' I accepted that condition with rapture. At the time I understood what that meant, but I swear to God I don't understand it now. 'I don't love you, but I will be true to you.' What does that mean? It's a fog, a darkness. I love her now as intensely as I did the day we were married, while she, I believe, is as indifferent as ever, and I believe she is glad when I go away from home. I don't know for certain whether she cares for me or not – I don't know, I don't know; but, as you see, we live under the same roof, call each other 'thou,' sleep together, have children, our property is in common. . . . What does it mean, what does it mean? What is the object of it? And do you understand it at all, my dear fellow? It's cruel torture! Because I don't understand our relations, I hate, sometimes her, sometimes myself, sometimes both at once. Everything is in a tangle in my brain; I torment myself and grow stupid. And as though to spite me, she grows more beautiful every day, she is getting more wonderful. . . I fancy her hair is marvellous, and her smile is like no other woman's. I love her, and I know that my love is hopeless. Hopeless love for a woman by whom one has two children! Is that intelligible? And isn't it terrible? Isn't it more terrible than ghosts?"

He was in the mood to have talked on a good deal longer, but luckily we heard the coachman's voice. Our horses had arrived. We got into the carriage, and Forty Martyrs, taking off his cap, helped us both into the carriage with an expression that suggested that he had long been waiting for an opportunity to come in contact with our precious persons.

"Dmitri Petrovitch, let me come to you," he said, blinking furiously and tilting his head on one side. "Show divine mercy! I am dying of hunger!"

"Very well," said Silin. "Come, you shall stay three days, and then we shall see."

"Certainly, sir," said Forty Martyrs, overjoyed. "I'll come today, sir."

It was a five miles' drive home. Dmitri Petrovitch, glad that he had at last opened his heart to his friend, kept his arm round my waist all the way; and speaking now, not with bitterness and not with apprehension, but quite cheerfully, told me that if everything had been satisfactory in his home life, he should have returned to Petersburg and taken up scientific work there. The movement which had driven so many gifted young men into the country was, he said, a deplorable movement. We had plenty of rye and wheat in Russia, but absolutely no cultured people. The strong and gifted among the young ought to take up science, art, and politics; to act otherwise meant being wasteful. He generalized with pleasure and expressed regret that he would be parting from me early next morning, as he had to go to a sale of timber.

And I felt awkward and depressed, and it seemed to me that I was deceiving the man. And at the same time it was pleasant to me. I gazed at the immense crimson moon which was rising, and pictured the tall, graceful, fair woman, with her pale face, always well-dressed and fragrant with some special scent, rather like musk, and for some reason it pleased me to think she did not love her husband.

On reaching home, we sat down to supper. Marya Sergeyevna, laughing, regaled us with our purchases, and I thought that she certainly had wonderful hair and that her smile was unlike any other woman's. I watched her, and I wanted to detect in every look and movement that she did not love her husband, and I fancied that I did see it.

Dmitri Petrovitch was soon struggling with sleep. After supper he sat with us for ten minutes and said:

"Do as you please, my friends, but I have to be up at three o'clock tomorrow morning. Excuse my leaving you."

He kissed his wife tenderly, pressed my hand with warmth and gratitude, and made me promise that I would certainly come the following week. That he might not oversleep next morning, he went to spend the night in the lodge.

Marya Sergeyevna always sat up late, in the Petersburg fashion, and for some reason on this occasion I was glad of it.

"And now," I began when we were left alone, "and now you'll be kind and play me something."

I felt no desire for music, but I did not know how to begin the conversation. She sat down to the piano and played, I don't remember what. I sat down beside her and looked at her plump white hands and tried to read something on her cold, indifferent face. Then she smiled at something and looked at me.

"You are dull without your friend," she said.

I laughed.

"It would be enough for friendship to be here once a month, but I turn up oftener than once a week."

Saying this, I got up and walked from one end of the room to the other. She too got up and walked away to the fireplace.

"What do you mean to say by that?" she said, raising her large, clear eyes and looking at me.

I made no answer.

"What you say is not true," she went on, after a moment's thought. "You only come here on account of Dmitri Petrovitch. Well, I am very glad. One does not often see such friendships nowadays."

"Aha!" I thought, and, not knowing what to say, I asked: "Would you care for a turn in the garden?"

I went out upon the verandah. Nervous shudders were running over my head and I felt chilly with excitement. I was convinced now that our conversation would be utterly trivial, and that there was nothing particular we should be able to say to one another, but that, that night, what I did not dare to dream of was bound to happen — that it was bound to be that night or never.

"What lovely weather!" I said aloud.

"It makes absolutely no difference to me," she answered.

I went into the drawing-room. Marya Sergeyevna was standing, as before, near the fireplace, with her hands behind her back, looking away and thinking of something.

"Why does it make no difference to you?" I asked.

"Because I am bored. You are only bored without your friend, but I am always bored. However . . . that is of no interest to you."

I sat down to the piano and struck a few chords, waiting to hear what she would say.

"Please don't stand on ceremony," she said, looking angrily at me, and she seemed as though on the point of crying with vexation. "If you are sleepy, go to bed. Because you are Dmitri Petrovitch's friend, you are not in duty bound to be bored with his wife's company. I don't want a sacrifice. Please go."

I did not, of course, go to bed. She went out on the verandah while I remained in the drawing-room and spent five minutes turning over the music. Then I went out, too. We stood close together in the shadow of the curtains, and below us were the steps bathed in moonlight. The black shadows of the trees stretched across the flower beds and the yellow sand of the paths.

"I shall have to go away tomorrow, too," I said.

"Of course, if my husband's not at home you can't stay here," she said sarcastically. "I can imagine how miserable you would be if you were in love with me! Wait a bit: one day I shall throw myself on your neck. . . . I shall see with what horror you will run away from me. That would be interesting."

Her words and her pale face were angry, but her eyes were full of tender passionate love. I already looked upon this lovely creature as my property, and then for the first time I noticed that she had golden eyebrows, exquisite eyebrows. I had never seen such eyebrows before. The thought that I might at once press her to my heart, caress her, touch her wonderful hair, seemed to me such a miracle that I laughed and shut my eyes.

"It's bed-time now. . . . A peaceful night," she said.

"I don't want a peaceful night," I said, laughing, following her into the drawing-room. "I shall curse this night if it is a peaceful one."

Pressing her hand, and escorting her to the door, I saw by her face that she understood me, and was glad that I understood her, too.

I went to my room. Near the books on the table lay Dmitri Petrovitch's cap, and that reminded me of his affection for me. I took my stick and went out into the garden. The mist had risen here, too, and the same tall, narrow, ghostly shapes which I had seen earlier on the river were trailing round the trees and bushes and wrapping about them. What a pity I could not talk to them!

In the extraordinarily transparent air, each leaf, each drop of dew stood out distinctly; it was all smiling at me in the stillness half asleep, and as I passed the green seats I recalled the words in some play of Shakespeare's: "How sweetly falls the moonlight on yon seat!"

There was a mound in the garden; I went up it and sat down. I was tormented by a delicious feeling. I knew for certain that in a moment I should hold in my arms, should press to my heart her magnificent body, should kiss her golden eyebrows; and I wanted to disbelieve it, to tantalize myself, and was sorry that she had cost me so little trouble and had yielded so soon.

But suddenly I heard heavy footsteps. A man of medium height appeared in the avenue, and I recognized him at once as Forty Martyrs. He sat down on the bench and heaved a deep sigh, then crossed himself three times and lay down. A minute later he got up and lay on the other side. The gnats and the dampness of the night prevented his sleeping.

"Oh, life!" he said. "Wretched, bitter life!"

Looking at his bent, wasted body and hearing his heavy, noisy sighs, I thought of an unhappy, bitter life of which the confession had been made to me that day, and I felt uneasy and frightened at my blissful mood. I came down the knoll and went to the house.

"Life, as he thinks, is terrible," I thought, "so don't stand on ceremony with it, bend it to your will, and until it crushes you, snatch all you can wring from it."

Marya Sergeyevna was standing on the verandah. I put my arms round her without a word, and began greedily kissing her eyebrows, her temples, her neck. . . .

In my room she told me she had loved me for a long time, more than a year. She vowed eternal love, cried and begged me to take her away with me. I repeatedly took her to the window to look at her face in the moonlight, and she seemed to me a lovely dream, and I made haste to hold her tight to convince myself of the truth of it. It was long since I had known such raptures. . . . Yet somewhere far away at the bottom of my heart I felt an awkwardness, and I was ill at ease. In her love for me there was something incongruous and burdensome, just as in Dmitri Petrovitch's friendship. It was a great, serious passion with tears and vows, and I wanted nothing serious in it – no tears, no vows, no talk of the future. Let that moonlight night flash through our lives like a meteor and – *basta!*

At three o'clock she went out of my room, and, while I was standing in the doorway, looking after her, at the end of the corridor Dmitri Petrovitch suddenly made his appearance; she started and stood aside to let him pass, and her whole figure was expressive of repulsion. He gave a strange smile, coughed, and came into my room.

"I forgot my cap here yesterday," he said without looking at me.

He found it and, holding it in both hands, put it on his head; then he looked at my confused face, at my slippers, and said in a strange, husky voice unlike his own:

"I suppose it must be my fate that I should understand nothing. . . . If you understand anything, I congratulate you. It's all darkness before my eyes."

And he went out, clearing his throat. Afterwards from the window I saw him by the stable, harnessing the horses with his own hands. His hands were trembling, he was in nervous haste and kept looking round at the house; probably he was feeling terror. Then he got into the gig, and, with a strange expression as though afraid of being pursued, lashed the horses.

Shortly afterwards I set off, too. The sun was already rising, and the mist of the previous day clung timidly to the bushes and the hillocks. On the box of the carriage was sitting Forty Martyrs; he had already succeeded in getting drunk and was muttering tipsy nonsense.

"I am a free man," he shouted to the horses. "Ah, my honeys, I am a nobleman in my own right, if you care to know!"

The terror of Dmitri Petrovitch, the thought of whom I could not get out of my head, infected me. I thought of what had happened and could make nothing of it. I looked at the rooks, and it seemed so strange and terrible that they were flying.

"Why have I done this?" I kept asking myself in bewilderment and despair. "Why has it turned out like this and not differently? To whom and for what was it necessary that she should love me in earnest, and that he should come into my room to fetch his cap? What had a cap to do with it?

I set off for Petersburg that day, and I have not seen Dmitri Petrovitch nor his wife since. I am told that they are still living together.

A PROBLEM

THE strictest measures were taken that the Uskovs' family secret might not leak out and become generally known. Half of the servants were sent off to the theatre or the circus; the other half were sitting in the kitchen and not allowed to leave it. Orders were given that no one was to be admitted. The wife of the Colonel, her sister, and the governess, though they had been initiated into the secret, kept up a pretence of knowing nothing; they sat in the dining-room and did not show themselves in the drawing-room or the hall.

Sasha Uskov, the young man of twenty-five who was the cause of all the commotion, had arrived some time before, and by the advice of kind-hearted Ivan Markovitch, his uncle, who was taking his part, he sat meekly in the hall by the door leading to the study, and prepared himself to make an open, candid explanation.

The other side of the door, in the study, a family council was being held. The subject under discussion was an exceedingly disagreeable and delicate one. Sasha Uskov had cashed at one of the banks a false promissory note, and it had become due for payment three days before, and now his two paternal uncles and Ivan Markovitch, the brother of his dead mother, were deciding the question whether they should pay the money and save the family honour, or wash their hands of it and leave the case to go for trial.

To outsiders who have no personal interest in the matter such questions seem simple; for those who are so unfortunate as to have to decide them in earnest they are extremely difficult. The uncles had been talking for a long time, but the problem seemed no nearer decision.

"My friends!" said the uncle who was a colonel, and there was a note of exhaustion and bitterness in his voice. "Who says that family honour is a mere convention? I don't say that at all. I am only warning you against a false view; I am pointing out the possibility of an unpardonable mistake. How can you fail to see it? I am not speaking Chinese; I am speaking Russian!"

"My dear fellow, we do understand," Ivan Markovitch protested mildly.

"How can you understand if you say that I don't believe in family honour? I repeat once more: fa-mil-y ho-nour falsely un-der-stood is a prejudice! Falsely understood! That's what I say: whatever may be the motives for screening a scoundrel, whoever he may be, and helping him to escape punishment, it is contrary to law and unworthy of a gentleman. It's not saving the family honour; it's civic cowardice! Take the army, for instance. . . . The honour of the army is more precious to us than any other honour, yet we don't screen our guilty members, but condemn them. And does the honour of the army suffer in consequence? Quite the opposite!"

The other paternal uncle, an official in the Treasury, a taciturn, dull-witted, and rheumatic man, sat silent, or spoke only of the fact that the Uskovs' name would get into the newspapers if the case went for trial. His opinion was that the case ought to be hushed up from the first and not become public property; but, apart from publicity in the newspapers, he advanced no other argument in support of this opinion.

The maternal uncle, kind-hearted Ivan Markovitch, spoke smoothly, softly, and with a tremor in his voice. He began with saying that youth has its rights and its peculiar temptations. Which of us has not been young, and who has not been led astray? To say nothing of ordinary mortals, even great men have not escaped errors and mistakes in their youth. Take, for instance, the biography of great writers. Did not every one of them gamble, drink, and draw down upon himself the anger of right-thinking people in his young days? If Sasha's error bordered upon crime, they must remember that Sasha had received practically no education; he had been expelled from the high school in the fifth class; he had lost his parents in early childhood, and so had been left at the tenderest age without guidance and good, benevolent influences. He was nervous, excitable, had no firm ground under his feet, and, above all, he had been unlucky. Even if he were guilty, anyway he deserved indulgence and the sympathy of all compassionate souls. He ought, of course, to be punished, but he was punished as it was by his conscience and the agonies he was enduring now while awaiting the sentence of his relations. The comparison with the army made by the Colonel was delightful, and did credit to his lofty intelligence; his appeal to their feeling of public duty spoke for the chivalry of his soul, but they must not forget that in each individual the citizen is closely linked with the Christian. . . .

"Shall we be false to civic duty," Ivan Markovitch exclaimed passionately, "if instead of punishing an erring boy we hold out to him a helping hand?"

Ivan Markovitch talked further of family honour. He had not the honour to belong to the Uskov family himself, but he knew their distinguished family went back to the thirteenth century; he did not forget for a minute, either, that his precious, beloved sister had been the wife of one of the representatives of that name. In short, the family was dear to him for many reasons, and he refused to admit the idea that, for the sake of a paltry fifteen hundred roubles, a blot should be cast on the escutcheon that was beyond all price. If all the motives he had brought forward were not sufficiently convincing, he, Ivan Markovitch, in conclusion, begged his listeners to ask themselves what was meant by crime? Crime is an immoral act founded upon ill-will. But is the will of man free? Philosophy has not yet given a positive answer to that question. Different views were held by the learned. The latest school of Lombroso, for instance, denies the freedom of the will, and considers every crime as the product of the purely anatomical peculiarities of the individual.

"Ivan Markovitch," said the Colonel, in a voice of entreaty, "we are talking seriously about an important matter, and you bring in Lombroso, you clever fellow. Think a little, what are you saying all this for? Can you imagine that all your thunderings and rhetoric will furnish an answer to the question?"

Sasha Uskov sat at the door and listened. He felt neither terror, shame, nor depression, but only weariness and inward emptiness. It seemed to him that it made absolutely no difference to him whether they forgave him or not; he had come here to hear his sentence and to explain himself simply because kind-hearted Ivan Markovitch had begged him to do so. He was not afraid of the future. It made no difference to him where he was: here in the hall, in prison, or in Siberia.

"If Siberia, then let it be Siberia, damn it all!"

He was sick of life and found it insufferably hard. He was inextricably involved in debt; he had not a farthing in his pocket; his family had become detestable to him; he would have to part from his friends and his women sooner or later, as they had begun to be too contemptuous of his sponging on them. The future looked black.

Sasha was indifferent, and was only disturbed by one circumstance; the other side of the door they were calling him a scoundrel and a criminal. Every minute he was on the point of jumping up, bursting into the study and shouting in answer to the detestable metallic voice of the Colonel:

"You are lying!"

"Criminal" is a dreadful word — that is what murderers, thieves, robbers are; in fact, wicked and morally hopeless people. And Sasha was very far from being all that. . . . It was true he owed a great deal and did not pay his debts. But debt is not a crime, and it is unusual for a man not to be in debt. The Colonel and Ivan Markovitch were both in debt. . . .

"What have I done wrong besides?" Sasha wondered.

He had discounted a forged note. But all the young men he knew did the same. Handrikov and Von Burst always forged IOU's from their parents or friends when their allowances were not paid at the regular time, and then when they got their money from home they redeemed them before they became due. Sasha had done the same, but had not redeemed the IOU because he had not got the money which Handrikov had promised to lend him. He was not to blame; it was the fault of circumstances. It was true that the use of another person's signature was considered reprehensible; but, still, it was not a crime but a generally accepted dodge, an ugly formality which injured no one and was quite harmless, for in forging the Colonel's signature Sasha had had no intention of causing anybody damage or loss.

"No, it doesn't mean that I am a criminal . . ." thought Sasha. "And it's not in my character to bring myself to commit a crime. I am soft, emotional. . . . When I have the money I help the poor...."

Sasha was musing after this fashion while they went on talking the other side of the door.

"But, my friends, this is endless," the Colonel declared, getting excited. "Suppose we were to forgive him and pay the money. You know he would not give up leading a dissipated life, squandering money, making debts, going to our tailors and ordering suits in our names! Can you guarantee that this will be his last prank? As far as I am concerned, I have no faith whatever in his reforming!"

The official of the Treasury muttered something in reply; after him Ivan Markovitch began talking blandly and suavely again. The Colonel moved his chair impatiently and drowned the other's words with his detestable metallic voice. At last the door opened and Ivan Markovitch came out of the study; there were patches of red on his lean shaven face.

"Come along," he said, taking Sasha by the hand. "Come and speak frankly from your heart. Without pride, my dear boy, humbly and from your heart."

Sasha went into the study. The official of the Treasury was sitting down; the Colonel was standing before the table with one hand in his pocket and one knee on a chair. It was smoky and stifling in the study. Sasha did not look at the official or the Colonel; he felt suddenly ashamed and uncomfortable. He looked uneasily at Ivan Markovitch and muttered:

"I'll pay it . . . I'll give it back. . . ."

"What did you expect when you discounted the IOU?" he heard a metallic voice.

"I . . . Handrikov promised to lend me the money before now."

Sasha could say no more. He went out of the study and sat down again on the chair near the door.

He would have been glad to go away altogether at once, but he was choking with hatred and he awfully wanted to remain, to tear the Colonel to pieces, to say something rude to him. He sat trying to think of something violent and effective to say to his hated uncle, and at that moment a woman's figure, shrouded in the twilight, appeared at the drawing-room door. It was the Colonel's wife. She beckoned Sasha to her, and, wringing her hands, said, weeping:

"*Alexandre,* I know you don't like me, but . . . listen to me; listen, I beg you. . . . But, my dear, how can this have happened? Why, it's awful, awful! For goodness' sake, beg them, defend yourself, entreat them."

Sasha looked at her quivering shoulders, at the big tears that were rolling down her cheeks, heard behind his back the hollow, nervous voices of worried and exhausted people, and shrugged his shoulders. He had not in the least expected that his aristocratic relations would raise such a tempest over a paltry fifteen hundred roubles! He could not understand her tears nor the quiver of their voices.

An hour later he heard that the Colonel was getting the best of it; the uncles were finally inclining to let the case go for trial.

"The matter's settled," said the Colonel, sighing. "Enough."

After this decision all the uncles, even the emphatic Colonel, became noticeably depressed. A silence followed.

"Merciful Heavens!" sighed Ivan Markovitch. "My poor sister!"

And he began saying in a subdued voice that most likely his sister, Sasha's mother, was present unseen in the study at that moment. He felt in his soul how the unhappy, saintly woman was weeping, grieving, and begging for her boy. For the sake of her peace beyond the grave, they ought to spare Sasha.

The sound of a muffled sob was heard. Ivan Markovitch was weeping and muttering something which it was impossible to catch through the door. The Colonel got up and paced from corner to corner. The long conversation began over again.

But then the clock in the drawing-room struck two. The family council was over. To avoid seeing the person who had moved him to such wrath, the Colonel went from the study, not into the hall, but into the vestibule. . . . Ivan Markovitch came out into the hall. . . . He was agitated and rubbing his hands joyfully. His tear-stained eyes looked good-humoured and his mouth was twisted into a smile.

"Capital," he said to Sasha. "Thank God! You can go home, my dear, and sleep tranquilly. We have decided to pay the sum, but on condition that you repent and come with me tomorrow into the country and set to work."

A minute later Ivan Markovitch and Sasha in their great-coats and caps were going down the stairs. The uncle was muttering something edifying. Sasha did not listen, but felt as though some uneasy weight were gradually slipping off his shoulders. They had forgiven him; he was free! A gust of joy sprang up within him and sent a sweet chill to his heart. He longed to breathe, to move swiftly, to live! Glancing at the street lamps and the black sky, he remembered that Von Burst was celebrating his name-day that evening at the "Bear," and again a rush of joy flooded his soul....

"I am going!" he decided.

But then he remembered he had not a farthing, that the companions he was going to would despise him at once for his empty pockets. He must get hold of some money, come what may!

"Uncle, lend me a hundred roubles," he said to Ivan Markovitch.

His uncle, surprised, looked into his face and backed against a lamp-post.

"Give it to me," said Sasha, shifting impatiently from one foot to the other and beginning to pant. "Uncle, I entreat you, give me a hundred roubles."

His face worked; he trembled, and seemed on the point of attacking his uncle. . . .

"Won't you?" he kept asking, seeing that his uncle was still amazed and did not understand. "Listen. If you don't, I'll give myself up tomorrow! I won't let you pay the IOU! I'll present another false note tomorrow!"

Petrified, muttering something incoherent in his horror, Ivan Markovitch took a hundred-rouble note out of his pocket-book and gave it to Sasha. The young man took it and walked rapidly away from him. . . .

Taking a sledge, Sasha grew calmer, and felt a rush of joy within him again. The "rights of youth" of which kind-hearted Ivan Markovitch had spoken at the family council woke up and asserted themselves. Sasha pictured the drinking-party before him, and, among the bottles, the women, and his friends, the thought flashed through his mind:

"Now I see that I am a criminal; yes, I am a criminal."

NOT WANTED

BETWEEN six and seven o'clock on a July evening, a crowd of summer visitors – mostly fathers of families – burdened with parcels, portfolios, and ladies' hat-boxes, was trailing along from the little station of Helkovo, in the direction of the summer villas. They all looked exhausted, hungry, and ill-humoured, as though the sun were not shining and the grass were not green for them.

Trudging along among the others was Pavel Matveyitch Zaikin, a member of the Circuit Court, a tall, stooping man, in a cheap cotton dust-coat and with a cockade on his faded cap. He was perspiring, red in the face, and gloomy. . . .

"Do you come out to your holiday home every day?" said a summer visitor, in ginger-coloured trousers, addressing him.

"No, not every day," Zaikin answered sullenly. "My wife and son are staying here all the while, and I come down two or three times a week. I haven't time to come every day; besides, it is expensive."

"You're right there; it is expensive," sighed he of the ginger trousers. "In town you can't walk to the station, you have to take a cab; and then, the ticket costs forty-two kopecks; you buy a paper for the journey; one is tempted to drink a glass of vodka. It's all petty expenditure not worth considering, but, mind you, in the course of the summer it will run up to some two hundred roubles. Of course, to be in the lap of Nature is worth any money – I don't dispute it . . . idyllic and all the rest of it; but of course, with the salary an official gets, as you know yourself, every farthing has to be considered. If you waste a halfpenny you lie awake all night. . . . Yes. . . I receive, my dear sir – I haven't the honour of knowing your name – I receive a salary of very nearly two thousand roubles a year. I am a civil councillor, I smoke second-rate tobacco, and I haven't a rouble to spare to buy Vichy water, prescribed me by the doctor for gall-stones."

"It's altogether abominable," said Zaikin after a brief silence. "I maintain, sir, that summer holidays are the invention of the devil and of woman. The devil was actuated in the present instance by malice, woman by excessive frivolity. Mercy on us, it is not life at all; it is hard labour, it is hell! It's hot and stifling, you can hardly breathe, and you wander about like a lost soul and can find no refuge. In town there is no furniture, no servants. . . everything has been carried off to the villa: you eat what you can get; you go without your tea because there is no one to heat the samovar; you can't wash yourself; and when you come down here into this 'lap of Nature' you have to walk, if you please, through the dust and heat. . . . Phew! Are you married?"

"Yes. . . three children," sighs Ginger Trousers.

"It's abominable altogether. . . . It's a wonder we are still alive."

At last the summer visitors reached their destination. Zaikin said good-bye to Ginger Trousers and went into his villa. He found a death-like silence in the house. He could hear nothing but the buzzing of the gnats, and the prayer for help of a fly destined for the dinner of a spider. The windows were hung with muslin curtains, through which the faded flowers of the geraniums showed red. On the unpainted wooden walls near the oleographs flies were slumbering. There was not a soul in the passage, the kitchen, or the dining-room. In the room which was called indifferently the parlour or the drawing-room, Zaikin found his son Petya, a little boy of six. Petya was sitting at the table, and breathing loudly with his lower lip stuck out, was engaged in cutting out the figure of a knave of diamonds from a card.

"Oh, that's you, father!" he said, without turning round. "Good-evening."

"Good-evening. . . . And where is mother?"

"Mother? She is gone with Olga Kirillovna to a rehearsal of the play. The day after tomorrow they will have a performance. And they will take me, too. . . . And will you go?"

"H'm! . . . When is she coming back?"

"She said she would be back in the evening."

"And where is Natalya?"

"Mamma took Natalya with her to help her dress for the performance, and Akulina has gone to the wood to get mushrooms. Father, why is it that when gnats bite you their stomachs get red?"

"I don't know. . . . Because they suck blood. So there is no one in the house, then?"

"No one; I am all alone in the house."

Zaikin sat down in an easy-chair, and for a moment gazed blankly at the window.

"Who is going to get our dinner?" he asked.

"They haven't cooked any dinner today, father. Mamma thought you were not coming today, and did not order any dinner. She is going to have dinner with Olga Kirillovna at the rehearsal."

"Oh, thank you very much; and you, what have you to eat?"

"I've had some milk. They bought me six kopecks' worth of milk. And, father, why do gnats suck blood?"

Zaikin suddenly felt as though something heavy were rolling down on his liver and beginning to gnaw it. He felt so vexed, so aggrieved, and so bitter, that he was choking and tremulous; he wanted to jump up, to bang something on the floor, and to burst into loud abuse; but then he remembered that his doctor had absolutely forbidden him all excitement, so he got up, and making an effort to control himself, began whistling a tune from "Les Huguenots."

"Father, can you act in plays?" he heard Petya's voice.

"Oh, don't worry me with stupid questions!" said Zaikin, getting angry. "He sticks to one like a leaf in the bath! Here you are, six years old, and just as silly as you were three years ago. . . . Stupid, neglected child! Why are you spoiling those cards, for instance? How dare you spoil them?"

"These cards aren't yours," said Petya, turning round. "Natalya gave them me."

"You are telling fibs, you are telling fibs, you horrid boy!" said Zaikin, growing more and more irritated. "You are always telling fibs! You want a whipping, you horrid little pig! I will pull your ears!

Petya leapt up, and craning his neck, stared fixedly at his father's red and wrathful face. His big eyes first began blinking, then were dimmed with moisture, and the boy's face began working.

"But why are you scolding?" squealed Petya. "Why do you attack me, you stupid? I am not interfering with anybody; I am not naughty; I do what I am told, and yet . . . you are cross! Why are you scolding me?"

The boy spoke with conviction, and wept so bitterly that Zaikin felt conscience-stricken.

"Yes, really, why am I falling foul of him?" he thought. "Come, come," he said, touching the boy on the shoulder. "I am sorry, Petya . . . forgive me. You are my good boy, my nice boy, I love you."

Petya wiped his eyes with his sleeve, sat down, with a sigh, in the same place and began cutting out the queen. Zaikin went off to his own room. He stretched himself on the sofa, and putting his hands behind his head, sank into thought. The boy's tears had softened his anger, and by degrees the oppression on his liver grew less. He felt nothing but exhaustion and hunger.

"Father," he heard on the other side of the door, "shall I show you my collection of insects?"

"Yes, show me."

Petya came into the study and handed his father a long green box. Before raising it to his ear Zaikin could hear a despairing buzz and the scratching of claws on the sides of the box. Opening the lid, he saw a number of butterflies, beetles, grasshoppers, and flies fastened to the bottom of the box with pins. All except two or three butterflies were still alive and moving.

"Why, the grasshopper is still alive!" said Petya in surprise. "I caught him yesterday morning, and he is still alive!"

"Who taught you to pin them in this way?"

"Olga Kirillovna."

"Olga Kirillovna ought to be pinned down like that herself!" said Zaikin with repulsion. "Take them away! It's shameful to torture animals."

"My God! How horribly he is being brought up!" he thought, as Petya went out.

Pavel Matveyitch forgot his exhaustion and hunger, and thought of nothing but his boy's future. Meanwhile, outside the light was gradually fading. . . . He could hear the summer visitors trooping back from the evening bathe. Some one was stopping near the open dining-room window and shouting: "Do you want any mushrooms?" And getting no answer, shuffled on with bare feet. . . . But at last, when the dusk was so thick that the outlines of the geraniums behind the muslin curtain were lost, and whiffs of the freshness of evening were coming in at the window, the door of the passage was thrown open noisily, and there came a sound of rapid footsteps, talk, and laughter. . . .

"Mamma!" shrieked Petya.

Zaikin peeped out of his study and saw his wife, Nadyezhda Stepanovna, healthy and rosy as ever; with her he saw Olga Kirillovna, a spare woman with fair hair and heavy freckles, and two unknown men: one a lanky young man with curly red hair and a big Adam's apple; the other, a short stubby man with a shaven face like an actor's and a bluish crooked chin.

"Natalya, set the samovar," cried Nadyezhda Stepanovna, with a loud rustle of her skirts. "I hear Pavel Matveyitch is come. Pavel, where are you? Good-evening, Pavel!" she said, running into the study breathlessly. "So you've come. I am so glad. . . . Two of our amateurs have come with me. . . . Come, I'll introduce you. . . . Here, the taller one is Koromyslov . . . he sings splendidly; and the other, the little one . . . is called Smerkalov: he is a real actor . . . he recites magnificently. Oh, how tired I am! We have just had a rehearsal. . . . It goes splendidly. We are acting 'The Lodger with the Trombone' and 'Waiting for Him.' . . . The performance is the day after tomorrow. . . ."

"Why did you bring them?" asked Zaikin.

"I couldn't help it, Poppet; after tea we must rehearse our parts and sing something. . . . I am to sing a duet with Koromyslov. . . . Oh, yes, I was almost forgetting! Darling, send Natalya to get some sardines, vodka, cheese, and something else. They will most likely stay to supper. . . . Oh, how tired I am!"

"H'm! I've no money."

"You must, Poppet! It would be awkward! Don't make me blush."

Half an hour later Natalya was sent for vodka and savouries; Zaikin, after drinking tea and eating a whole French loaf, went to his bedroom and lay down on the bed, while Nadyezhda Stepanovna and her visitors, with much noise and laughter, set to work to rehearse their parts. For a long time Pavel Matveyitch heard Koromyslov's nasal reciting and Smerkalov's theatrical exclamations. . . . The rehearsal was followed by a long conversation, interrupted by the shrill laughter of Olga Kirillovna. Smerkalov, as a real actor, explained the parts with aplomb and heat. . . .

Then followed the duet, and after the duet there was the clatter of crockery. . . . Through his drowsiness Zaikin heard them persuading Smerkalov to read "The Woman who was a Sinner," and heard him, after affecting to refuse, begin to recite. He hissed, beat himself on the breast, wept, laughed in a husky bass. . . . Zaikin scowled and hid his head under the quilt.

"It's a long way for you to go, and it's dark," he heard Nadyezhda Stepanovna's voice an hour later. "Why shouldn't you stay the night here? Koromyslov can sleep here in the drawing-room on the sofa, and you, Smerkalov, in Petya's bed. . . . I can put Petya in my husband's study. . . . Do stay, really!"

At last when the clock was striking two, all was hushed, the bedroom door opened, and Nadyezhda Stepanovna appeared.

"Pavel, are you asleep?" she whispered.

"No; why?"

"Go into your study, darling, and lie on the sofa. I am going to put Olga Kirillovna here, in your bed. Do go, dear! I would put her to sleep in the study, but she is afraid to sleep alone. . . . Do get up!"

Zaikin got up, threw on his dressing-gown, and taking his pillow, crept wearily to the study. . . . Feeling his way to his sofa, he lighted a match, and saw Petya lying on the sofa. The boy was not asleep, and, looking at the match with wide-open eyes:

"Father, why is it gnats don't go to sleep at night?" he asked.

"Because . . . because . . . you and I are not wanted. . . . We have nowhere to sleep even."

"Father, and why is it Olga Kirillovna has freckles on her face?"

"Oh, shut up! I am tired of you."

After a moment's thought, Zaikin dressed and went out

into the street for a breath of air. . . . He looked at the grey morning sky, at the motionless clouds, heard the lazy call of the drowsy corncrake, and began dreaming of the next day, when he would go to town, and coming back from the court would tumble into bed. . . . Suddenly the figure of a man appeared round the corner.

"A watchman, no doubt," thought Zaikin. But going nearer and looking more closely he recognized in the figure the summer visitor in the ginger trousers.

"You're not asleep?" he asked.

"No, I can't sleep," sighed Ginger Trousers. "I am enjoying Nature. . . . A welcome visitor, my wife's mother, arrived by the night train, you know. She brought with her our nieces . . . splendid girls! I was delighted to see them, although . . . it's very damp! And you, too, are enjoying Nature?"

"Yes," grunted Zaikin, "I am enjoying it, too. . . . Do you know whether there is any sort of tavern or restaurant in the neighbourhood?"

Ginger Trousers raised his eyes to heaven and meditated profoundly.

TYPHUS

A YOUNG lieutenant called Klimov was travelling from Petersburg to Moscow in a smoking carriage of the mail train. Opposite him was sitting an elderly man with a shaven face like a sea captain's, by all appearances a well-to-do Finn or Swede. He pulled at his pipe the whole journey and kept talking about the same subject:

"Ha, you are an officer! I have a brother an officer too, only he is a naval officer. . . . He is a naval officer, and he is stationed at Kronstadt. Why are you going to Moscow?"

"I am serving there."

"Ha! And are you a family man?"

"No, I live with my sister and aunt."

"My brother's an officer, only he is a naval officer; he has a wife and three children. Ha!"

The Finn seemed continually surprised at something, and gave a broad idiotic grin when he exclaimed "Ha!" and continually puffed at his stinking pipe. Klimov, who for some reason did not feel well, and found it burdensome to answer questions, hated him with all his heart. He dreamed of how nice it would be to snatch the wheezing pipe out of his hand and fling it under the seat, and drive the Finn himself into another compartment.

"Detestable people these Finns and . . . Greeks," he thought. "Absolutely superfluous, useless, detestable people. They simply fill up space on the earthly globe. What are they for?"

And the thought of Finns and Greeks produced a feeling akin to sickness all over his body. For the sake of comparison he tried to think of the French, of the Italians, but his efforts to think of these people evoked in his mind, for some reason, nothing but images of organ-grinders, naked women, and the foreign oleographs which hung over the chest of drawers at home, at his aunt's.

Altogether the officer felt in an abnormal state. He could not arrange his arms and legs comfortably on the seat, though he had the whole seat to himself. His mouth felt dry and sticky; there was a heavy fog in his brain; his thoughts seemed to be straying, not only within his head, but outside his skull, among the seats and the people that were shrouded in the darkness of night. Through the mist in his brain, as through a dream, he heard the murmur of voices, the rumble of wheels, the slamming of doors. The sounds of the bells, the whistles, the guards, the running to and fro of passengers on the platforms, seemed more frequent than usual. The time flew by rapidly, imperceptibly, and so it seemed as though the train were stopping at stations every minute, and metallic voices crying continually:

"Is the mail ready?"

"Yes!" was repeatedly coming from outside.

It seemed as though the man in charge of the heating came in too often to look at the thermometer, that the noise of trains going in the opposite direction and the rumble of the wheels over the bridges was incessant. The noise, the whistles, the Finn, the tobacco smoke — all this mingling with the menace and flickering of the misty images in his brain, the shape and character of which a man in health can never recall, weighed upon Klimov like an unbearable nightmare. In horrible misery he lifted his heavy head, looked at the lamp in the rays of which shadows and misty blurs seemed to be dancing. He wanted to ask for water, but his parched tongue would hardly move, and he scarcely had strength to answer the Finn's questions. He tried to lie down more comfortably and go to sleep, but he could not succeed. The Finn several times fell asleep, woke up again, lighted his pipe, addressed him with his "Ha!" and went to sleep again; and still the lieutenant's legs could not get into a comfortable position, and still the menacing images stood facing him.

At Spirovo he went out into the station for a drink of water. He saw people sitting at the table and hurriedly eating.

"And how can they eat!" he thought, trying not to sniff the air, that smelt of roast meat, and not to look at the munching mouths — they both seemed to him sickeningly disgusting.

A good-looking lady was conversing loudly with a military man in a red cap, and showing magnificent white teeth as she smiled; and the smile, and the teeth, and the lady herself made on Klimov the same revolting impression as the ham and the rissoles. He could not understand how it was the military man in the red cap was not ill at ease, sitting beside her and looking at her healthy, smiling face.

When after drinking some water he went back to his carriage, the Finn was sitting smoking; his pipe was wheezing and squelching like a golosh with holes in it in wet weather.

"Ha!" he said, surprised; "what station is this?"

"I don't know," answered Klimov, lying down and shutting his mouth that he might not breathe the acrid tobacco smoke.

"And when shall we reach Tver?"

"I don't know. Excuse me, I . . . I can't answer. I am ill. I caught cold today."

The Finn knocked his pipe against the window-frame and began talking of his brother, the naval officer. Klimov no longer heard him; he was thinking miserably of his soft, comfortable bed, of a bottle of cold water, of his sister Katya, who was so good at making one comfortable, soothing, giving one water. He even smiled when the vision of his orderly Pavel, taking off his heavy stifling boots and putting water on the little table, flitted through his imagination. He fancied that if he could only get into his bed, have a drink of water, his nightmare would give place to sound healthy sleep.

"Is the mail ready?" a hollow voice reached him from the distance.

"Yes," answered a bass voice almost at the window.

It was already the second or third station from Spirovo.

The time was flying rapidly in leaps and bounds, and it seemed as though the bells, whistles, and stoppings would never end. In despair Klimov buried his face in the corner of the seat, clutched his head in his hands, and began again thinking of his sister Katya and his orderly Pavel, but his sister and his orderly were mixed up with the misty images in his brain, whirled round, and disappeared. His burning breath, reflected from the back of the seat, seemed to scald his face; his legs were uncomfortable; there was a draught from the window on his back; but, however wretched he was, he did not want to change his position. . . . A heavy nightmarish lethargy gradually gained possession of him and fettered his limbs.

When he brought himself to raise his head, it was already light in the carriage. The passengers were putting on their fur coats and moving about. The train was stopping. Porters in white aprons and with discs on their breasts were bustling among the passengers and snatching up their boxes. Klimov put on his great-coat, mechanically followed the other passengers out of the carriage, and it seemed to him that not he, but some one else was moving, and he felt that his fever, his thirst, and the menacing images which had not let him sleep all night, came out of the carriage with him. Mechanically he took his luggage and engaged a sledge-driver. The man asked him for a rouble and a quarter to drive to Povarsky Street, but he did not haggle, and without protest got submissively into the sledge. He still understood the difference of numbers, but money had ceased to have any value to him.

At home Klimov was met by his aunt and his sister Katya, a girl of eighteen. When Katya greeted him she had a pencil and exercise book in her hand, and he remembered that she was preparing for an examination as a teacher. Gasping with fever, he walked aimlessly through all the rooms without answering their questions or greetings, and when he reached his bed he sank down on the pillow. The Finn, the red cap, the lady with the white teeth, the smell of roast meat, the flickering blurs, filled his consciousness, and by now he did not know where he was and did not hear the agitated voices.

When he recovered consciousness he found himself in bed, undressed, saw a bottle of water and Pavel, but it was no cooler, nor softer, nor more comfortable for that. His arms and legs, as before, refused to lie comfortably; his tongue stuck to the roof of his mouth, and he heard the wheezing of the Finn's pipe. . . . A stalwart, black-bearded doctor was busy doing something beside the bed, brushing against Pavel with his broad back.

"It's all right, it's all right, young man," he muttered. "Excellent, excellent . . . goo-od, goo-od . . . !"

The doctor called Klimov "young man," said "goo-od" instead of "good" and "so-o" instead of "so."

"So-o . . . so-o . . . so-o," he murmured. "Goo-od, goo-od . . . ! Excellent, young man. You mustn't lose heart!"

The doctor's rapid, careless talk, his well-fed countenance, and condescending "young man," irritated Klimov.

"Why do you call me 'young man'?" he moaned. "What familiarity! Damn it all!"

And he was frightened by his own voice. The voice was so dried up, so weak and peevish, that he would not have known it.

"Excellent, excellent!" muttered the doctor, not in the least offended. . . . "You mustn't get angry, so-o, so-o, so-s. . . ."

And the time flew by at home with the same startling swiftness as in the railway carriage. The daylight was continually being replaced by the dusk of evening. The doctor seemed never to leave his bedside, and he heard at every moment his "so-o, so-o, so-o." A continual succession of people was incessantly crossing the bedroom. Among them were: Pavel, the Finn, Captain Yaroshevitch, Lance-Corporal Maximenko, the red cap, the lady with the white teeth, the doctor. They were all talking and waving their arms, smoking and eating. Once by daylight Klimov saw the chaplain of the regiment, Father Alexandr, who was standing before the bed, wearing a stole and with a prayer-book in his hand. He was muttering something with a grave face such as Klimov had never seen in him before. The lieutenant remembered that Father Alexandr used in a friendly way to call all the Catholic officers "Poles," and wanting to amuse him, he cried:

"Father, Yaroshevitch the Pole has climbed up a pole!"

But Father Alexandr, a light-hearted man who loved a joke, did not smile, but became graver than ever, and made the sign of the cross over Klimov. At night-time by turn two shadows came noiselessly in and out; they were his aunt and sister. His sister's shadow knelt down and prayed; she bowed down to the ikon, and her grey shadow on the wall bowed down too, so that two shadows were praying. The whole time there was a smell of roast meat and the Finn's pipe, but once Klimov smelt the strong smell of incense. He felt so sick he could not lie still, and began shouting:

"The incense! Take away the incense!"

There was no answer. He could only hear the subdued singing of the priest somewhere and some one running upstairs.

When Klimov came to himself there was not a soul in his bedroom. The morning sun was streaming in at the window through the lower blind, and a quivering sunbeam, bright and keen as the sword's edge, was flashing on the glass bottle. He heard the rattle of wheels — so there was no snow now in the street. The lieutenant looked at the ray, at the familiar furniture, at the door, and the first thing he did was to laugh. His chest and stomach heaved with delicious, happy, tickling laughter. His whole body from head to foot was overcome by a sensation of infinite happiness and joy in life, such as the first man must have felt when he was created and first saw the world. Klimov felt a passionate desire for movement, people, talk. His body lay a motionless block; only his hands stirred, but that he hardly noticed, and his whole attention was concentrated on trifles. He rejoiced in his breathing, in his laughter, rejoiced in the existence of the water-bottle, the ceiling, the sunshine, the tape on the curtains. God's world, even in the narrow space of his bedroom, seemed beautiful, varied, grand. When the doctor made his appearance, the lieutenant was thinking what a delicious thing medicine was, how charming and pleasant the doctor was, and how nice and interesting people were in general.

"So-o, so, so. . . Excellent, excellent! . . . Now we are well again. . . . Goo-od, goo-od!" the doctor pattered.

The lieutenant listened and laughed joyously; he remembered the Finn, the lady with the white teeth, the train, and he longed to smoke, to eat.

"Doctor," he said, "tell them to give me a crust of rye bread and salt, and . . . and sardines."

The doctor refused; Pavel did not obey the order, and did not go for the bread. The lieutenant could not bear this and began crying like a naughty child.

"Baby!" laughed the doctor. "Mammy, bye-bye!"

Klimov laughed, too, and when the doctor went away he fell into a sound sleep. He woke up with the same joyfulness and sensation of happiness. His aunt was sitting near the bed.

"Well, aunt," he said joyfully. "What has been the matter?"

"Spotted typhus."

"Really. But now I am well, quite well! Where is Katya?"

"She is not at home. I suppose she has gone somewhere from her examination."

The old lady said this and looked at her stocking; her lips began quivering, she turned away, and suddenly broke into sobs. Forgetting the doctor's prohibition in her despair, she said:

"Ah, Katya, Katya! Our angel is gone! Is gone!"

She dropped her stocking and bent down to it, and as she did so her cap fell off her head. Looking at her grey head and understanding nothing, Klimov was frightened for Katya, and asked:

"Where is she, aunt?"

The old woman, who had forgotten Klimov and was thinking only of her sorrow, said:

"She caught typhus from you, and is dead. She was buried the day before yesterday."

This terrible, unexpected news was fully grasped by Klimov's consciousness; but terrible and startling as it was, it could not overcome the animal joy that filled the convalescent. He cried and laughed, and soon began scolding because they would not let him eat.

Only a week later when, leaning on Pavel, he went in his dressing-gown to the window, looked at the overcast spring sky and listened to the unpleasant clang of the old iron rails which were being carted by, his heart ached, he burst into tears, and leaned his forehead against the window-frame.

"How miserable I am!" he muttered. "My God, how miserable!"

And joy gave way to the boredom of everyday life and the feeling of his irrevocable loss.

⊕⊕

A MISFORTUNE

SOFYA PETROVNA, the wife of Lubyantsev the notary, a handsome young woman of five-and-twenty, was walking slowly along a track that had been cleared in the wood, with Ilyin, a lawyer who was spending the summer in the neighbourhood. It was five o'clock in the evening. Feathery-white masses of cloud stood overhead; patches of bright blue sky peeped out between them. The clouds stood motionless, as though they had caught in the tops of the tall old pine-trees. It was still and sultry.

Farther on, the track was crossed by a low railway embankment on which a sentinel with a gun was for some reason pacing up and down. Just beyond the embankment there was a large white church with six domes and a rusty roof.

"I did not expect to meet you here," said Sofya Petrovna,

looking at the ground and prodding at the last year's leaves with the tip of her parasol, "and now I am glad we have met. I want to speak to you seriously and once for all. I beg you, Ivan Mihalovitch, if you really love and respect me, please make an end of this pursuit of me! You follow me about like a shadow, you are continually looking at me not in a nice way, making love to me, writing me strange letters, and . . . and I don't know where it's all going to end! Why, what can come of it?"

Ilyin said nothing. Sofya Petrovna walked on a few steps and continued:

"And this complete transformation in you all came about in the course of two or three weeks, after five years' friendship. I don't know you, Ivan Mihalovitch!"

Sofya Petrovna stole a glance at her companion. Screwing up his eyes, he was looking intently at the fluffy clouds. His face looked angry, ill-humoured, and preoccupied, like that of a man in pain forced to listen to nonsense.

"I wonder you don't see it yourself," Madame Lubyantsev went on, shrugging her shoulders. "You ought to realize that it's not a very nice part you are playing. I am married; I love and respect my husband. . . . I have a daughter . . . . Can you think all that means nothing? Besides, as an old friend you know my attitude to family life and my views as to the sanctity of marriage."

Ilyin cleared his throat angrily and heaved a sigh.

"Sanctity of marriage . . ." he muttered. "Oh, Lord!"

Yes, yes. . . . I love my husband, I respect him; and in any case I value the peace of my home. I would rather let myself be killed than be a cause of unhappiness to Andrey and his daughter. . . . And I beg you, Ivan Mihalovitch, for God's sake, leave me in peace! Let us be as good, true friends as we used to be, and give up these sighs and groans, which really don't suit you. It's settled and over! Not a word more about it. Let us talk of something else."

Sofya Petrovna again stole a glance at Ilyin's face. Ilyin was looking up; he was pale, and was angrily biting his quivering lips. She could not understand why he was angry and why he was indignant, but his pallor touched her.

"Don't be angry; let us be friends," she said affectionately. "Agreed? Here's my hand."

Ilyin took her plump little hand in both of his, squeezed it, and slowly raised it to his lips.

"I am not a schoolboy," he muttered. "I am not in the least tempted by friendship with the woman I love."

"Enough, enough! It's settled and done with. We have reached the seat; let us sit down."

Sofya Petrovna's soul was filled with a sweet sense of relief: the most difficult and delicate thing had been said, the painful question was settled and done with. Now she could breathe freely and look Ilyin straight in the face. She looked at him, and the egoistic feeling of the superiority of the woman over the man who loves her, agreeably flattered her. It pleased her to see this huge, strong man, with his manly, angry face and his big black beard – clever, cultivated, and, people said, talented – sit down obediently beside her and bow his head dejectedly. For two or three minutes they sat without speaking.

"Nothing is settled or done with," began Ilyin. "You repeat copy-book maxims to me. 'I love and respect my husband . . . the sanctity of marriage. . . .' I know all that without your help, and I could tell you more, too. I tell you truthfully and honestly that I consider the way I am behaving as criminal and immoral. What more can one say than that? But what's the good of saying what everybody knows? Instead of feeding nightingales with paltry words, you had much better tell me what I am to do."

"I've told you already – go away."

"As you know perfectly well, I have gone away five times, and every time I turned back on the way. I can show you my through tickets – I've kept them all. I have not will enough to run away from you! I am struggling. I am struggling horribly; but what the devil am I good for if I have no backbone, if I am weak, cowardly! I can't struggle with Nature! Do you understand? I cannot! I run away from here, and she holds on to me and pulls me back. Contemptible, loathsome weakness!"

Ilyin flushed crimson, got up, and walked up and down by the seat.

"I feel as cross as a dog," he muttered, clenching his fists. "I hate and despise myself! My God! like some depraved schoolboy, I am making love to another man's wife, writing idiotic letters, degrading myself . . . ugh!"

Ilyin clutched at his head, grunted, and sat down. "And then your insincerity!" he went on bitterly. "If you do dislike my disgusting behaviour, why have you come here? What drew you here? In my letters I only ask you for a direct, definite answer – yes or no; but instead of a direct answer, you contrive every day these 'chance' meetings with me and regale me with copy-book maxims!"

Madame Lubyantsev was frightened and flushed. She suddenly felt the awkwardness which a decent woman feels when she is accidentally discovered undressed.

"You seem to suspect I am playing with you," she muttered. "I have always given you a direct answer, and . . . only today I've begged you . . ."

"Ough! as though one begged in such cases! If you were to say straight out 'Get away,' I should have been gone long ago; but you've never said that. You've never once given me a direct answer. Strange indecision! Yes, indeed; either you are playing with me, or else . . ."

Ilyin leaned his head on his fists without finishing. Sofya Petrovna began going over in her own mind the way she had behaved from beginning to end. She remembered that not only in her actions, but even in her secret thoughts, she had always been opposed to Ilyin's love-making; but yet she felt there was a grain of truth in the lawyer's words. But not knowing exactly what the truth was, she could not find answers to make to Ilyin's complaint, however hard she thought. It was awkward to be silent, and, shrugging her shoulders, she said:

So I am to blame, it appears."

"I don't blame you for your insincerity," sighed Ilyin. "I did not mean that when I spoke of it. . . . Your insincerity is natural and in the order of things. If people agreed together and suddenly became sincere, everything would go to the devil."

Sofya Petrovna was in no mood for philosophical reflections, but she was glad of a chance to change the conversation, and asked:

"But why?"

"Because only savage women and animals are sincere. Once civilization has introduced a demand for such comforts as, for instance, feminine virtue, sincerity is out of place. . . ."

Ilyin jabbed his stick angrily into the sand. Madame Lubyantsev listened to him and liked his conversation, though a great deal of it she did not understand. What gratified her most was that she, an ordinary woman, was talked to by a talented man on "intellectual" subjects; it afforded her great pleasure, too, to watch the working of his mobile, young face, which was still pale and angry. She failed to understand a great deal that he said, but what was clear to her in his words was the attractive boldness with which the modern man without hesitation or doubt decides great questions and draws conclusive deductions.

She suddenly realized that she was admiring him, and was alarmed.

"Forgive me, but I don't understand," she said hurriedly. "What makes you talk of insincerity? I repeat my request again: be my good, true friend; let me alone! I beg you most earnestly!"

"Very good; I'll try again," sighed Ilyin. "Glad to do my best. . . . Only I doubt whether anything will come of my efforts. Either I shall put a bullet through my brains or take to drink in an idiotic way. I shall come to a bad end! There's a limit to everything – to struggles with Nature, too. Tell me, how can one struggle against madness? If you drink wine, how are you to struggle against intoxication? What am I to do if your image has grown into my soul, and day and night stands persistently before my eyes, like that pine there at this moment? Come, tell me, what hard and difficult thing can I do to get free from this abominable, miserable condition, in which all my thoughts, desires, and dreams are no longer my own, but belong to some demon who has taken possession of me? I love you, love you so much that I am completely thrown out of gear; I've given up my work and all who are dear to me; I've forgotten my God! I've never been in love like this in my life."

Sofya Petrovna, who had not expected such a turn to their conversation, drew away from Ilyin and looked into his face in dismay. Tears came into his eyes, his lips were quivering, and there was an imploring, hungry expression in his face.

"I love you!" he muttered, bringing his eyes near her big, frightened eyes. "You are so beautiful! I am in agony now, but I swear I would sit here all my life, suffering and looking in your eyes. But . . . be silent, I implore you!"

Sofya Petrovna, feeling utterly disconcerted, tried to think as quickly as possible of something to say to stop him. "I'll go away," she decided, but before she had time to make a movement to get up, Ilyin was on his knees before her. . . . He was clasping her knees, gazing into her face and speaking passionately, hotly, eloquently. In her terror and confusion she did not hear his words; for some reason now, at this dangerous moment, while her knees were being agreeably squeezed and felt as though they were in a warm bath, she was trying, with a sort of angry spite, to interpret her own sensations. She was angry that instead of brimming over with protesting virtue, she was entirely overwhelmed with weakness, apathy, and emptiness, like a drunken man utterly reckless; only at the bottom of her soul a remote bit of herself was malignantly taunting her: "Why don't you go? Is this as it should be? Yes?"

Seeking for some explanation, she could not understand how it was she did not pull away the hand to which Ilyin was clinging like a leech, and why, like Ilyin, she hastily glanced to right and to left to see whether any one was looking. The clouds and the pines stood motionless, looking at them severely, like old ushers seeing mischief, but bribed not to tell the school authorities. The sentry stood like a post on the embankment and seemed to be looking at the seat.

"Let him look," thought Sofya Petrovna.

"But . . . but listen," she said at last, with despair in her voice. "What can come of this? What will be the end of this?"

"I don't know, I don't know," he whispered, waving off the disagreeable questions.

They heard the hoarse, discordant whistle of the train. This cold, irrelevant sound from the everyday world of prose made Sofya Petrovna rouse herself.

"I can't stay . . . it's time I was at home," she said, getting up quickly. "The train is coming in. . . Andrey is coming by it! He will want his dinner."

Sofya Petrovna turned towards the embankment with a burning face. The engine slowly crawled by, then came the carriages. It was not the local train, as she had supposed, but a goods train. The trucks filed by against the background of the white church in a long string like the days of a man's life, and it seemed as though it would never end.

But at last the train passed, and the last carriage with the guard and a light in it had disappeared behind the trees. Sofya Petrovna turned round sharply, and without looking at Ilyin, walked rapidly back along the track. She had regained her self-possession. Crimson with shame, humiliated not by Ilyin – no, but by her own cowardice, by the shamelessness with which she, a chaste and high-principled woman, had allowed a man, not her husband, to hug her knees – she had only one thought now: to get home as quickly as possible to her villa, to her family. The lawyer could hardly keep pace with her. Turning from the clearing into a narrow path, she turned round and glanced at him so quickly that she saw nothing but the sand on his knees, and waved to him to drop behind.

Reaching home, Sofya Petrovna stood in the middle of her room for five minutes without moving, and looked first at the window and then at her writing-table.

"You low creature!" she said, upbraiding herself. "You low creature!"

To spite herself, she recalled in precise detail, keeping nothing back – she recalled that though all this time she had been opposed to Ilyin's lovemaking, something had impelled her to seek an interview with him; and what was more, when he was at her feet she had enjoyed it enormously. She recalled it all without sparing herself, and now, breathless with shame, she would have liked to slap herself in the face.

"Poor Andrey!" she said to herself, trying as she thought of her husband to put into her face as tender an expression as she could. "Varya, my poor little girl, doesn't know what a mother she has! Forgive me, my dear ones! I love you so much . . . so much!"

And anxious to prove to herself that she was still a good wife and mother, and that corruption had not yet touched that "sanctity of marriage" of which she had spoken to Ilyin, Sofya Petrovna ran to the kitchen and abused the cook for not having yet laid the table for Andrey Ilyitch. She tried to picture her husband's hungry and exhausted appearance, commiserated him aloud, and laid the table for him with her own hands, which she had never done before. Then she found her daughter Varya, picked her up in her arms and hugged her warmly; the child seemed to her cold and heavy, but she was unwilling to acknowledge this to herself, and she began explaining to the child how good, kind, and honourable her papa was.

But when Andrey Ilyitch arrived soon afterwards she hardly greeted him. The rush of false feeling had already passed off without proving anything to her, only irritating and exasperating her by its falsity. She was sitting by the window, feeling miserable and cross. It is only by being in trouble that people can understand how far from easy it is to be the master of one's feelings and thoughts. Sofya Petrovna said afterwards that there was a tangle within her which it was as difficult to unravel as to count a flock of sparrows rapidly flying by. From the fact that she was not overjoyed to see her husband, that she did not like his manner at dinner, she concluded all of a sudden that she was beginning to hate her husband

Andrey Ilyitch, languid with hunger and exhaustion, fell upon the sausage while waiting for the soup to be brought in, and ate it greedily, munching noisily and moving his temples.

"My goodness!" thought Sofya Petrovna. "I love and respect him, but . . . why does he munch so repulsively?"

The disorder in her thoughts was no less than the disorder in her feelings. Like all persons inexperienced in combating unpleasant ideas, Madame Lubyantsev did her utmost not to think of her trouble, and the harder she tried the more vividly Ilyin, the sand on his knees, the fluffy clouds, the train, stood out in her imagination.

"And why did I go there this afternoon like a fool?" she thought, tormenting herself. "And am I really so weak that I cannot depend upon myself?"

Fear magnifies danger. By the time Andrey Ilyitch was finishing the last course, she had firmly made up her mind to tell her husband everything and to flee from danger!

"I've something serious to say to you, Andrey," she began after dinner while her husband was taking off his coat and boots to lie down for a nap.

"Well?"

"Let us leave this place!"

" H'm! . . . Where shall we go? It's too soon to go back to town."

"No; for a tour or something of that sort.

"For a tour . . ." repeated the notary, stretching. "I dream of that myself, but where are we to get the money, and to whom am I to leave the office?"

And thinking a little he added:

"Of course, you must be bored. Go by yourself if you like."

Sofya Petrovna agreed, but at once reflected that Ilyin would be delighted with the opportunity, and would go with her in the same train, in the same compartment. . . . She thought and looked at her husband, now satisfied but still languid. For some reason her eyes rested on his feet – miniature, almost feminine feet, clad in striped socks; there was a thread standing out at the tip of each sock.

Behind the blind a bumble-bee was beating itself against the window-pane and buzzing. Sofya Petrovna looked at the threads on the socks, listened to the bee, and pictured how she would set off. . . . *vis-à-vis* Ilyin would sit, day and night, never taking his eyes off her, wrathful at his own weakness and pale with spiritual agony. He would call himself an immoral schoolboy, would abuse her, tear his hair, but when darkness came on and the passengers were asleep or got out at a station, he would seize the opportunity to kneel before her and embrace her knees as he had at the seat in the wood. . . .

She caught herself indulging in this day-dream.

"Listen. I won't go alone," she said. "You must come with me."

"Nonsense, Sofotchka!" sighed Lubyantsev. "One must be sensible and not want the impossible."

"You will come when you know all about it," thought Sofya Petrovna.

Making up her mind to go at all costs, she felt that she was out of danger. Little by little her ideas grew clearer; her spirits rose and she allowed herself to think about it all, feeling that however much she thought, however much she dreamed, she would go away. While her husband was asleep, the evening gradually came on. She sat in the drawing-room and played the piano. The greater liveliness out of doors, the sound of music, but above all the thought that she was a sensible person, that she had surmounted her difficulties, completely restored her spirits. Other women, her appeased conscience told her, would probably have been carried off their feet in her position, and would have lost their balance, while she had almost died of shame, had been miserable, and was now running out of the danger which perhaps did not exist! She was so touched by her own virtue and determination that she even looked at herself two or three times in the looking-glass.

When it got dark, visitors arrived. The men sat down in the dining-room to play cards; the ladies remained in the drawing-room and the verandah. The last to arrive was Ilyin. He was gloomy, morose, and looked ill. He sat down in the corner of the sofa and did not move the whole evening. Usually good-humoured and talkative, this time he remained silent, frowned, and rubbed his eyebrows. When he had to answer some question, he gave a forced smile with his upper lip only, and answered jerkily and irritably. Four or five times he made some jest, but his jests sounded harsh and cutting. It seemed to Sofya Petrovna that he was on the verge of hysterics. Only now, sitting at the piano, she recognized fully for the first time that this unhappy man was in deadly earnest, that his soul was sick, and that he could find no rest. For her sake he was wasting the best days of his youth and his career, spending the last of his money on a summer villa, abandoning his mother and sisters, and, worst of all, wearing himself out in an agonizing struggle with himself. From mere common humanity he ought to be treated seriously.

She recognized all this clearly till it made her heart ache, and if at that moment she had gone up to him and said to him, "No," there would have been a force in her voice hard to disobey. But she did not go up to him and did not speak — indeed, never thought of doing so. The pettiness and egoism of youth had never been more patent in her than that evening. She realized that Ilyin was unhappy, and that he was sitting on the sofa as though he were on hot coals; she felt sorry for him, but at the same time the presence of a man who loved her to distraction, filled her soul with triumph and a sense of her own power. She felt her youth, her beauty, and her unassailable virtue, and, since she had decided to go away, gave herself full licence for that evening. She flirted, laughed incessantly, sang with peculiar feeling and gusto. Everything delighted and amused her. She was amused at the memory of what had happened at the seat in the wood, of the sentinel who had looked on. She was amused by her guests, by Ilyin's cutting jests, by the pin in his cravat, which she had never noticed before. There was a red snake with diamond eyes on the pin; this snake struck her as so amusing that she could have kissed it on the spot.

Sofya Petrovna sang nervously, with defiant recklessness as though half intoxicated, and she chose sad, mournful songs which dealt with wasted hopes, the past, old age, as though in mockery of another's grief. " 'And old age comes nearer and nearer' . . ." she sang. And what was old age to her?

"It seems as though there is something going wrong with me," she thought from time to time through her laughter and singing.

The party broke up at twelve o'clock. Ilyin was the last to leave. Sofya Petrovna was still reckless enough to accompany him to the bottom step of the verandah. She wanted to tell him that she was going away with her husband, and to watch the effect this news would produce on him.

The moon was hidden behind the clouds, but it was light enough for Sofya Petrovna to see how the wind played with the skirts of his overcoat and with the awning of the verandah. She could see, too, how white Ilyin was, and how he twisted his upper lip in the effort to smile.

"Sonia, Sonitchka . . . my darling woman!" he muttered, preventing her from speaking. "My dear! my sweet!"

In a rush of tenderness, with tears in his voice, he showered caressing words upon her, that grew tenderer and tenderer, and even called her "thou," as though she were his wife or mistress. Quite unexpectedly he put one arm round her waist and with the other hand took hold of her elbow.

"My precious! my delight!" he whispered, kissing the nape of her neck; "be sincere; come to me at once!"

She slipped out of his arms and raised her head to give vent to her indignation and anger, but the indignation did not come off, and all her vaunted virtue and chastity was only sufficient to enable her to utter the phrase used by all ordinary women on such occasions:

"You must be mad."

"Come, let us go," Ilyin continued. "I felt just now, as well as at the seat in the wood, that you are as helpless as I am, Sonia. . . . You are in the same plight! You love me and are fruitlessly trying to appease your conscience. . . ."

Seeing that she was moving away, he caught her by her lace cuff and said rapidly:

"If not today, then tomorrow you will have to give in! Why, then, this waste of time? My precious, darling Sonia, the sentence is passed; why put off the execution? Why deceive yourself?"

Sofya Petrovna tore herself from him and darted in at the door. Returning to the drawing-room, she mechanically shut the piano, looked for a long time at the music-stand, and sat down. She could not stand up nor think. All that was left of her excitement and recklessness was a fearful weakness, apathy, and dreariness. Her conscience whispered to her that she had behaved badly, foolishly, that evening, like some madcap girl – that she had just been embraced on the verandah, and still had an uneasy feeling in her waist and her elbow. There was not a soul in the drawing-room; there was only one candle burning. Madame Lubyantsev sat on the round stool before the piano, motionless, as though expecting something. And as though taking advantage of the darkness and her extreme lassitude, an oppressive, overpowering desire began to assail her. Like a boa-constrictor it gripped her limbs and her soul, and grew stronger every second, and no longer menaced her as it had done, but stood clear before her in all its nakedness.

She sat for half an hour without stirring, not restraining herself from thinking of Ilyin, then she got up languidly and dragged herself to her bedroom. Andrey Ilyitch was already in bed. She sat down by the open window and gave herself up to desire. There was no "tangle" now in her head; all her thoughts and feelings were bent with one accord upon a single aim. She tried to struggle against it, but instantly gave it up. . . . She understood now how strong and relentless was the foe. Strength and fortitude were needed to combat him, and her birth, her education, and her life had given her nothing to fall back upon.

"Immoral wretch! Low creature!" she nagged at herself for her weakness. "So that's what you're like!"

Her outraged sense of propriety was moved to such indignation by this weakness that she lavished upon herself every term of abuse she knew, and told herself many offensive and humiliating truths. So, for instance, she told herself that she never had been moral, that she had not come to grief before simply because she had had no opportunity, that her inward conflict during that day had all been a farce. . . .

"And even if I have struggled," she thought, "what sort of struggle was it? Even the woman who sells herself struggles before she brings herself to it, and yet she sells herself. A fine struggle! Like milk, I've turned in a day! In one day!"

She convicted herself of being tempted, not by feeling, not by Ilyin personally, but by sensations which awaited her . . . an idle lady, having her fling in the summer holidays, like so many!

" 'Like an unfledged bird when the mother has been slain,' " sang a husky tenor outside the window.

"If I am to go, it's time," thought Sofya Petrovna. Her heart suddenly began beating violently.

"Andrey!" she almost shrieked. "Listen! we . . . we are going? Yes?"

"Yes, I've told you already: you go alone."

"But listen," she began. "If you don't go with me, you are in danger of losing me. I believe I am . . . in love already."

"With whom?" asked Andrey Ilyitch.

"It can't make any difference to you who it is!" cried Sofya

Petrovna.

Andrey Ilyitch sat up with his feet out of bed and looked wonderingly at his wife's dark figure.

"It's a fancy!" he yawned.

He did not believe her, but yet he was frightened. After thinking a little and asking his wife several unimportant questions, he delivered himself of his opinions on the family, on infidelity . . . spoke listlessly for about ten minutes and got into bed again. His moralizing produced no effect. There are a great many opinions in the world, and a good half of them are held by people who have never been in trouble!

In spite of the late hour, summer visitors were still walking outside. Sofya Petrovna put on a light cape, stood a little, thought a little. . . . She still had resolution enough to say to her sleeping husband:

"Are you asleep? I am going for a walk. . . . Will you come with me?"

That was her last hope. Receiving no answer, she went out. . . . It was fresh and windy. She was conscious neither of the wind nor the darkness, but went on and on. . . . An overmastering force drove her on, and it seemed as though, if she had stopped, it would have pushed her in the back.

"Immoral creature!" she muttered mechanically. "Low wretch!"

She was breathless, hot with shame, did not feel her legs under her, but what drove her on was stronger than shame, reason, or fear.

A TRIFLE FROM LIFE

A WELL-FED, red-cheeked young man called Nikolay Ilyitch Belyaev, of thirty-two, who was an owner of house property in Petersburg, and a devotee of the race-course, went one evening to see Olga Ivanovna Irnin, with whom he was living, or, to use his own expression, was dragging out a long, wearisome romance. And, indeed, the first interesting and enthusiastic pages of this romance had long been perused; now the pages dragged on, and still dragged on, without presenting anything new or of interest.

Not finding Olga Ivanovna at home, my hero lay down on the lounge chair and proceeded to wait for her in the drawing-room.

"Good-evening, Nikolay Ilyitch!" he heard a child's voice. "Mother will be here directly. She has gone with Sonia to the dressmaker's."

Olga Ivanovna's son, Alyosha — a boy of eight who looked graceful and very well cared for, who was dressed like a picture, in a black velvet jacket and long black stockings — was lying on the sofa in the same room. He was lying on a satin cushion and, evidently imitating an acrobat he had lately seen at the circus, stuck up in the air first one leg and then the other. When his elegant legs were exhausted, he brought his arms into play or jumped up impulsively and went on all fours, trying to stand with his legs in the air. All this he was doing with the utmost gravity, gasping and groaning painfully as though he regretted that God had given him such a restless body.

"Ah, good-evening, my boy," said Belyaev. "It's you! I did not notice you. Is your mother well?"

Alyosha, taking hold of the tip of his left toe with his right hand and falling into the most unnatural attitude, turned over, jumped up, and peeped at Belyaev from behind the big fluffy lampshade.

"What shall I say?" he said, shrugging his shoulders. "In reality mother's never well. You see, she is a woman, and women, Nikolay Ilyitch, have always something the matter with them."

Belyaev, having nothing better to do, began watching Alyosha's face. He had never before during the whole of his intimacy with Olga Ivanovna paid any attention to the boy, and had completely ignored his existence; the boy had been before his eyes, but he had not cared to think why he was there and what part he was playing.

In the twilight of the evening, Alyosha's face, with his

white forehead and black, unblinking eyes, unexpectedly reminded Belyaev of Olga Ivanovna as she had been during the first pages of their romance. And he felt disposed to be friendly to the boy.

"Come here, insect," he said; "let me have a closer look at you."

The boy jumped off the sofa and skipped up to Belyaev.

"Well," began Nikolay Ilyitch, putting a hand on the boy's thin shoulder. "How are you getting on?"

"How shall I say! We used to get on a great deal better."

"Why?"

"It's very simple. Sonia and I used only to learn music and reading, and now they give us French poetry to learn. Have you been shaved lately?"

"Yes."

"Yes, I see you have. Your beard is shorter. Let me touch it.... Does that hurt?"

"No."

"Why is it that if you pull one hair it hurts, but if you pull a lot at once it doesn't hurt a bit? Ha, ha! And, you know, it's a pity you don't have whiskers. Here ought to be shaved . . . but here at the sides the hair ought to be left. . . ."

The boy nestled up to Belyaev and began playing with his watch-chain.

"When I go to the high-school," he said, "mother is going to buy me a watch. I shall ask her to buy me a watch-chain like this. . . . Wh-at a lo-ket! Father's got a locket like that, only yours has little bars on it and his has letters. . . . There's mother's portrait in the middle of his. Father has a different sort of chain now, not made with rings, but like ribbon. . . ."

"How do you know? Do you see your father?"

"I? M'm . . . no . . . I . . ."

Alyosha blushed, and in great confusion, feeling caught in a lie, began zealously scratching the locket with his nail. . . . Belyaev looked steadily into his face and asked:

"Do you see your father?"

"N-no!"

"Come, speak frankly, on your honour. . . . I see from your face you are telling a fib. Once you've let a thing slip out it's no good wriggling about it. Tell me, do you see him? Come, as a friend."

Alyosha hesitated.

"You won't tell mother?" he said.

"As though I should!"

"On your honour?"

"On my honour."

"Do you swear?"

"Ah, you provoking boy! What do you take me for?"

Alyosha looked round him, then with wide-open eyes, whispered to him:

"Only, for goodness' sake, don't tell mother. . . . Don't tell any one at all, for it is a secret. I hope to goodness mother won't find out, or we should all catch it – Sonia, and I, and Pelagea. . . . Well, listen. . . Sonia and I see father every Tuesday and Friday. When Pelagea takes us for a walk before dinner we go to the Apfel Restaurant, and there is father waiting for us. . . . He is always sitting in a room apart, where you know there's a marble table and an ash-tray in the shape of a goose without a back. . . ."

"What do you do there?"

"Nothing! First we say how-do-you-do, then we all sit round the table, and father treats us with coffee and pies. You know Sonia eats the meat-pies, but I can't endure meat-pies! I like the pies made of cabbage and eggs. We eat such a lot that we have to try hard to eat as much as we can at dinner, for fear mother should notice."

"What do you talk about?"

"With father? About anything. He kisses us, he hugs us, tells us all sorts of amusing jokes. Do you know, he says when we are grown up he is going to take us to live with him. Sonia does not want to go, but I agree. Of course, I should miss mother; but, then, I should write her letters! It's a queer idea, but we could come and visit her on holidays – couldn't we? Father says, too, that he will buy me a horse. He's an awfully kind man! I can't understand why mother does not ask him to come and live with us, and why she forbids us to see him. You know he loves mother very much. He is always asking us how she is and what she is doing. When she was ill he clutched his head like this, and . . . and kept running about. He always tells us to be obedient and respectful to her. Listen. Is it true that we are unfortunate?"

"H'm! . . . Why?"

"That's what father says. 'You are unhappy children,' he says. It's strange to hear him, really. 'You are unhappy,' he says, 'I am unhappy, and mother's unhappy. You must pray to God,' he says; 'for yourselves and for her.' "

Alyosha let his eyes rest on a stuffed bird and sank into thought.

"So . . ." growled Belyaev. "So that's how you are going on. You arrange meetings at restaurants. And mother does not know?"

"No-o. . . . How should she know? Pelagea would not tell her for anything, you know. The day before yesterday he gave us some pears. As sweet as jam! I ate two."

"H'm! . . . Well, and I say . . Listen. Did father say anything about me?"

"About you? What shall I say?"

Alyosha looked searchingly into Belyaev's face and shrugged his shoulders.

"He didn't say anything particular."

"For instance, what did he say?"

"You won't be offended?"

"What next? Why, does he abuse me?"

"He doesn't abuse you, but you know he is angry with you. He says mother's unhappy owing to you . . . and that you have ruined mother. You know he is so queer! I explain to him that you are kind, that you never scold mother; but he only shakes his head."

"So he says I have ruined her?"

"Yes; you mustn't be offended, Nikolay Ilyitch."

Belyaev got up, stood still a moment, and walked up and down the drawing-room.

"That's strange and . . . ridiculous!" he muttered, shrugging his shoulders and smiling sarcastically. "He's entirely to blame, and I have ruined her, eh? An innocent lamb, I must say. So he told you I ruined your mother?"

"Yes, but . . . you said you would not be offended, you know."

"I am not offended, and . . . and it's not your business. Why, it's . . . why, it's positively ridiculous! I have been thrust into it like a chicken in the broth, and now it seems I'm to blame!"

A ring was heard. The boy sprang up from his place and ran out. A minute later a lady came into the room with a little girl; this was Olga Ivanovna, Alyosha's mother. Alyosha followed them in, skipping and jumping, humming aloud and waving his hands. Belyaev nodded, and went on walking up and down.

"Of course, whose fault is it if not mine?" he muttered with a snort. "He is right! He is an injured husband."

"What are you talking about?" asked Olga Ivanovna.

"What about? . . . Why, just listen to the tales your lawful spouse is spreading now! It appears that I am a scoundrel and a villain, that I have ruined you and the children. All of you are unhappy, and I am the only happy one! Wonderfully, wonderfully happy!"

"I don't understand, Nikolay. What's the matter?"

"Why, listen to this young gentleman!" said Belyaev, pointing to Alyosha.

Alyosha flushed crimson, then turned pale, and his whole face began working with terror.

"Nikolay Ilyitch," he said in a loud whisper. "Sh-sh!"

Olga Ivanovna looked in surprise at Alyosha, then at Belyaev, then at Alyosha again.

"Just ask him," Belyaev went on. "Your Pelagea, like a regular fool, takes them about to restaurants and arranges meetings with their papa. But that's not the point: the point is that their dear papa is a victim, while I'm a wretch who has broken up both your lives. . ."

"Nikolay Ilyitch," moaned Alyosha. "Why, you promised

on your word of honour!"

"Oh, get away!" said Belyaev, waving him off. "This is more important than any word of honour. It's the hypocrisy revolts me, the lying! . . ."

"I don't understand it," said Olga Ivanovna, and tears glistened in her eyes. "Tell me, Alyosha," she turned to her son. "Do you see your father?"

Alyosha did not hear her; he was looking with horror at Belyaev.

"It's impossible," said his mother; "I will go and question Pelagea."

Olga Ivanovna went out.

"I say, you promised on your word of honour!" said Alyosha, trembling all over.

Belyaev dismissed him with a wave of his hand, and went on walking up and down. He was absorbed in his grievance and was oblivious of the boy's presence, as he always had been. He, a grownup, serious person, had no thought to spare for boys. And Alyosha sat down in the corner and told Sonia with horror how he had been deceived. He was trembling, stammering, and crying. It was the first time in his life that he had been brought into such coarse contact with lying; till then he had not known that there are in the world, besides sweet pears, pies, and expensive watches, a great many things for which the language of children has no expression.

JOY

IT was twelve o'clock at night.

Mitya Kuldarov, with excited face and ruffled hair, flew into his parents' flat, and hurriedly ran through all the rooms. His parents had already gone to bed. His sister was in bed, finishing the last page of a novel. His schoolboy brothers were asleep.

"Where have you come from?" cried his parents in amazement. "What is the matter with you?

"Oh, don't ask! I never expected it; no, I never expected it! It's... it's positively incredible!"

Mitya laughed and sank into an armchair, so overcome by happiness that he could not stand on his legs.

"It's incredible! You can't imagine! Look!"

His sister jumped out of bed and, throwing a quilt round her, went in to her brother. The schoolboys woke up.

"What's the matter? You don't look like yourself."

"It's because I am so delighted, Mamma! Do you know, now all Russia knows of me! All Russia! Till now only you knew that there was a registration clerk called Dmitry Kuldarov, and now all Russia knows it! Mamma! Oh, Lord!"

Mitya jumped up, ran up and down all the rooms, and then sat down again.

"Why, what has happened? Tell us sensibly!"

"You live like wild beasts, you don't read the newspapers and take no notice of what's published, and there's so much that is interesting in the papers. If anything happens it's all known at once, nothing is hidden! How happy I am! Oh, Lord! You know it's only celebrated people whose names are published in the papers, and now they have gone and published mine!"

"What do you mean? Where?"

The papa turned pale. The mamma glanced at the holy image and crossed herself. The schoolboys jumped out of bed and, just as they were, in short nightshirts, went up to their brother.

"Yes! My name has been published! Now all Russia knows of me! Keep the paper, mamma, in memory of it! We will read it sometimes! Look!"

Mitya pulled out of his pocket a copy of the paper, gave it to his father, and pointed with his finger to a passage marked with blue pencil.

"Read it!"

The father put on his spectacles.

"Do read it!"

The mamma glanced at the holy image and crossed herself. The papa cleared his throat and began to read: "At eleven o'clock on the evening of the 29th of December, a registration clerk of the name of Dmitry Kuldarov..."

"You see, you see! Go on!"

"... a registration clerk of the name of Dmitry Kuldarov, coming from the beershop in Kozihin's buildings in Little Bronnaia in an intoxicated condition..."

"That's me and Semyon Petrovitch.. . . It's all described exactly! Go on! Listen!"

". . . intoxicated condition, slipped and fell under a horse belonging to a sledge-driver, a peasant of the village of Durikino in the Yuhnovsky district, called Ivan Drotov. The frightened horse, stepping over Kuldarov and drawing the sledge over him, together with a Moscow merchant of the second guild called Stepan Lukov, who was in it, dashed along the street and was caught by some house-porters. Kuldarov, at first in an unconscious condition, was taken to the police station and there examined by the doctor. The blow he had received on the back of his head..."

"It was from the shaft, papa. Go on! Read the rest!"

"... he had received on the back of his head turned out not to be serious. The incident was duly reported. Medical aid was given to the injured man...."

"They told me to foment the back of my head with cold water. You have read it now? Ah! So you see. Now it's all over Russia! Give it here!"

Mitya seized the paper, folded it up and put it into his pocket.

"I'll run round to the Makarovs and show it to them.... I must show it to the Ivanitskys too, Natasya Ivanovna, and Anisim Vassilyitch.... I'll run! Good-bye!"

Mitya put on his cap with its cockade and, joyful and triumphant, ran into the street.

CHORISTERS

THE Justice of the Peace, who had received a letter from Petersburg, had set the news going that the owner of Yefremovo, Count Vladimir Ivanovitch, would soon be arriving. When he would arrive —there was no saying.

"Lake a thief in the night," said Father Kuzma, a grey-headed little priest in a lilac cassock. "And when he does come the place will be crowded with the nobility and other high gentry. All the neighbours will flock here. Mind now, do your best, Alexey Alexeitch.... I beg you most earnestly."

"You need not trouble about me," said Alexey Alexeitch, frowning. "I know my business. If only my enemy intones the litany in the right key. He may. . out of sheer spite...."

"There, there.... I'll persuade the deacon... I'll persuade him."

Alexey Alexeitch was the sacristan of the Yefremovo church. He also taught the schoolboys church and secular singing, for which he received sixty roubles a year from the revenues of the Count's estate. The schoolboys were bound to sing in church in return for their teaching. Alexey Alexeitch was a tall, thickset man of dignified deportment, with a fat, clean-shaven face that reminded one of a cow's udder. His imposing figure and double chin made him look like a man occupying an important position in the secular hierarchy rather than a sacristan. It was strange to see him, so dignified and imposing, flop to the ground before the bishop and, on one occasion, after too loud a squabble with the deacon Yevlampy Avdiessov, remain on his knees for two hours by order of the head priest of the district. Grandeur was more in keeping with his figure than humiliation.

On account of the rumours of the Count's approaching visit he had a choir practice every day, morning and evening. The choir practice was held at the school. It did not interfere much with the school work. During the practice the schoolmaster,

Sergey Makaritch, set the children writing copies while he joined the tenors as an amateur.

This is how the choir practice was conducted. Alexey Alexeitch would come into the school-room, slamming the door and blowing his nose. The trebles and altos extricated themselves noisily from the school-tables. The tenors and basses, who had been waiting for some time in the yard, came in, tramping like horses. They all took their places. Alexey Alexeitch drew himself up, made a sign to enforce silence, and struck a note with the tuning fork.

"To-to-li-to-tom... Do-mi-sol-do!"

"Adagio, adagio.... Once more"

After the "Amen" there followed "Lord have mercy upon us" from the Great Litany. All this had been learned long ago, sung a thousand times and thoroughly digested, and it was gone through simply as a formality. It was sung indolently, unconsciously. Alexey Alexeitch waved his arms calmly and chimed in now in a tenor, now in a bass voice. It was all slow, there was nothing interesting. . . . But before the "Cherubim" hymn the whole choir suddenly began blowing their noses, coughing and zealously turning the pages of their music. The sacristan turned his back on the choir and with a mysterious expression on his face began tuning his violin. The preparations lasted a couple of minutes.

'Take your places. Look at your music carefully.... Basses, don't overdo it ... rather softly."

Bortnyansky's "Cherubim" hymn, No. 7, was selected. At a given signal silence prevailed. All eyes were fastened on the music, the trebles opened their mouths. Alexey Alexeitch softly lowered his arm.

"Piano... piano.... You see 'piano' is written there.... More lightly, more lightly."

When they had to sing "piano" an expression of benevolence and amiability overspread Alexey Alexeitch's face, as though he was dreaming of a dainty morsel.

"Forte... forte! Hold it!"

And when they had to sing "forte" the sacristan's fat face expressed alarm and even horror.

The "Cherubim" hymn was sung well, so well that the school-children abandoned their copies and fell to watching the movements of Alexey Alexeitch. People stood under the windows. The schoolwatchman, Vassily, came in wearing an apron and carrying a dinner-knife in his hand and stood listening. Father Kuzma, with an anxious face appeared suddenly as though he had sprung from out of the earth. . . . After 'Let us lay aside all earthly cares' Alexey Alexeitch wiped the sweat off his brow and went up to Father Kuzma in excitement.

"It puzzles me, Father Kuzma," he said, shrugging his shoulders, "why is it that the Russian people have no understanding? It puzzles me, may the Lord chastise me! Such an uncultured people that you really cannot tell whether they have a windpipe in their throats or some other sort of internal arrangement. Were you choking, or what?" he asked, addressing the bass Gennady Semitchov, the innkeeper's brother.

"Why?"

"What is your voice like? It rattles like a saucepan. I bet you were boozing yesterday! That's what it is! Your breath smells like a tavern.... E-ech! You are a clodhopper, brother! You are a lout! How can you be a chorister if you keep company with peasants in the tavern? Ech, you are an ass, brother!"

"It's a sin, it's a sin, brother," muttered Father Kuzma. "God sees everything ... through and through...."

"That's why you have no idea of singing — because you care more for vodka than for godliness, you fool."

"Don't work yourself up," said Father Kuzma. "Don't be cross. ... I will persuade him."

Father Kuzma went up to Gennady Semitchov and began "persuading" him: "What do you do it for? Try and put your mind to it. A man who sings ought to restrain himself, because his throat is... er.. tender."

Gennady scratched his neck and looked sideways towards the window as though the words did not apply to him.

After the "Cherubim" hymn they sang the Creed, then "It is meet and right"; they sang smoothly and with feeling, and so right on to "Our Father."

"To my mind. Father Kuzma," said the sacristan, "the old "Our Father is better than the modem. That's what we ought to sing before the Count."

"No, no.... Sing the modern one. For the Count hears nothing but modern music when he goes to Mass in Petersburg or Moscow.... In the churches there, I imagine ... there's very different sort of music there, brother 1"

After "Our Father" there was again a great blowing of noses, coughing and turning over of pages. The most difficult part of the performance came next: the "concert." Alexey Alexeitch was practising two pieces, "Who is the God of glory" and "Universal Praise." Whichever the choir learned best would be sung before the Count. During the "concert" the sacristan rose to a pitch of enthusiasm. The expression of benevolence was continually alternating with one of alarm.

"Forte!" he muttered. "Andante! let yourselves go! Sing, you image! Tenors, you don't bring it off! To-to-ti-to-tom. ... Sol... si... sol, I tell you, you blockhead! Glory! Basses, glo... o... ry.

His bow travelled over the heads and shoulders of the erring trebles and altos. His left hand was continually pulling the ears of the young singers. On one occasion, carried away by his feelings he flipped the bass Gennady under the chin with his bent thumb. But the choristers were not moved to tears or to anger at his blows: they realised the fall gravity of their task.

After the "concert" came a minute of silence. Alexey Alexeitch, red, perspiring and exhausted, sat down on the window-sill, and turned upon the company lustreless, wearied, but triumphant eyes. In the listening crowd he observed to his immense annoyance the deacon Avdiessov. The deacon, a tall thick-set man with a red pock-marked face, and straw in his hair, stood leaning against the stove and grinning contemptuously.

"That's right, sing away! Perform your music!" he muttered in a deep bass. "Much the Count will care for your singing! He doesn't care whether you sing with music or without.... For he is an atheist."

Father Kuzma looked round in a scared way and twiddled his fingers.

"Come, come," he muttered. "Hush, deacon, I beg."

After the "concert" they sang "May our lips be filled with praise," and the choir practice was over. The choir broke up to reassemble in the evening for another practice. And so it went on every day.

One month passed and then a second.... The steward, too, had by then received a notice that the Count would soon be coming. At last the dusty sun-blinds were taken off the windows of the big house, and Yefremovo heard the strains of the broken-down, out-of-tune piano. Father Kuzma was pining, though he could not himself have said why, or whether it was from delight or alarm.... The deacon went about grinning.

The following Saturday evening Father Kuzma went to the sacristan's lodgings. His face was pale, his shoulders drooped, the lilac of his cassock looked faded.

"I have just been at his Excellency's," he said to the sacristan, stammering. "He is a cultivated gentleman with refined ideas. But... er... it's mortifying, brother.... 'At what o'clock, your Excellency, do you desire us to ring for Mass to-morrow?' And he said: 'As you think best. Only, couldn't it be as short and quick as possible without a choir.' Without a choir! Er... do you understand, without, without a choir...."

Alexey Alexeitch turned crimson. He would rather have spent two hours on his knees again than have heard those words! He did not sleep all night. He was not so much mortified at the waste of his labours as at the fact that the deacon would give him no peace now with his jeers. The deacon was delighted at his discomfiture. Next day all through the service he was casting disdainful glances towards the choir where Alexey Alexeitch was booming responses in solitude. When he passed by the choir with the censer he muttered:

"Perform your music! Do your utmost! The Count will give a ten-rouble note to the choir!"

After the service the sacristan went home, crushed and ill with mortification. At the gate he was overtaken by the red-faced deacon.

"Stop a minute, Alyosha!" said the deacon. "Stop a minute, silly, don't be cross! You are not the only one, I am in for it too! Immediately after the Mass Father Kuzma went up to the Count and asked: 'And what did you think of the deacon's voice, your Excellency. He has a deep bass, hasn't he?' And the Count — do you know what he answered by way of compliment? 'Anyone can bawl,' he said. 'A man's voice is not as important as his brains.' A learned gentleman from Petersburg! An atheist is an atheist, and that's all about it! Come, brother in misfortune, let us go and have a drop to drown our troubles!"

And the enemies went out of the gate arm-in-arm.

THE MARSHAL'S WIDOW

ON the first of February every year, St. Trifon's day, there is an extraordinary commotion on the estate of Madame Zavzyatov, the widow of Trifon Lvovitch, the late marshal of the district. On that day, the nameday of the deceased marshal, the widow Lyubov Petrovna has a requiem service celebrated in his memory, and after the requiem a thanksgiving to the Lord. The whole district assembles for the service. There you will see Hrumov the present marshal, Marfutkin, the president of the Zemstvo, Potrashkov, the permanent member of the Rural Board, the two justices of the peace of the district, the police captain, Krinolinov, two police-superintendents, the district doctor, Dvornyagin, smelling of iodoform, all the landowners, great and small, and so on. There are about fifty people assembled in all.

Precisely at twelve o'clock, the visitors, with long faces, make their way from all the rooms to the big hall. There are carpets on the floor and their steps are noiseless, but the solemnity of the occasion makes them instinctively walk on tip-toe, holding out their hands to balance themselves. In the hall everything is already prepared. Father Yevmeny, a little old man in a high faded cap, puts on his black vestments. Konkordiev, the deacon, already in his vestments, and as red as a crab, is noiselessly turning over the leaves of his missal and putting slips of paper in it. At the door leading to the vestibule, Luka, the sacristan, puffing out his cheeks and making round eyes, blows up the censer. The hall is gradually filled with bluish transparent smoke and the smell of incense.

Gelikonsky, the elementary schoolmaster, a young man with big pimples on his frightened face, wearing a new greatcoat like a sack, carries round wax candles on a silver-plated tray. The hostess, Lyubov Petrovna, stands in the front by a little table with a dish of funeral rice on it, and holds her handkerchief in readiness to her face. There is a profound stillness, broken from time to time by sighs. Everybody has a long, solemn face....

The requiem service begins. The blue smoke curls up from the censer and plays in the slanting sunbeams, the lighted candles faintly splutter. The singing, at first harsh and deafening, soon becomes quiet and musical as the choir gradually adapt themselves to the acoustic conditions of the rooms.... The tunes are all mournful and sad.... The guests are gradually brought to a melancholy mood and grow pensive. Thoughts of the brevity of human life, of mutability, of worldly vanity stray through their brains.... They recall the deceased Zavzyatov, a thick-set, red-cheeked man who used to drink off a bottle of champagne at one gulp and smash looking-glasses with his forehead. And when they sing "With Thy Saints, 0 Lord," and the sobs of their hostess are audible, the guests shift uneasily from one foot to the other. The more emotional begin to feel a tickling in their throat and about their eyelids. Marfutkin, the president of the Zemstvo, to stifle the unpleasant feeling, bends down to the police captain's ear and whispers:

"I was at Ivan Fyodoritch's yesterday.... Pyotr Petrovitch and I took all the tricks, playing no trumps. . . . Yes, indeed. . . . Olga Andreyevna was so exasperated that her false tooth fell out of her mouth."

But at last the "Eternal Memory" is sung. Gelikonsky respectfully takes away the candles, and the memorial service is over. Thereupon there follows a momentary commotion; there is a changing of vestments and a thanksgiving service. After the thanksgiving, while Father Yevmeny is disrobing, the visitors rub their hands and cough, while their hostess tells some anecdote of the good-heartedness of the deceased Trifon Lvovitch.

"Pray come to lunch, friends," she says, concluding her story with a sigh.

The visitors, trying not to push or tread on each other's feet, hasten into the dining-room. . . . There the luncheon is awaiting them. The repast is so magnificent that the deacon Konkordiev thinks it his duty every year to fling up his hands as he looks at it and, shaking his head in amazement, say:

"Supernatural! It's not so much like human fare, Father Yevmeny, as offerings to the gods."

The lunch is certainly exceptional. Everything that the flora and fauna of the country can furnish is on the table, but the only thing supernatural about it, perhaps, is that on the table there is everything except... alcoholic beverages. Lyubov Petrovna has taken a vow never to have in her house cards or spirituous liquors – the two sources of her husband's ruin. And the only bottles contain oil and vinegar, as though in mockery and chastisement of the guests who are to a man desperately fond of the bottle, and given to tippling.

Please help yourselves, gentlemen!" the marshal's widow presses them. "Only you must excuse me, I have no vodka.... I have none in the house."

The guests approach the table and hesitatingly attack the pie. But the progress with eating is slow. In the plying of forks, in the cutting up and munching, there is a certain sloth and apathy. . . . Evidently something is wanting.

"I feel as though I had lost something," one of the justices of the peace whispers to the other. "I feel as I did when my wife ran away with the engineer. ... I can't eat."

Marfutkin, before beginning to eat, rumbles for a long time in his pocket and looks for his handkerchief.

"Oh, my handkerchief must be in my greatcoat," he recalls in a loud voice, "and here I am looking for it," and he goes into the vestibule where the fur coats are hanging up.

He returns from the vestibule with glistening eyes, and at once attacks the pie with relish.

"I say, it's horrid munching away with a dry mouth, isn't it?" he whispers to Father Yevmeny. "Go into the vestibule, Father. There's a bottle there in my fur coat.... Only mind you are careful; don't make a clatter with the bottle."

Father Yevmeny recollects that he has some direction to give to Luka, and trips off to the vestibule.

"Father, a couple of words in confidence," says Dvornyagin, overtaking him.

"You should see the fur coat I've bought myself, gentlemen," Hrumov boasts. "It's worth a thousand, and I gave... you won't believe it... two hundred and fifty! Not a farthing more."

At any other time the guests would have greeted this information with indifference, but now they display surprise and incredulity. In the end they all troop out into the vestibule to look at the *far* coat, and go on looking at it till the doctor's man Mikeshka carries five empty bottles out on the sly. When the steamed sturgeon is served, Marfutkin remembers that he has left his cigar case in his sledge and goes to the stable. That he may not be lonely on this expedition, he takes with him the deacon, who appropriately feels it necessary to have a look at his horse....

On the evening of the same day, Lyubov Petrovna is sitting in her study, writing a letter to an old friend in Petersburg:

'To-day, as in past years," she writes among other things, "I had a memorial service for my dear husband. All my neighbours came to the service. They are a simple, rough set, but what hearts! I gave them a splendid lunch, but of course, as in previous years, without a drop of alcoholic liquor. Ever since he died from excessive drinking I have vowed to establish temperance in this district and thereby to expiate his sins. I have begun the campaign for temperance at my own house. Father Yevmeny is delighted with my efforts, and helps me both in word and deed. Oh, *ma chèiv,* if you knew how fond my bears are of me! The president of the Zemstvo, Marfutkin, kissed my hand after lunch, held it a long while to his lips, and, wagging his head in an absurd way, burst into tears: so much feeling but no words! Father Yevmeny, that delightful little old man, sat down by me, and looking tearfully at me kept babbling something like a child. I did not understand what he said, but I know how to understand true feeling. The police captain, the handsome man of whom I wrote to you, went down on his knees to me, tried to read me some verses of his own composition (he is a poet), but... his feelings were too much for him, he lurched and fell over... that huge giant went into hysterics, you can imagine my delight! The day did not pass without a hitch, however. Poor Alalykin, the president of the judges' assembly, a stout and apoplectic man, was overcome by illness and lay on the sofa in a state of unconsciousness for two hours. We had to pour water on him .... I am thankful to Doctor Dvornyagin: he had brought a bottle of brandy from his dispensary and he moistened the patient's temples, which quickly revived him, and he was able to be moved...."

BOOTS

A PIANO-TUNER called Murkin, a close-shaven man with a yellow face, with a nose stained with snuff, and cotton-wool in his ears, came out of his hotel-room into the passage, and in a cracked voice cried: "Semyon! Waiter!"

And looking at his frightened face one might have supposed that the ceiling had fallen in on him or that he had just seen a ghost in his room.

"Upon my word, Semyon!" he cried, seeing the attendant running towards him. "What is the meaning of it? I am a rheumatic, delicate man and you make me go barefoot! Why is it you don't give me my boots all this time? Where are they?"

Semyon went into Murkin's room, looked at the place where he was in the habit of putting the boots he had cleaned, and scratched his head: the boots were not there.

"Where can they be, the damned things?" Semyon brought out. "I fancy I cleaned them in the evening and put them here.... H'm!... Yesterday, I must own, I had a drop.... I must have put them in another room, I suppose. That must be it, Afanasy Yegoritch, they are in another room! There are lots of boots, and how the devil is one to know them apart when one is drunk and does not know what one is doing?... I must have taken them in to the lady that's next door... the actress...."

"And now, if you please, I am to go in to a lady and disturb her all through you! Here, if you please, through this foolishness I am to wake up a respectable woman."

Sighing and coughing, Murkin went to the door of the next room and cautiously tapped.

"Who's there?" he heard a woman's voice a minute later.

"It's I!" Murkin began in a plaintive voice, standing in the attitude of a cavalier addressing a lady of the highest society. "Pardon my disturbing you, madam, but I am a man in delicate health, rheumatic.... The doctors, madam, have ordered me to keep my feet warm, especially as I have to go at once to tune the piano at Madame la Générate Shevelitsyn's. I can't go to her barefoot."

"But what do you want? What piano?"

"Not a piano, madam; it is in reference to boots! Semyon, stupid fellow, cleaned my boots and put them by mistake in your room. Be so extremely kind, madam, as to give me my boots!"

There was a sound of rustling, of jumping off the bed and the flapping of slippers, after which the door opened slightly and a plump feminine hand flung at Murkin's feet a pair of boots. The piano-tuner thanked her and went into his own room.

"Odd..." he muttered, putting on the boots, it seems as though this is not the right boot. Why, here are two left boots! Both are for the left foot! I say, Semyon, these are not my boots! My boots have red tags and no patches on them, and these are in holes and have no tags."

Semyon picked up the boots, turned them over several times before his eyes, and frowned.

"Those are Pavel Alexandritch's boots," he grumbled, squinting at them. He squinted with the left eve.

"What Pavel Alexandritch?"

"The actor; he comes here every Tuesday.... He must have put on yours instead of his own.... So I must have put both pairs in her room, his and yours. Here's a go!"

"Then go and change them!"

"That's all right!" sniggered Semyon, "go and change them.... Where am I to find him now? He went off an hour ago.... Go and look for the wind in the fields!"

"Where does he live then?"

"Who can tell? He comes here every Tuesday, and where he lives I don't know. He comes and stays the night, and then you may wait till next Tuesday...."

"There, do you see, you brute, what you have done? Why, what am I to do now? It is time I was at Madame la Générale Shevelitsyn's, you anathema! My feet are frozen!"

"You can change the boots before long. Put on these boots, go about in them till the evening, and in the evening go to the theatre.... Ask there for Blistanov, the actor.... If you don't care to go to the theatre, you will have to wait till next Tuesday; he only comes here on Tuesdays... ."

"But why are there two boots for the left foot?' asked the piano-tuner, picking up the boots with an air of disgust.

"What God has sent him, that he wears. Through poverty... where is an actor to get boots? I said to him "What boots, Pavel Alexandritch! They are a positive disgrace!' and he said: 'Hold your peace,' says he, 'and turn pale! In those very boots,' says he, 'I have played counts and princes.' A queer lot! Artists, that's the only word for them! If I were the governor or anyone in command, I would get all these actors together and clap them all in prison."

Continually sighing and groaning and knitting his brows, Murkin drew the two left boots on to his feet, and set off, limping, to Madame la Générale Shevelitsyn's. He went about the town all day long tuning pianos, and all day long it seemed to him that everyone was looking at his feet and seeing his patched boots with heels worn down at the sides! Apart from his moral agonies he had to suffer physically also; the boots gave him a corn.

In the evening he was at the theatre. There was a performance of *Bluebeard.* It was only just before the last act, and then only thanks to the good offices of a man he knew who played a flute in the orchestra, that he gained admittance behind the scenes. Going to the men's dressing-room, he found there all the male performers. Some were changing their clothes, others were painting their faces, others were smoking. Bluebeard was standing with King Bobesh, showing him a revolver.

"You had better buy it," said Bluebeard. "I bought it at Kursk, a bargain, for eight roubles, but, there! I will let you have it for six.... A wonderfully good one!"

"Steady.... It's loaded, you know!"

"Can I see Mr. Blistanov?" the piano-tuner asked as he went in.

"I am he!" said Bluebeard, turning to him. "What do you want?"

"Excuse my troubling you, sir," began the piano-tuner in an imploring voice, "but, believe me, I am a man in delicate health, rheumatic. The doctors have ordered me to keep my feet warm..." "But, speaking plainly, what do you want?"

"You see," said the piano-tuner, addressing Bluebeard. "Er... you stayed last night at Buhteyev's furnished apartments... No. 64..."

"What's this nonsense?" said King Bobesh with a grin. "My wife is at No. 64."

"Your wife, sir? Delighted...." Murkin smiled. "It was she, your good lady, who gave me this gentleman's boots.... After this gentleman – the piano-tuner indicated Blistanov–" had gone away I missed my boots.... I called the waiter, you know, and he said: 'I left your boots in the next room!' By mistake, being in a state of intoxication, he left my boots as well as yours at 64," said Murkin, turning to Blistanov, "and when you left this gentleman's lady you put on mine."

"What are you talking about?" said Blistanov, and he scowled." Have you come here to libel me?"

"Not at all, sir – God forbid! You misunderstand me. What am I talking about? About boots! You did stay the night at No. 64, didn't you?" "When?" "Last night!" "Why, did you see me there?"

"No, sir, I didn't see you," said Murkin in great confusion, sitting down and taking off the boots. "I did not see you, but this gentleman's lady threw out your boots here to me ... instead of mine."

"What right have you, sir, to make such assertions? I say nothing about myself, but you are slandering a woman, and in the presence of her husband, too!"

A fearful hubbub arose behind the scenes. King Bobesh, the injured husband, suddenly turned crimson and brought his fist down upon the table with such violence that two actresses in the next dressing-room felt faint.

"And you believe it?' cried Bluebeard. "You believe this worthless rascal? O-oh! Would you like me to kill him like a dog? Would you like it? I will turn him into a beefsteak! I'll blow his brains out!"

And all the persons who were promenading that evening in the town park by the Summer theatre describe to this day how just before the fourth act they saw a man with bare feet, a yellow face, and terror-stricken eyes dart out of the theatre and dash along the principal avenue. He was pursued by a man in the costume of Bluebeard, armed with a revolver. What happened later no one saw. All that is known is that Murkin was confined to his bed for a fortnight after his acquaintance with Blistanov, and that to the words "I am a man in delicate health, rheumatic" he took to adding, "I am a wounded man...."

ART

A GLOOMY winter morning.

On the smooth and glittering surface of the river Bystryanka, sprinkled here and there with snow, stand two peasants, scrubby little Seryozhka and the church beadle, Matvey. Seryozhka, a short-legged, ragged, mangy-looking fellow of thirty, stares angrily at the ice. Tufts of wool hang from his shaggy sheepskin like a mangy dog. In his hands he holds a compass made of two pointed sticks. Matvey, a fine-looking old man in a new sheepskin and high felt boots, looks with mild blue eyes upwards where on the high sloping bank a village nestles picturesquely. In his hands there is a heavy crowbar.

"Well, are we going to stand like this till evening with our arms folded?" says Seryozhka, breaking the silence and turning his angry eyes on Matvey. "Have you come here to stand about, old fool, or to work?"

"Well, you... er... show me..." Matvey mutters, blinking mildly.

"Show you.... It's always me: me to show you, and me to do it. They have no sense of their own! Mark it out with the compasses, that's what's wanted! You can't break the ice without marking it out. Mark it! Take the compass."

Matvey takes the compasses from Seryozhka's hands, and, shuffling heavily on the same spot and jerking with his elbows in all directions, he begins awkwardly trying to describe a circle on the ice. Seryozhka screws up his eyes contemptuously and obviously enjoys his awkwardness and incompetence.

"Eh-eh-eh!" he mutters angrily. "Even that you can't do! The fact is you are a stupid peasant, a wooden-head! You ought to be grazing geese and not making a Jordan! Give the compasses here! Give them here, I say!"

Seryozhka snatches the compasses out of the hands of the perspiring Matvey, and in an instant, jauntily twirling round on one heel, he describes a circle on the ice. The outline of the new Jordan is ready now, all that is left to do is to break the ice...

But before proceeding to the work Seryozhka spends a long time in airs and graces, whims and reproaches...

"I am not obliged to work for you! You are employed in the church, you do it!

He obviously enjoys the peculiar position in which he has been placed by the fate that has bestowed on him the rare talent of surprising the whole parish once a year by his art. Poor mild Matvey has to listen to many venomous and contemptuous words from him. Seryozhka sets to work with vexation, with anger. He is lazy. He has hardly described the circle when he is already itching to go up to the village to drink tea, lounge about, and babble...

"I'll be back directly," he says, lighting his cigarette, "and meanwhile you had better bring something to sit on and sweep up, instead of standing there counting the crows."

Matvey is left alone. The air is grey and harsh but still. The white church peeps out genially from behind the huts scattered on the river bank. Jackdaws are incessantly circling round its golden crosses. On one side of the village where the river bank breaks off and is steep a hobbled horse is standing at the very edge, motionless as a stone, probably asleep or deep in thought.

Matvey, too, stands motionless as a statue, waiting patiently. The dreamily brooding look of the river, the circling of the jackdaws, and the sight of the horse make him drowsy. One hour passes, a second, and still Seryozhka does not come. The river has long been swept and a box brought to sit on, but the drunken fellow does not appear. Matvey waits and merely yawns. The feeling of boredom is one of which he knows nothing. If he were told to stand on the river for a day, a month, or a year he would stand there.

At last Seryozhka comes into sight from behind the huts. He walks with a lurching gait, scarcely moving. He is too lazy to go the long way round, and he comes not by the road, but prefers a short cut in a straight line down the bank, and sticks in the snow, hangs on to the bushes, slides on his back as he comes — and all this slowly, with pauses.

"What are you about?" he cries, falling on Matvey at once. "Why are you standing there doing nothing! When are you going to break the ice?"

Matvey crosses himself, takes the crowbar in both hands, and begins breaking the ice, carefully keeping to the circle that has been drawn. Seryozhka sits down on the box and watches the heavy clumsy movements of his assistant.

"Easy at the edges! Easy there!" he commands. "If you can't do it properly, you shouldn't undertake it, once you have undertaken it you should do it. You!"

A crowd collects on the top of the bank. At the sight of the spectators Seryozhka becomes even more excited.

"I declare I am not going to do it..." he says, lighting a stinking cigarette and spitting on the ground. "I should like to see how you get on without me. Last year at Kostyukovo, Styopka Gulkov undertook to make a Jordan as I do. And what did it amount to — it was a laughing-stock. The Kostyukovo folks came to ours — crowds and crowds of them! The people flocked from all the villages."

"Because except for ours there is nowhere a proper Jordan ..."

"Work, there is no time for talking. . . . Yes, old man . . . you won't find another Jordan like it in the whole province. The soldiers say you would look in vain, they are not so good even in the towns. Easy, easy!"

Matvey puns and groans. The work is not easy. The ice is firm and thick; and he has to break it and at once take the pieces away that the open space may not be blocked up.

But, hard as the work is and senseless as Seryozhka's commands are, by three o'clock there is a large circle of dark water in the Bystryanka.

"It was better last year," says Seryozhka angrily. 'You can't do even that! Ah, dummy! To keep such fools in the temple of God! Go and bring a board to make the pegs! Bring the ring, you crow! And er... get some bread somewhere. .. and some cucumbers, or something."

Matvey goes off and soon afterwards comes back, carrying on his shoulders an immense wooden ring which had been painted in previous years in patterns of various colours. In the centre of the ring is a red cross, at the circumference holes for the pegs. Seryozhka takes the ring and covers the hole in the ice with it.

"Just right... it fits.... We have only to renew the paint and it will be first-rate. ... Come, why are you standing still? Make the lectern. Or—er—go and get logs to make the cross..."

Matvey, who has not tasted food or drink all day, trudges up the hill again. Lazy as Seryozhka is, he makes the pegs with his own hands. He knows that those pegs have a miraculous power: whoever gets hold of a peg after the blessing of the water will be lucky for the whole year. Such work is really worth doing.

But the real work begins the following day. Then Seryozhka displays himself before the ignorant Matvey in all the greatness of his talent. There is no end to his babble, his fault-finding, his whims and fancies. If Matvey nails two big pieces of wood to make a cross, he is dissatisfied and tells him to do it again. If Matvey stands still, Seryozhka asks him angrily why he does not go; if he moves, Seryozhka shouts to him not to go away but to do his work. He is not satisfied with his tools, with the weather, or with his own talent; nothing pleases him.

Matvey saws out a great piece of ice for a lectern. "Why have you broken off the corner?' cries Seryozhka, and glares at him furiously. "Why have you broken off the corner? I ask you." "Forgive me, for Christ's sake." "Do it over again!"

Matvey saws again... and there is no end to his sufferings. A lectern is to stand by the hole in the ice that is covered by the painted ring; on the lectern is to be carved the cross and the open gospel. But that is not all. Behind the lectern there is to be a high cross to be seen by all the crowd and to glitter in the sun as though sprinkled with diamonds and rubies. On the cross is to be a dove carved out of ice. The path from the church to the Jordan is to be strewn with branches of fir and juniper. All this is their task.

First of all Seryozhka sets to work on the lectern. He works with a file, a chisel, and an awl. He is perfectly successful in the cross on the lectern, the gospel, and the drapery that hangs down from the lectern. Then he begins on the dove. While he is trying to carve an expression of meekness and humility on the face of the dove, Matvey, lumbering about like a bear, is coating with ice the cross he has made of wood. He takes the cross and dips it in the hole. Waiting till the water has frozen on the cross he dips it in a second time, and so on till the cross is covered with a thick layer of ice. It is a difficult job, calling for a great deal of strength and patience.

But now the delicate work is finished. Seryozhka races about the village like one possessed. He swears and vows he will go at once to the river and smash all his work. He is looking for suitable paints.

His pockets are full of ochre, dark blue, red lead, and verdigris; without paying a farthing he rushes headlong from one shop to another. The shop is next door to the tavern. Here he has a drink; with a wave of his hand he darts off without paying. At one hut he gets beetroot leaves, at another an onion skin, out of which he makes a yellow colour. He swears, shoves, threatens, and not a soul murmurs! They all smile at him, they sympathise with him, call him Sergey

Nikititch; they all feel that his art is not his personal affair but something that concerns them all, the whole people. One creates, the others help him. Seryozhka in himself is a nonentity, a sluggard, a drunkard, and a wastrel, but when he has his red lead or compasses in his hand he is at once something higher, a servant of God.

Epiphany morning comes. The precincts of the church and both banks of the river for a long distance are swarming with people. Everything that makes up the Jordan is scrupulously concealed under new mats. Seryozhka is meekly moving about near the mats, trying to control his emotion. He sees thousands of people. There are many here from other parishes; these people have come many a mile on foot through the frost and the snow merely to see his celebrated Jordan. Matvey, who had finished his coarse, rough work, is by now back in the church, there is no sight, no sound of him; he is already forgotten.... The weather is lovely.... There is not a cloud in the sky. The sunshine is dazzling.

The church bells ring out on the hill. . . Thousands of heads are bared, thousands of hands are moving, there are thousands of signs of the cross!

And Seryozhka does not know what to do with himself for impatience. But now they are ringing the bells for the Sacrament; then half an hour later a certain agitation is perceptible in the belfry and among the people. Banners are borne out of the church one after the other, while the bells peal in joyous haste. Seryozhka, trembling, pulls away the mat... and the people behold something extraordinary. The lectern, the wooden ring, the pegs, and the cross in the ice are iridescent with thousands of colors. The cross and the dove glitter so dazzlingly that it hurts the eyes to look at them. Merciful God, how fine it is! A murmur of wonder and delight runs through the crowd; the bells peal more loudly still, the day grows brighter; the banners oscillate and move over the crowd as over the waves. The procession, guttering with the settings of the ikons and the vestments of the clergy, comes slowly down the road and turns towards the Jordan. Hands are waved to the belfry for the ringing to cease, and the blessing of the water begins. The priests conduct the service slowly, deliberately, evidently trying to prolong the ceremony and the joy of praying all gathered together. There is perfect stillness.

But now they plunge the cross in, and the air echoes with an extraordinary din. Guns are fired, the bells peal furiously, loud exclamations of delight, shouts, and a rush to get the pegs. Seryozhka listens to this uproar, sees thousands of eyes fixed upon him, and the lazy fellow's soul is filled with a sense of glory and triumph.

LOVE

"THREE o'clock in the morning. The soft April night is looking in at my windows and caressingly winking at me with its stars. I can't sleep, I am so happy!

"My whole being from head to heels is bursting with a strange, incomprehensible feeling. I can't analyse it just now – I haven't the time, I'm too lazy, and there – hang analysis! Why, is a man likely to interpret his sensations when he is flying head foremost from a belfry, or has just learned that he has won two hundred thousand? Is he in a state to do it?"

This was more or less how I began my love-letter to Sasha, a girl of nineteen with whom I had fallen in love. I began it five times, and as often tore up the sheets, scratched out whole pages, and copied it all over again. I spent as long over the letter as if it had been a novel I had to write to order. And it was not because I tried to make it longer, more elaborate, and more fervent, but because I wanted endlessly to prolong the process of this writing, when one sits in the stillness of one's study and communes with one's own day-dreams while the spring night looks in at one's window. Between the lines I saw a beloved image, and it seemed to me that there were, sitting at the same table writing with me, spirits as naïvely happy, as foolish, and as blissfully smiling as I. I wrote continually, looking at my hand, which still ached deliciously where hers had lately pressed it, and if I turned my eyes away I had a vision of the green trellis of the little gate. Through that trellis Sasha gazed at me after I had said goodbye to her. When I was saying good-bye to Sasha I was thinking of nothing and was simply admiring her figure as every decent man admires a pretty woman; when I saw through the trellis two big eyes, I suddenly, as though by inspiration, knew that I was in love, that it was all settled between us, and fully decided already, that I had nothing left to do but to carry out certain formalities.

It is a great delight also to seal up a love-letter, and, slowly putting on one's hat and coat, to go softly out of the house and to cany the treasure to the post. There are no stars in the sky now: in their place there is a long whitish streak in the east, broken here and there by clouds above the roofs of the dingy houses; from that streak the whole sky is flooded with pale light. The town is asleep, but already the water-carts have come out, and somewhere in a far-away factory a whistle sounds to wake up the workpeople. Beside the postbox, slightly moist with dew, you are sure to see the clumsy figure of a house porter, wearing a bell-shaped sheepskin and carrying a stick. He is in a condition akin to catalepsy: he is not asleep or awake, but something between.

If the boxes knew how often people resort to them for the decision of their fate, they would not have such a humble air. I, anyway, almost kissed my postbox, and as I gazed at it I reflected that the post is the greatest of blessings.

I beg anyone who has ever been in love to remember how one usually hurries home after dropping the letter in the box, rapidly gets into bed and pulls up the quilt in the full conviction that as soon as one wakes up in the morning one will be overwhelmed with memories of the previous day and look with rapture at the window, where the daylight will be eagerly making its way through the folds of the curtain.

Well, to facts.... Next morning at midday, Sasha's maid brought me the following answer: "I am delited be sure to come to us to day please I shall expect you. Your S."

Not a single comma. This lack of punctuation, and the misspelling of the word "delighted," the whole letter, and even the long, narrow envelope in which it was put filled my heart with tenderness. In the sprawling but diffident handwriting I recognised Sasha's walk, her way of raising her eyebrows when she laughed, the movement of her lips.... But the contents of the letter did not satisfy me. In the first place, poetical letters are not answered in that way, and in the second, why should I go to Sasha's house to wait till it should occur to her stout mamma, her brothers, and poor relations to leave us alone together? It would never enter their heads, and nothing is more hateful than to have to restrain one's raptures simply because of the intrusion of some animate trumpery in the shape of a half-deaf old woman or little girl pestering one with questions. I sent an answer by the maid asking Sasha to select some park or boulevard for a rendezvous. My suggestion was readily accepted. I had struck the right chord, as the saying is.

Between four and five o'clock in the afternoon I made my way to the furthest and most overgrown part of the park. There was not a soul in the park, and the tryst might have taken place somewhere nearer in one of the avenues or arbours, but women don't like doing it by halves in romantic affairs; in for a penny, in for a pound – if you are in for a tryst, let it be in the farthest and most impenetrable thicket, where one runs the risk of stumbling upon some rough or drunken man. When I went up to Sasha she was standing with her back to me, and in that back I could read a devilish lot of mystery. It seemed as though that back and the nape of her neck, and the black spots on her dress were saying: Hush!... The girl was wearing a simple cotton dress over which she had thrown a light cape. To add to the air of mysterious secrecy, her face was covered with a white veil. Not to spoil the effect, I had to approach on tiptoe and speak in a half whisper.

From what I remember now, I was not so much the essential point of the rendezvous as a detail of it. Sasha was not so much absorbed in the interview itself as in its romantic mysteriousness. my kisses, the silence of the gloomy trees, my vows.... There was not a minute in which she forgot herself, was overcome, or let the mysterious expression drop from her face, and really if there had been any Ivan Sidoritch or Sidor Ivanitch in my place she would have felt just as happy. How is one to make out in such circumstances whether one is loved or not? Whether the love is "the real thing" or not?

From the park I took Sasha home with me. The presence

of the beloved woman in one's bachelor quarters affects one like wine and music. Usually one begins to speak of the future, and the confidence and self-reliance with which one does so is beyond bounds. You make plans and projects, talk fervently of the rank of general though you have not yet reached the rank of a lieutenant, and altogether you fire off such high-flown nonsense that your listener must have a great deal of love and ignorance of life to assent to it. Fortunately for men, women in love are always blinded by their feelings and never know anything of life. Far from not assenting, they actually turn pale with holy awe, are full of reverence and hang greedily on the maniac's words. Sasha listened to me with attention, but I soon detected an absent-minded expression on her face, she did not understand me. The future of which I talked interested her only in its external aspect and I was wasting time in displaying my plans and projects before her. She was keenly interested in knowing which would be her room, what paper she would have in the room, why I had an upright piano instead of a grand piano, and so on. She examined carefully all the little things on my table, looked at the photographs, sniffed at the bottles, peeled the old stamps off the envelopes, saying she wanted them for something.

"Please collect old stamps for me!" she said, making a grave face. "Please do."

Then she found a nut in the window, noisily cracked it and ate it.

"Why don't you stick little labels on the backs of your books?" she asked, taking a look at the bookcase.

"What for?"

"Oh, so that each book should have its number. And where am I to put my books? I've got books too, you know."

"What books have you got?" I asked.

Sasha raised her eyebrows, thought a moment and said:

"All sorts."

And if it had entered my head to ask her what thoughts, what convictions, what aims she had, she would no doubt have raised her eyebrows, thought a minute, and have said in the same way: "All sorts."

Later I saw Sasha home and left her house regularly,

officially engaged, and was so reckoned till our wedding. If the reader will allow me to judge merely from my personal experience, I maintain that to be engaged is very dreary, far more so than to be a husband or nothing at all. An engaged man is neither one thing nor the other, he has left one side of the river and not reached the other, he is not married and yet he can't be said to be a bachelor, but is in something not unlike the condition of the porter whom I have mentioned above

Every day as soon as I had a free moment I hastened to my fiancee. As I went I usually bore within me a multitude of hopes, desires, intentions, suggestions, phrases. I always fancied that as soon as the maid opened the door I should, from feeling oppressed and stifled, plunge at once up to my neck into a sea of refreshing happiness. But it always turned out otherwise in fact. Every time I went to see my fiancee I found all her family and other members of the household busy over the silly trousseau. (And by the way, they were hard at work sewing for two months and then they had less than a hundred roubles' worth of things). There was a smell of irons, candle grease and fames. Bugles scrunched under one's feet. The two most important rooms were piled up with billows of linen, calico, and muslin and from among the billows peeped out Sasha's little head with a thread between her teeth. All the sewing party welcomed me with cries of delight but at once led me off into the dining-room where I could not hinder them nor see what only husbands are permitted to behold. In spite of my feelings, I had to sit in the dining-room and converse with Pimenovna, one of the poor relations. Sasha, looking worried and excited, kept running by me with a thimble, a skein of wool or some other boring object.

"Wait, wait, I shan't be a minute," she would say when I raised imploring eyes to her. "Only fancy that wretch Stepanida has spoilt the bodice of the barège dress!"

And after waiting in vain for this grace, I lost my temper, went out of the house and walked about the streets in the company of the new cane I had bought. Or I would want to go for a walk or a drive with my fiancee, would go round and find her already standing in the hall with her mother, dressed to go out and playing with her parasol.

"Oh, we are going to the Arcade," she would say. "We

have got to buy some; more cashmere and change the hat."

My outing is knocked on the head. I join the ladies and go with them to the Arcade. It is revoltingly dull to listen to women shopping, haggling and trying to outdo the sharp shopman. I felt ashamed when Sasha, after turning over masses of material and knocking down the prices to a minimum, walked out of the shop without buying anything, or else told the shopman to cut her some half rouble's worth.

When they came out of the shop, Sasha and her mamma with scared and worried faces would discuss at length having made a mistake, having bought the wrong thing, the flowers in the chintz being too dark, and so on.

Yes, it is a bore to be engaged! I'm glad it's over.

Now I am married. It is evening. I am sitting in my study reading. Behind me on the sofa Sasha is sitting munching something noisily. I want a glass of beer.

"Sasha, look for the corkscrew...." I say. "It's lying about somewhere."

Sasha leaps up, rummages in a disorderly way among two or three heaps of papers, drops the matches, and without finding the corkscrew, sits down in silence.... Five minutes pass – ten... I begin to be fretted both by thirst and vexation.

"Sasha, do look for the corkscrew," I say.

Sasha leaps up again and rummages among the papers near me. Her munching and rustling of the papers affects me like the sound of sharpening knives against each other.... I get up and begin looking for the corkscrew myself. At last it is found and the beer is uncorked. Sasha remains by the table and begins telling me something at great length.

'You'd better read something, Sasha," I say.

She takes up a book, sits down facing me and begins moving her lips.... I look at her little forehead, moving lips, and sink into thought.

"She is getting on for twenty...." I reflect. "If one takes a boy of the educated class and of that age and compares them, what a difference! The boy would have knowledge and convictions and some intelligence."

But I forgive that difference just as the low forehead and moving lips are forgiven. I remember in my old Lovelace days

I have cast off women for a stain on their stockings, or for one foolish word, or for not cleaning their teeth, and now I forgive everything: the munching, the muddling about after the corkscrew, the slovenliness, the long talking about nothing that matters; I forgive it all almost unconsciously, with no effort of will, as though Sasha's mistakes were my mistakes, and many things which would have made me wince in old days move me to tenderness and even rapture. The explanation of this forgiveness of everything lies in my love for Sasha, but what is the explanation of the love itself, I really don't know.

⊕⊕

LADIES

FYODOR PETROVITCH the Director of Elementary Schools in the N. District, who considered himself a just and generous man, was one day interviewing in his office a schoolmaster called Vremensky.

"No, Mr. Vremensky," he was saying, "your retirement is inevitable. You cannot continue your work as a schoolmaster with a voice like that! How did you come to lose it?"

"I drank cold beer when I was in a perspiration..." hissed the schoolmaster.

"What a pity! After a man has served fourteen years, such a calamity all at once! The idea of a career being ruined by such a trivial thing. What are you intending to do now?"

The schoolmaster made no answer.

"Are you a family man?" asked the director.

"A wife and two children, your Excellency..." hissed the schoolmaster.

A silence followed. The director got up from the table and walked to and fro in perturbation.

"I cannot think what I am going to do with you!" he said. "A teacher you cannot be, and you are not yet entitled to a pension.... To abandon you to your fate, and leave you to do the best you can, is rather awkward. We look on you as one of our men, you have served fourteen years, so it is our business to help you.... But how are we to help you? What can I do for you? Put yourself in my place: what can I do for you?"

A silence followed; the director walked up and down, still thinking, and Vremensky, overwhelmed by his trouble, sat on the edge of his chair, and he, too, thought. All at once the director began beaming, and even snapped his fingers.

"I wonder I did not think of it before!" he began rapidly. "Listen, this is what I can offer you. Next week our secretary at the Home is retiring. If you like, you can have his place! There you are!"

Vremensky, not expecting such good fortune, beamed too.

"That's capital," said the director. "Write the application to-day."

Dismissing Vremensky, Fyodor Petrovitch felt relieved and even gratified: the bent figure of the hissing schoolmaster was no longer confronting him, and it was agreeable to recognize that in offering a vacant post to Vremensky he had acted fairly and conscientiously, like a good-hearted and thoroughly decent person. But this agreeable state of mind did not last long. When he went home and sat down to dinner his wife, Nastasya Ivanovna, said suddenly:

"Oh yes, I was almost forgetting! Nina Sergeyevna came to see me yesterday and begged for your interest on behalf of a young man. I am told there is a vacancy in our Home...."

Yes, but the post has already been promised to someone else," said the director, and he frowned. "And you know my rule: I never give posts through patronage."

"I know, but for Nina Sergeyevna, I imagine, you might make an exception. She loves us as though we were relations, and we have never done anything for her. And don't think of refusing, Fedya! You will wound both her and me with your whims."

"Who is it that she is recommending?"

"Polzuhin!"

"What Polzuhin? Is it that fellow who played Tchatsky at the party on New Year's Day? Is it that gentleman? Not on any account!"

The director left off eating.

"Not on any account!" he repeated. "Heaven preserve us!"

"But why not?"

"Understand, my dear, that if a young man does not set to work directly, but through women, he must be good for nothing! Why doesn't he come to me himself?"

After dinner the director lay on the sofa in his study and began reading the letters and newspapers he had received.

"Dear Fyodor Petrovitch," wrote the wife of the Mayor of the town. "You once said that I knew the human heart and understood people. Now you have an opportunity of verifying this in practice. K. N. Polzuhin, whom I know to be an excellent young man, will call upon you in a day or two to ask you for the post of secretary at our Home. He is a very nice youth. If you take an interest in him you will be convinced of it." And so on.

"On no account!" was the director's comment. "Heaven preserve me!"

After that, not a day passed without the director's receiving letters recommending Polzuhin. One fine morning Polzuhin himself, a stout young man with a close-shaven face like a jockey's, in a new black suit, made his appearance....

"I see people on business not here but at the office," said the director drily, on hearing his request.

"Forgive me, your Excellency, but our common acquaintances advised me to come here."

"H'm!" growled the director, looking with hatred at the pointed toes of the young man's shoes. 'To the best of my belief your father is a man of property and you are not in want," he said. "What induces you to ask for this post? The salary is very trifling!"

"It's not for the sake of the salary.... It's a government post, any way..."

"H'm.... It strikes me that within a month you will be sick of the job and you will give it up, and meanwhile there are candidates for whom it would be a career for life. There are poor men for whom ..."

"I shan't get sick of it, your Excellency," Polzuhin interposed. "Honour bright, I will do my best!"

It was too much for the director.

"Tell me," he said, smiling contemptuously, "why was it you didn't apply to me direct but thought fitting instead to trouble ladies as a preliminary?"

"I didn't know that it would be disagreeable to you," Polzuhin answered, and he was embarrassed. "But, your Excellency, if you attach no significance to letters of recommendation, I can give you a testimonial...."

He drew from his pocket a letter and handed it to the director. At the bottom of the testimonial, which was written in official language and handwriting, stood the signature of the Governor. Everything pointed to the Governor's having signed it unread, simply to get rid of some importunate lady.

"There's nothing for it, I bow to his authority... I obey..." said the director, reading the testimonial, and he heaved a sigh.

"Send in your application to-morrow.... There's nothing to be done...."

And when Polzuhin had gone out, the director abandoned himself to a feeling of repulsion.

"Sneak!" he hissed, pacing from one corner to the other. "He has got what he wanted, one way or the other, the good-for-nothing toady! Making up to the ladies! Reptile! Creature!"

The director spat loudly in the direction of the door by which Polzuhin had departed, and was immediately overcome with embarrassment, for at that moment a lady, the wife of the Superintendent of the Provincial Treasury, walked in at the door.

"I've come for a tiny minute... a tiny minute..." began the lady. "Sit down, friend, and listen to me attentively.... Well, I've been told you have a post vacant.. . . To-day or to-morrow you will receive a visit from a young man called Polzuhin...."

The lady chattered on, while the director gazed at her with lustreless, stupefied eyes like a man on the point of fainting, gazed and smiled from politeness.

And the next day when Vremensky came to his office it was a long time before the director could bring himself to tell the truth. He hesitated, was incoherent, and could not think how to begin or what to say. He wanted to apologize to the schoolmaster, to tell him the whole truth, but his tongue halted like a drunkard's, his ears burned, and he was suddenly overwhelmed with vexation and resentment that he should have to play such an absurd part — in his own office, before his subordinate. He suddenly brought his fist down on the table, leaped up, and shouted angrily:

"I have no post for you! I have not, and that's all about it! Leave me in peace! Don't worry me! Be so good as to leave me alone!"

And he walked out of the office.

STRONG IMPRESSIONS

IT happened not so long ago in the Moscow circuit court. The jurymen, left in the court for the night, before lying down to sleep fell into conversation about strong impressions. They were led to this discussion by recalling a witness who, by his own account, had begun to stammer and had gone grey owing to a terrible moment. The jurymen decided that before going to sleep, each one of them should ransack among his memories and tell something that had happened to him. Man's life is brief, but yet there is no man who cannot boast that there have been terrible moments in his past.

One juryman told the story of how he was nearly drowned; another described how, in a place where there were neither doctors nor chemists, he had one night poisoned his own son through giving him zinc vitriol by mistake for soda. The child did not die, but the father nearly went out of his mind. A third, a man not old but in bad health, told how he had twice attempted to commit suicide: the first time by shooting himself and the second time by throwing himself before a train.

The fourth, a foppishly dressed, fat little man, told us the following story:

"I was not more than twenty-two or twenty-three when I fell head over ears in love with my present wife and made her an oner. Now I could with pleasure thrash myself for my early marriage, but at the time, I don't know what would have become of me if Natasha had refused me. My love was absolutely the real thing, just as it is described in novels – frantic, passionate, and so on. My happiness overwhelmed me and I did not know how to get away from

it, and I bored my father and my friends and the servants, continually talking about the fervour of my passion. Happy people are the most sickening bores. I was a fearful bore: I feel ashamed of it even now....

"Among my friends there was in those days a young man who was beginning! his career as a lawyer. Now he is a lawyer known all over Russia; in those days he was only just beginning to gain recognition and was not rich and famous enough to be entitled to cut an old friend when he met him. I used to go and see him once or twice a week. We used to loll on sofas and begin discussing philosophy.

"One day I was lying on his sofa, arguing that there was no more ungrateful profession than that of a lawyer. I tried to prove that as soon as the examination of witnesses is over the court can easily dispense with both the counsels for the prosecution and for the defence, because they are neither of them necessary and are only in the way. If a grown-up juryman, morally and mentally sane, is convinced that the ceiling is white, or that Ivanov is guilty, to struggle with that conviction and to vanquish it is beyond the power of any Demosthenes. Who can convince me that I have a red moustache when I know that it is black? As I listen to an orator I may perhaps grow sentimental and weep, but my fundamental conviction, based for the most part on unmistakable evidence and fact, is not changed in the least. My lawyer maintained that I was young and foolish and that I was talking childish nonsense. In his opinion, for one thing, an obvious fact becomes still more obvious through light being thrown upon it by conscientious, well-informed people; for another, talent is an elemental force, a hurricane capable of turning even stones to dust, let alone such trifles as the convictions of artis Eans and merchants of the second guild. It is as hard for human weakness to struggle against talent as to look at the sun without winking, or to stop the wind. One simple mortal by the power of the word turns thousands of convinced savages to Christianity; Odysseus was a man of the firmest convictions, but he succumbed to the Syrens, and so on. All history consists of similar examples, and in life they are met with at every turn; and so it is bound to be, or the intelligent and talented man would have no superiority over the stupid and incompetent.

"I stuck to my point, and went on maintaining that convictions are stronger than any talent, though, frankly speaking, I could not have defined exactly what I meant by conviction or what I meant by talent. Most likely I simply talked for the sake of talking.

" Take you, for example,' said the lawyer. You are convinced &t this moment that your fiancee is an angel and that there is not a man in the whole town happier than you. But I tell you: ten or twenty minutes would be enough for me to make you sit down to this table and write to your fiancee, breaking off your engagement.

"I laughed.

" 'Don't laugh, I am speaking seriously,' said my friend. 'If I choose, in twenty minutes you will be happy at the thought that you need not get married. Goodness knows what talent I have, but you are not one of the strong sort.'

"'Well, try it on!' said I.

" 'No, what for? I am only telling you this. You are a good boy and it would be cruel to subject you to such an experiment And besides I am not in good form to-day.'

"We sat down to supper. The wine and the thought of Natasha, my beloved flooded my whole being with youth and happiness. My happiness was so boundless that the lawyer sitting opposite to me with his green eyes seemed to me an unhappy man, so small, so grey.... "

'Do try!' I persisted. 'Come, I entreat you!

"The lawyer shook his head and frowned. Evidently I was beginning to bore him.

" 'I know,' he said, 'after my experiment you will say, thank you, and will call me your saviour; but you see I must think of your fiancee too. She loves you; your jilting her would make her suffer. And what a charming creature she is! I envy you.'

"The lawyer sighed, sipped his wine, and began talking of how charming my Natasha was. He had an extraordinary gift of description. He could knock you off a regular string of words about a woman's eyelashes or her little finger. I listened to him with relish.

" 'I have seen a great many women in my day,' he said, 'but I give you my word of honour, I speak as a friend, your Natasha Andreyevna is a pearl, a rare girl. Of course she has her defects — many of them, in fact, if you like — but still she is fascinating.'

"And the lawyer began talking of my fiancee's defects. Now I understand very well that he was talking of women in general, of their weak points in general, but at the time it seemed to me that he was talking only of Natasha. He went into ecstasies over her turn-up nose, her shrieks, her shrill laugh, her airs and graces, precisely all the things I so disliked in her. All that was, to his thinking, infinitely sweet, graceful, and feminine.

"Without my noticing it, he quickly passed from his enthusiastic tone to one of fatherly admonition, and then to a light and derisive one.... There was no presiding judge and no one to check the diffusiveness of the lawyer. I had not time to open my mouth, besides, what could I say? What my friend said was not new, it was what everyone has known for ages, and the whole venom lay not in what he said, but in the damnable form he put it in. It really was beyond anything!

"As I listened to him then I learned that the same word has thousands of shades of meaning according to the tone in which it is pronounced, and the form which is given to the sentence. Of course I cannot reproduce the tone or the form; I can only say that as I listened to my friend and walked up and down the room, I was moved to resentment, indignation, and contempt together with him. I even believed him when with tears in his eyes he informed me that I was a great man, that I was worthy of a better fate, that I was destined to achieve something in the future which marriage would hinder!

" 'My friend!' he exclaimed, pressing my hand. 'I beseech you, I adjure you: stop before it is too late. Stop! May Heaven preserve you from this strange, cruel mistake! My friend, do not ruin your youth!'

"Believe me or not, as you choose, but the long and the short of it was that I sat down to the table and wrote to my fiancee, breaking off the engagement. As I wrote I felt relieved that it was not yet too late to rectify my mistake. Sealing the letter, I hastened out into the street to post it. The lawyer himself came with me.

" 'Excellent! Capital!' he applauded me as my letter to Natasha disappeared into the darkness of the box. 'I congratulate you with all my heart. I am glad for you.'

"After walking a dozen paces with me the lawyer went on:

" 'Of course, marriage has its good points. I, for instance, belong to the class of people to whom marriage and home life is everything.'

"And he proceeded to describe his life, and lay before me all the hideousness of a solitary bachelor existence.

"He spoke with enthusiasm of his future wife, of the sweets of ordinary family life, and was so eloquent, so sincere in his ecstasies that by the time we had reached his door, I was in despair.

" 'What are you doing to me, you horrible man?' I said, gasping. You have ruined me! Why did you make me write that cursed letter? I love her, I love her!'

"And I protested my love. I was horrified at my conduct which now seemed to me wild and senseless. It is impossible, gentlemen, to imagine a more violent emotion than I experienced at that moment. Oh, what I went through, what I suffered! If some kind person had thrust a revolver into my hand at that moment, I should have put a bullet through my brains with pleasure.

" 'Come, come ...' said the lawyer, slapping me on the shoulder, and he laughed. 'Give over crying. The letter won't reach your fiancee. It was not you who wrote the address but I, and I muddled it so they won't be able to make it out at the post-office. It will be a lesson to you not to argue about what you don't understand.'

"Now, gentlemen, I leave it to the next to speak."

The fifth juryman settled himself more comfortably, and had just opened his mouth to begin his story when we heard the clock strike on Spassky Tower.

'Twelve..." one of the jurymen counted. "And into which class, gentlemen, would you put the emotions that are being experienced now by the man we are trying? He, that murderer, is spending the night in a convict cell here in the court, sitting or lying down and of course not sleeping, and throughout the whole sleepless night listening to that chime. What is he thinking of? What visions are haunting him?"

And the jurymen all suddenly forgot about strong impressions; what their companion who had once written a letter to his Natasha had suffered seemed unimportant, even not amusing; and no one said anything more; they began quietly and in silence lying down to sleep.

AT CHRISTMAS TIME

I

"WHAT shall I write?" said Yegor, and he dipped his pen in the ink.

Vasilisa had not seen her daughter for four years. Her daughter Yefimya had gone after her wedding to Petersburg, had sent them two letters, and since then seemed to vanish out of their lives; there had been no sight nor sound of her. And whether the old woman were milking her cow at dawn, or heating her stove, or dozing at night, she was always thinking of one and the same thing – what was happening to Yefimya, whether she were alive out yonder. She ought to have sent a letter, but the old father could not write, and there was no one to write.

But now Christmas had come, and Vasilisa could not bear it any longer, and went to the tavern to Yegor, the brother of the innkeeper's wife, who had sat in the tavern doing nothing ever since he came back from the army; people said that he could write letters very well if he were properly paid. Vasilisa talked to the cook at the tavern, then to the mistress of the house, then to Yegor himself. They agreed upon fifteen kopecks.

And now — it happened on the second day of the holidays, in the tavern kitchen — Yegor was sitting at the table, holding the pen in his hand. Vasilisa was standing before him, pondering with an expression of anxiety and woe on her face. Pyotr, her husband, a very thin old man with a brownish bald patch, had come with her; he stood looking straight before him like a blind man. On the stove a piece of pork was being braised in a saucepan; it was spurting and hissing, and seemed to be actually saying: "Flu-flu-flu." It was stifling.

"What am I to write?" Yegor asked again.

"What?" asked Vasilisa, looking at him angrily and suspiciously. "Don't worry me! You are not writing for nothing; no fear, you'll be paid for it. Come, write: 'To our dear son-in-law, Andrey Hrisanfitch, and to our only beloved daughter, Yefimya Petrovna, with our love we send a low bow and our parental blessing abiding for ever.' "

"Written; fire away."

" 'And we wish them a happy Christmas; we are alive and well, and I wish you the same, please the Lord . . . the Heavenly King.' "

Vasilisa pondered and exchanged glances with the old man.

" 'And I wish you the same, please the Lord the Heavenly King,' " she repeated, beginning to cry.

She could say nothing more. And yet before, when she lay awake thinking at night, it had seemed to her that she could not get all she had to say into a dozen letters. Since the time when her daughter had gone away with her husband much water had flowed into the sea, the old people had lived feeling bereaved, and sighed heavily at night as though they had buried their daughter. And how many events had occurred in the village since then, how many marriages and deaths! How long the winters had been! How long the nights!

"It's hot," said Yegor, unbuttoning his waistcoat. "It must be seventy degrees. What more?" he asked.

The old people were silent.

"What does your son-in-law do in Petersburg?" asked Yegor.

"He was a soldier, my good friend," the old man answered in a weak voice. " He left the service at the same time as you did. He was a soldier, and now, to be sure, he is at Petersburg at a hydropathic establishment. The doctor treats the sick with water. So he, to be sure, is house-porter at the doctor's."

"Here it is written down," said the old woman, taking a letter out of her pocket. "We got it from Yefimya, goodness knows when. Maybe they are no longer in this world."

Yegor thought a little and began writing rapidly:

"At the present time" — he wrote — "since your destiny through your own doing allotted you to the Military Career, we counsel you to look into the Code of Disciplinary Offences and Fundamental Laws of the War Office, and you will see in that law the Civilization of the Officials of the War Office."

He wrote and kept reading aloud what was written, while Vasilisa considered what she ought to write: how great had been their want the year before, how their corn had not lasted even till Christmas, how they had to sell their cow. She ought to ask for money, ought to write that the old father was often ailing and would soon no doubt give up his soul to God . . . but how to express this in words? What must be said first and what afterwards?

"Take note," Yegor went on writing, "in volume five of the Army Regulations soldier is a common noun and a proper one, a soldier of the first rank is called a general, and of the last a private. . . ."

The old man stirred his lips and said softly:

"It would be all right to have a look at the grandchildren."

"What grandchildren?" asked the old woman, and she looked angrily at him; "perhaps there are none."

"Well, but perhaps there are. Who knows?"

"And thereby you can judge," Yegor hurried on, "what is the enemy without and what is the enemy within. The foremost of our enemies within is Bacchus." The pen squeaked, executing upon the paper flourishes like fish-hooks. Yegor hastened and read over every line several times. He sat on a stool sprawling his broad feet under the table, well-fed, bursting with health, with a coarse animal face and a red bull neck. He was vulgarity itself: coarse, conceited, invincible, proud of having been born and bred in a pot-house; and Vasilisa quite understood the vulgarity, but could not express it in words, and could only look angrily and suspiciously at Yegor. Her head was beginning to ache, and her thoughts were in confusion from the sound of his voice and his unintelligible words, from the heat and the stuffiness, and she said nothing and thought nothing, but simply waited for him to finish scribbling. But the old man looked with full confidence. He believed in his old woman who had brought him there, and in Yegor; and when he had mentioned the hydropathic establishment it could be seen that he believed in the establishment and the healing efficacy of water.

Having finished the letter, Yegor got up and read the whole of it through from the beginning. The old man did not understand, but he nodded his head trustfully.

"That's all right; it is smooth . . ." he said. "God give you health. That's all right. . . ."

They laid on the table three five-kopeck pieces and went out of the tavern; the old man looked immovably straight before him as though he were blind, and perfect trustfulness was written on his face; but as Vasilisa came out of the tavern she waved angrily at the dog, and said angrily:

"Ugh, the plague."

The old woman did not sleep all night; she was disturbed by thoughts, and at daybreak she got up, said her prayers, and went to the station to send off the letter.

It was between eight and nine miles to the station.

II

Dr. B. O. Mozelweiser's hydropathic establishment worked on New Year's Day exactly as on ordinary days; the only difference was that the porter, Andrey Hrisanfitch, had on a uniform with new braiding, his boots had an extra polish, and he greeted every visitor with "A Happy New Year to you!"

It was the morning; Andrey Hrisanfitch was standing at the door, reading the newspaper. Just at ten o'clock there arrived a general, one of the habitual visitors, and directly after him the postman; Andrey Hrisanfitch helped the general off with his great-coat, and said:

"A Happy New Year to your Excellency!"

"Thank you, my good fellow; the same to you."

And at the top of the stairs the general asked, nodding towards the door (he asked the same question every day and always forgot the answer):

"And what is there in that room?"

"The massage room, your Excellency."

When the general's steps had died away Andrey Hrisanfitch looked at the post that had come, and found one addressed to himself. He tore it open, read several lines, then, looking at the newspaper, he walked without haste to his own room, which was downstairs close by at the end of the passage. His wife Yefimya was sitting on the bed, feeding her baby; another child, the eldest, was standing by, laying its curly head on her knee; a third was asleep on the bed.

Going into the room, Andrey gave his wife the letter and said:

"From the country, I suppose."

Then he walked out again without taking his eyes from the paper. He could hear Yefimya with a shaking voice reading the first lines. She read them and could read no more; these lines were enough for her. She burst into tears, and hugging her eldest child, kissing him, she began saying – and it was hard to say whether she were laughing or crying:

"It's from granny, from grandfather," she said. "From the country. . . . The Heavenly Mother, Saints and Martyrs! The snow lies heaped up under the roofs now . . . the trees are as white as white. The boys slide on little sledges . . . and dear old bald grandfather is on the stove . . . and there is a little yellow dog. . . . My own darlings!"

Andrey Hrisanfitch, hearing this, recalled that his wife had on three or four occasions given him letters and asked him to send them to the country, but some important business had always prevented him; he had not sent them, and the letters somehow got lost.

"And little hares run about in the fields," Yefimya went on chanting, kissing her boy and shedding tears. "Grandfather is kind and gentle; granny is good, too – kind-hearted. They are warm-hearted in the country, they are God-fearing . . . and there is a little church in the village; the peasants sing in the choir. Queen of Heaven, Holy Mother and Defender, take us away from here!"

Andrey Hrisanfitch returned to his room to smoke a little till there was another ring at the door, and Yefimya ceased speaking, subsided, and wiped her eyes, though her lips were still quivering. She was very much frightened of him – oh, how frightened of him! She trembled and was reduced to terror by the sound of his steps, by the look in his eyes, and dared not utter a word in his presence.

Andrey Hrisanfitch lighted a cigarette, but at that very moment there was a ring from upstairs. He put out his cigarette, and, assuming a very grave face, hastened to his front door.

The general was coming downstairs, fresh and rosy from his bath.

"And what is there in that room?" he asked, pointing to a door.

Andrey Hrisanfitch put his hands down swiftly to the seams of his trousers, and pronounced loudly:

"Charcot douche, your Excellency!"

A HAPPY MAN

THE passenger train is just starting from Bologoe, the junction on the Petersburg-Moscow line. In a second-class smoking compartment five passengers sit dozing, shrouded in the twilight of the carriage. They had just had a meal, and now, snugly ensconced in their seats, they are trying to go to sleep. Stillness.

The door opens and in there walks a tall, lanky figure straight as a poker, with a ginger-coloured hat and a smart overcoat, wonderfully suggestive of a journalist in Jules Verne or on the comic stage.

The figure stands still in the middle of the compartment for a long while, breathing heavily, screwing up his eyes and peering at the seats.

"No, wrong again!" he mutters. "What the deuce! It's positively revolting! No, the wrong one again!"

One of the passengers stares at the figure and utters a shout of joy:

"Ivan Alexyevitch! what brings you here? Is it you?"

The poker-like gentleman starts, stares blankly at the passenger, and recognizing him claps his hands with delight.

"Ha! Pyotr Petrovitch," he says. "How many summers, how many winters! I didn't know you were in this train."

"How are you getting on?"

"I am all right; the only thing is, my dear fellow, I've lost my compartment and I simply can't find it. What an idiot I am! I ought to be thrashed!"

The poker-like gentleman sways a little unsteadily and sniggers.

"Queer things do happen!" he continues. "I stepped out just after the second bell to get a glass of brandy. I got it, of course. Well, I thought, since it's a long way to the next station, it would be as well to have a second glass. While I was thinking about it and drinking it the third bell rang.... I ran like mad and jumped into the first carriage. I am an idiot! I am the son of a hen!"

"But you seem in very good spirits," observes Pyotr Petrovitch. "Come and sit down! There's room and a welcome."

"No, no.... I'm off to look for my carriage. Good-bye!"

"You'll fall between the carriages in the dark if you don't look out! Sit down, and when we get to a station you'll find your own compartment. Sit down!"

Ivan Alexyevitch heaves a sigh and irresolutely sits down facing Pyotr Petrovitch. He is visibly excited, and fidgets as though he were sitting on thorns.

"Where are you travelling to?" Pyotr Petrovitch enquires.

"I? Into space. There is such a turmoil in my head that I couldn't tell where I am going myself. I go where fate takes me. Ha-ha! My dear fellow, have you ever seen a happy fool? No? Well, then, take a look at one. You behold the happiest of mortals! Yes! Don't you see something from my face?"

"Well, one can see you're a bit... a tiny bit so-so."

"I dare say I look awfully stupid just now. Ach! it's a pity I haven't a looking-glass, I should like to look at my counting-house. My dear fellow, I feel I am turning into an idiot, honour bright. Ha-ha! Would you believe it, I'm on my honeymoon. Am I not the son of a hen?"

"You? Do you mean to say you are married?"

"To-day, my dear boy. We came away straight after the wedding."

Congratulations and the usual questions follow. "Well, you are a fellow!" laughs Pyotr Petrovitch. "That's why you are rigged out such a dandy."

"Yes, indeed.... To complete the illusion, I've even sprinkled myself with scent. I am over my ears in vanity! No care, no thought, nothing but a sensation of something or other... deuce knows what to call it... beatitude or something? I've never felt so grand in my life!"

Ivan Alexyevitch shuts his eyes and waggles his head.

"I'm revoltingly happy," he says. "Just think; in a minute I shall go to my compartment. There on the seat near the window is sitting a being who is, so to say, devoted to you with her whole being. A little blonde with a little nose ... little fingers.... My little darling! My angel! My little poppet! Phylloxera of my soul! And her little foot! Good God! A little foot not like our beetle-crushers, but something miniature, fairylike, allegorical. I could pick it up and eat it, that little foot! Oh, but you don't understand! You're a materialist, of course, you begin analyzing at once, and one thing and another. You are cold-hearted bachelors, that's what you are! When you get married you'll think of me. 'Where's Ivan Alexyevitch now?' you'll say. Yes; so in a minute I'm going to my compartment. There she is waiting for me with impatience

... in joyful anticipation of my appearance. She'll have a smile to greet me. I sit down beside her and take her chin with my two fingers.

Ivan Alexyevitch waggles his head and goes off into a chuckle of delight.

"Then I lay my noddle on her shoulder and put my arm round her waist. Around all is silence, you know... poetic twilight. I could embrace the whole world at such a moment. Pyotr Petrovitch, allow me to embrace you!"

"Delighted, I'm sure." The two friends embrace while the passengers laugh in chorus. And the happy bridegroom continues:

"And to complete the idiocy, or, as the novelists say, to complete the illusion, one goes to the refreshment-room and tosses off two or three glasses. And then something happens in your head and your heart, finer than you can read of in a fairy tale. I am a man of no importance, but I feel as though I were limitless: I embrace the whole world!"

The passengers, looking at the tipsy and blissful bridegroom, are infected by his cheerfulness and no longer feel sleepy. Instead of one listener, Ivan Alexyevitch has now an audience of five. He wriggles and splutters, gesticulates, and prattles on without ceasing. He laughs and they all laugh.

"Gentlemen, gentlemen, don't think so much! Damn all this analysis! If you want a drink, drink, no need to philosophize as to whether it's bad for you or not.... Damn all this philosophy and psychology!"

The guard walks through the compartment.

"My dear fellow," the bridegroom addresses him, "when you pass through the carriage No. 209 look out for a lady in a grey hat with a white bird and tell her I'm here!"

'Yes, sir. Only there isn't a No. 209 in this train; there's 219!"

"Well, 219, then! It's all the same. Tell that lady, then, that her husband is all right!"

Ivan Alexyevitch suddenly clutches his head and groans:

"Husband.... Lady.... All in a minute! Husband.... Ha-ha! I am a puppy that needs thrashing, and here I am a husband!

Ach, idiot! But think of her! ... Yesterday she was a little girl, a midget... it s simply incredible!"

"Nowadays it really seems strange to see a happy man," observes one of the passengers; "one as soon expects to see a white elephant."

"Yes, and whose fault is it?" says Ivan Alexyevitch, stretching his long legs and thrusting out his feet with their very pointed toes. "If you are not happy it's your own fault! Yes, what else do you suppose it is? Man is the creator of his own happiness. If you want to be happy you will be, but you don't want to be! You obstinately turn away from happiness."

"Why, what next! How do you make that out?"

"Very simply. Nature has ordained that at a certain stage in his life man should love. When that time comes you should love like a house on fire, but you won't heed the dictates of nature, you keep waiting for something. What's more, it's laid down by law that the normal man should enter upon matrimony. There's no happiness without marriage. When the propitious moment has come, get married. There's no use in shilly-shallying. .. . But you don't get married, you keep waiting for something! Then the Scriptures tell us that 'wine maketh glad the heart of man.'... If you feel happy and you want to feel better still, then go to the refreshment bar and have a drink. The great thing is not to be too clever, but to follow the beaten track! The beaten track is a grand thing!"

"You say that man is the creator of his own happiness. How the devil is he the creator of it when a toothache or an ill-natured mother-in-law is enough to scatter his happiness to the winds? Everything depends on chance. If we had an accident at this moment you'd sing a different tune."

"Stuff and nonsense!" retorts the bridegroom. "Railway accidents only happen once a year. I'm not afraid of an accident, for there is no reason for one. Accidents are exceptional! Confound them! I don't want to talk of them! Oh, I believe we're stopping at a station."

"Where are you going now?" asks Pyotr Petrovitch. "To Moscow or somewhere further south?

"Why, bless you! How could I go somewhere further south, when I'm on my way to the north?"

"But Moscow isn't in the north."

"I know that, but we're on our way to Petersburg," says Ivan Alexyevitch.

"We are going to Moscow, mercy on us!"

"To Moscow? What do you mean?" says the bridegroom in amazement.

"It's queer.... For what station did you take your ticket?"

"For Petersburg."

"In that case I congratulate you. You've got into the wrong train."

There follows a minute of silence. The bridegroom gets up and looks blankly round the company.

"Yes, yes," Pyotr Petrovitch explains. "You must have jumped into the wrong train at Bologoe.... After your glass of brandy you succeeded in getting into the down-train."

Ivan Alexyevitch turns pale, clutches his head, and begins pacing rapidly about the carriage.

"Ach, idiot that I am!" he says in indignation. "Scoundrel! The devil devour me! Whatever am I to do now? Why, my wife is in that train! She's there all alone, expecting me, consumed by anxiety. Ach, I'm a motley fool!"

The bridegroom falls on the seat and writhes as though someone had trodden on his corns.

"I am un-unhappy man!" he moans. "What am I to do, What am I to do?"

"There, there!" the passengers try to console him. "It's all right. .. . You must telegraph to your wife and try to change into the Petersburg express. In that way you'll overtake her."

"The Petersburg express!" weeps the bridegroom, the creator of his own happiness. "And how am I to get a ticket for the Petersburg express? All my money is with my wife."

The passengers, laughing and whispering together, make a collection and furnish the happy man with funds.

A DAY IN THE COUNTRY

BETWEEN eight and nine o'clock in the morning.

A dark leaden-coloured mass is creeping over the sky towards the sun. Red zigzags of lightning gleam here and there across it. There is a sound of far-away rumbling. A warm wind frolics over the grass, bends the trees, and stirs up the dust. In a minute there will be a spurt of May rain and a real storm will begin.

Fyokla, a little beggar-girl of six, is running through the village, looking for Terenty the cobbler. The white-haired, barefoot child is pale. Her eyes are wide-open, her lips are trembling.

"Uncle, where is Terenty?" she asks every one she meets. No one answers. They are all preoccupied with the approaching storm and take refuge in their huts. At last she meets Silanty Silitch, the sacristan, Terenty's bosom friend. He is coming along, staggering from the wind.

"Uncle, where is Terenty?"

"At the kitchen-gardens," answers Silanty.

The beggar-girl runs behind the huts to the kitchen-gardens and there finds Terenty; the tall old man with a thin, pock-marked face, very long legs, and bare feet, dressed in a woman's tattered jacket, is standing near the vegetable plots, looking with drowsy, drunken eyes at the dark storm-cloud. On his long crane-like legs he sways in the wind like a starling-cote.

"Uncle Terenty!" the white-headed beggar-girl addresses him. "Uncle, darling!"

Terenty bends down to Fyokla, and his grim, drunken face is overspread with a smile, such as come into people's faces when they look at something little, foolish, and absurd, but warmly loved.

"Ah! servant of God, Fyokla," he says, lisping tenderly, "where have you come from?"

"Uncle Terenty," says Fyokla, with a sob, tugging at the lapel of the cobbler's coat. "Brother Danilka has had an accident! Come along!"

"What sort of accident? Ough, what thunder! Holy, holy, holy.... What sort of accident?"

"In the count's copse Danilka stuck his hand into a hole in a tree, and he can't get it out. Come along, uncle, do be kind and pull his hand out!"

"How was it he put his hand in? What for?"

"He wanted to get a cuckoo's egg out of the hole for me."

"The day has hardly begun and already you are in trouble...." Terenty shook his head and spat deliberately. "Well, what am I to do with you now? I must come ... I must, may the wolf gobble you up, you naughty children! Come, little orphan!"

Terenty comes out of the kitchen-garden and, lifting high his long legs, begins striding down the village street. He walks quickly without stopping or looking from side to side, as though he were shoved from behind or afraid of pursuit. Fyokla can hardly keep up with him.

They come out of the village and turn along the dusty road towards the count's copse that lies dark blue in the distance. It is about a mile and a half away. The clouds have by now covered the sun, and soon afterwards there is not a speck of blue left in the sky. It grows dark.

"Holy, holy, holy . . ."whispers Fyokla, hurrying after Terenty. The first rain-drops, big and heavy, lie, dark dots on the dusty road. A big drop falls on Fyokla's cheek and glides like a tear down her chin.

"The rain has begun," mutters the cobbler, kicking up the dust with his bare, bony feet. "That's fine, Fyokla, old girl. The grass and the trees are fed by the rain, as we are by bread. And as for the thunder, don't you be frightened, little orphan. Why should it kill a little thing like you?"

As soon as the rain begins, the wind drops. The only sound is the patter of rain dropping like fine shot on the young rye and the parched road.

"We shall get soaked, Fyolka," mutters Terenty. "There won't be a dry spot left on us.... Ho-ho, my girl! It's run down my neck! But don't be frightened, silly.... The grass will be dry again, the earth will be dry again, and we shall be dry again. There is the same sun for us all."

A flash of lightning, some fourteen feet long, gleams above their heads. There is a loud peal of thunder, and it seems to Fyokla that something big, heavy, and round is rolling over the sky and tearing it open, exactly over her head.

"Holy, holy, holy..." says Terenty, crossing himself. "Don't be afraid, little orphan! It is not from spite that it thunders."

Terenty's and Fyokla's feet are covered with lumps of heavy, wet clay. It is slippery and difficult to walk, but Terenty strides on more and more rapidly. The weak little beggar-girl is breathless and ready to drop.

But at last they go into the count's copse. The washed trees, stirred by a gust of wind, drop a perfect waterfall upon them. Terenty stumbles over stumps and begins to slacken his pace.

"Whereabouts is Danilka?" he asks. "Lead me to him."

Fyokla leads him into a thicket, and, after going a quarter of a mile, points to Danilka. Her brother, a little fellow of eight, with hair as red as ochre and a pale sickly face, stands leaning against a tree, and, with his head on one side, looking sideways at the sky. In one hand he holds his shabby old cap, the other is hidden in an old lime tree. The boy is gazing at the stormy sky, and apparently not thinking of his trouble. Hearing footsteps and seeing the cobbler he gives a sickly smile and says:

"A terrible lot of thunder, Terenty.... I've never heard so much thunder in all my life."

"And where is your hand?"

"In the hole.... Pull it out, please, Terenty!"

The wood had broken at the edge of the hole and jammed Danilka's hand: he could push it farther in, but could not pull it out. Terenty snaps off the broken piece, and the boy's hand, red and crushed, is released.

"It's terrible how it's thundering," the boy says again, rubbing his hand. "What makes it thunder, Terenty?"

"One cloud runs against the other," answers the cobbler. The party come out of the copse, and walk along the edge of it towards the darkened road. The thunder gradually abates, and its rumbling is heard far away beyond the village.

"The ducks flew by here the other day, Terenty," says Danilka, still rubbing his hand. "They must be nesting in the Gniliya Zaimishtcha marshes.. . . Fyolka, would you like me to show you a nightingale's nest?"

"Don't touch it, you might disturb them," says Terenty, wringing the water out of his cap. "The nightingale is a singing-bird, without sin. He has had a voice given him in his throat, to praise God and gladden the heart of man. It's a sin to disturb him."

"What about the sparrow?"

"The sparrow doesn't matter, he's a bad, spiteful bird. He is like a pickpocket in his ways. He doesn't like man to be happy. When Christ was crucified it was the sparrow brought nails to the Jews, and called 'alive! alive!'"

A bright patch of blue appears in the sky.

"Look!" says Terenty. "An ant-heap burst open by the rain! They've been flooded, the rogues!"

They bend over the ant-heap. The downpour has damaged it; the insects are scurrying to and fro in the mud, agitated, and busily trying to carry away their drowned companions.

"You needn't be in such a taking, you won't die of it!" says Terenty, grinning. "As soon as the sun warms you, you'll come to your senses again.... It's a lesson to you, you stupids. You won't settle on low ground another time."

They go on.

"And here are some bees," cries Danilka, pointing to the branch of a young oak tree.

The drenched and chilled bees are huddled together on the branch. There are so many of them that neither bark nor leaf can be seen. Many of them are settled on one another.

"That's a swarm of bees," Terenty informs them. 'They were flying looking for a home, and when the rain came down upon them they settled. If a swarm is flying, you need only sprinkle water on them to make them settle. Now if, say, you wanted to take the swarm, you would bend the branch with them into a sack and shake it, and they all fall in."

Little Fyokla suddenly frowns and rubs her neck vigorously. Her brother looks at her neck, and sees a big swelling on it.

"Hey-hey!" laughs the cobbler. "Do you know where you got that from, Fyokla, old girl? There are Spanish flies on some tree in the wood. The rain has trickled off them, and a drop has fallen on your neck – that's what has made the swelling,"

The sun appears from behind the clouds and floods the wood, the fields, and the three friends with its warm light. The dark menacing cloud has gone far away and taken the storm with it. The air is warm and fragrant. There is a scent of bird-cherry, meadowsweet, and lilies-of-the-valley.

"That herb is given when your nose bleeds," says Terenty, pointing to a woolly-looking flower. "It does good."

They hear a whistle and a rumble, but not such a rumble as the storm-clouds carried away. A goods train races by before the eyes of Terenty, Danilka, and Fyokla. The engine, panting and puffing out black smoke, drags more than twenty vans after it. Its power is tremendous. The children are interested to know how an engine, not alive and without the help of horses, can move and drag such weights, and Terenty undertakes to explain it to them:

"It's all the steam's doing, children.... The steam does the work.... You see, it shoves under that thing near the wheels, and it... you see... it works...."

They cross the railway line, and, going down from the embankment, walk towards the river. They walk not with any object, but just at random, and talk all the way.... Danilka asks questions, Terenty answers them....

Terenty answers all his questions, and there is no secret in Nature which baffles him. He knows everything. Thus, for example, he knows the names of all the wild flowers, animals, and stones. He knows what herbs cure diseases, he has no difficulty in telling the age of a horse or a cow. Looking at the sunset, at the moon, or the birds, he can tell what sort of weather it will be next day. And indeed, it is not only Terenty who is so wise. Silanty Silitch, the innkeeper, the market-gardener, the shepherd, and all the villagers, generally speaking, know as much as he does. These people have learned not from books, but in the fields, in the wood, on the river bank. Their teachers have been the birds themselves, when they sang to them, the sun when it left a glow of crimson behind it at setting, the very trees, and wild herbs.

Danilka looks at Terenty and greedily drinks in every word. In spring, before one is weary of the warmth and the monotonous green of the fields, when everything is fresh and full of fragrance, who would not want to hear about the golden may-beetles, about the cranes, about the gurgling streams, and the corn mounting into ear?

The two of them, the cobbler and the orphan, walk about the fields, talk unceasingly, and are not weary. They could wander about the world endlessly. They walk, and in their talk of the beauty of the earth do not notice the frail little beggar-girl tripping after them. She is breathless and moves with a lagging step. There are tears in her eyes; she would be glad to stop these inexhaustible wanderers, but to whom and where can she go? She has no home or people of her own; whether she likes it or not, she must walk and listen to their talk.

Towards midday, all three sit down on the river bank. Danilka takes out of his bag a piece of bread, soaked and reduced to a mash, and they begin to eat. Terenty says a prayer when he has eaten the bread, then stretches himself on the sandy bank and falls asleep. While he is asleep, the boy gazes at the water, pondering. He has many different things to think of. He has just seen the storm, the bees, the ants, the train. Now, before his eyes, fishes are whisking about. Some are two inches long and more, others are no bigger than one's nail. A viper, with its head held high, is swimming from one bank to the other.

Only towards the evening our wanderers return to the village. The children go for the night to a deserted barn, where the corn of the commune used to be kept, while Terenty, leaving them, goes to the tavern. The children lie huddled together on the straw, dozing.

The boy does not sleep. He gazes into the darkness, and it seems to him that he is seeing all that he has seen in the day: the storm-clouds, the bright sunshine, the birds, the fish, lanky Terenty. The number of his impressions, together with exhaustion and hunger, are too much for him; he is as hot as though he were on fire, and tosses from, side to side. He longs to tell someone all that is haunting him now in the darkness and agitating his soul, but there is no one to tell. Fyokla is too little and could not understand.

I'll tell Terenty to-morrow," thinks the boy.

The children fall asleep thinking of the homeless cobbler, and, in the night, Terenty comes to them, makes the sign of the cross over them, and puts bread under their heads. And no one sees his love. It is seen only by the moon which floats in the sky and peeps caressingly through the holes in the wall of the deserted barn.

VANKA

VANKA ZHUKOV, a boy of nine, who had been for three months apprenticed to Alyahin the shoemaker, was sitting up on Christmas Eve. Waiting till his master and mistress and their workmen had gone to the midnight service, he took out of his master's cupboard a bottle of ink and a pen with a rusty nib, and, spreading out a crumpled sheet of paper in front of him, began writing. Before forming the first letter he several times looked round fearfully at the door and the windows, stole a glance at the dark ikon, on both sides of which stretched shelves full of lasts, and heaved a broken sigh. The paper lay on the bench while he knelt before it.

"Dear grandfather, Konstantin Makaritch," he wrote, "I am writing you a letter. I wish you a happy Christmas, and all blessings from God Almighty. I have neither father nor mother, you are the only one left me."

Vanka raised his eyes to the dark ikon on which the light of his candle was reflected, and vividly recalled his grandfather, Konstantin Makaritch, who was night watchman to a family called Zhivarev. He was a thin but extraordinarily nimble and lively little old man of sixty-five, with an everlastingly laughing face and drunken eyes. By day he slept in the servants' kitchen, or made jokes with the cooks; at night, wrapped in an ample sheepskin, he walked round the grounds and tapped with his little mallet. Old Kashtanka and Eel, so-called on account of his dark colour and his long body like a weasel's, followed him with hanging heads. This Eel was exceptionally polite and affectionate, and looked with equal kindness on strangers and his own masters, but had not a very good reputation. Under his politeness and meekness was hidden the most Jesuitical cunning. No one knew better how to creep up on occasion and snap at one's legs, to slip into the store-room, or steal a hen from a peasant. His hind legs had been nearly pulled off more than once, twice he had been hanged, every week he was thrashed till he was half dead, but he always revived.

At this moment grandfather was, no doubt, standing at the gate, screwing up his eyes at the red windows of the church, stamping with his high felt boots, and joking with the servants. His little mallet was hanging on his belt.

He was clasping his hands, shrugging with the cold, and, with an aged chuckle, pinching first the housemaid, then the cook.

"How about a pinch of snuff?" he was saying, offering the women his snuff-box.

The women would take a sniff and sneeze. Grandfather would be indescribably delighted, go off into a merry chuckle, and cry:

'Tear it off, it has frozen on!"

They give the dogs a sniff of snuff too. Kashtanka sneezes, wriggles her head, and walks away offended. Eel does not sneeze, from politeness, but wags his tail And the weather is glorious. The air is still, fresh, and transparent. The night is dark, but one can see the whole village with its white roofs and coils of smoke coming from the chimneys, the trees silvered with hoar frost, the snowdrifts. The whole sky spangled with gay twinkling stars, and the Milky Way is as distinct as though it had been washed and rubbed with snow for a holiday.... Vanka sighed, dipped his pen, and went on writing:

"And yesterday I had a wigging. The master pulled me out into the yard by my hair, and whacked me with a boot-stretcher because I accidentally fell asleep while I was rocking their brat in the cradle. And a week ago the mistress told me to clean a herring, and I began from the tail end, and she took the herring and thrust its head in my face. The workmen laugh at me and send me to the tavern for vodka, and tell me to steal the master's cucumbers for them, and the master beats me with anything that comes to hand. And there is nothing to eat. In the morning they give me bread, for dinner, porridge, and in the evening, bread again; but as for tea, or soup, the master and mistress gobble it all up themselves. And I am put to sleep in the passage, and when their wretched brat cries I get no sleep at all, but have to rock the cradle. Dear grandfather, show the divine mercy, take me away from here, home to the village. It's more than I can bear. I bow down to your feet, and will pray to God for you for ever, take me away from here or I shall die."

Vanka's mouth worked, he rubbed his eyes with his black fist, and gave a sob. "I will powder your snuff for you," he went on. "I will pray for you, and if I do anything you can thrash me like Sidor's goat. And if you think I've no job, then I will beg the steward for Christ's sake to let me clean his boots, or I'll go for a shepherd-boy instead of Fedka. Dear grandfather, it is more than I can bear, it's simply no life at all. I wanted to run away to the village, but I have no boots, and I am afraid of the frost. When I grow up big I will take care of you for this, and not let anyone annoy you, and when you die I will pray for the rest of your soul, just as for my mammy's.

Moscow is a big town. It's all gentlemen's houses, and there are lots of horses, but there are no sheep, and the dogs are not spiteful. The lads here don't go out with the star, and they don't let anyone go into the choir, and once I saw in a shop window fishing-hooks for sale, fitted ready with the line and for all sorts of fish, awfully good ones, there was even one hook that would hold a forty-pound sheat-fish. And I have seen shops where there are guns of all sorts, after the pattern of the master's guns at home, so that I shouldn't wonder if they are a hundred roubles each. ... And in the butchers' shops there are grouse and woodcocks and fish and hares, but the shopmen don't say where they shoot them.

"Dear grandfather, when they have the Christmas tree at the big house, get me a gilt walnut, and put it away in the green trunk. Ask the young lady Olga Ignatyevna, say it's for Vanka."

Vanka gave a tremulous sigh, and again stared at the window. He remembered how his grandfather always went into the forest to get the Christmas tree for his master's family, and took his grandson with him. It was a merry time! Grandfather made a noise in his throat, the forest crackled with the frost, and looking at them Vanka chortled too. Before chopping down the Christmas tree, grandfather would smoke a pipe, slowly take a pinch of snuff and laugh at frozen Vanka.... The young fir trees, covered with hoar frost, stood motionless, waiting to see which of them was to die. Wherever one looked, a hare flew like an arrow over the snowdrifts.... Grandfather could not refrain from shouting: "Hold him, hold him ... hold him! Ah, the bob-tailed devil!"

When he had cut down the Christmas tree, grandfather used to drag it to the big house, and there set to work to decorate it.... The young lady, who was Vanka's favourite, Olga Ignatyevna, was the busiest of all. When Vanka's mother Pelageya was alive, and a servant in the big house, Olga Ignatyevna used to give him goodies, and having nothing better to do, taught him to read and write, to count up to a hundred, and even to dance a quadrille. When Pelageya died, Vanka had been transferred to the servants' kitchen to be with his grandfather, and from the kitchen to the shoemaker's in Moscow.

"Do come, dear grandfather," Vanka went on with his letter. "For Christ's sake, I beg you, take me away. Have pity on an unhappy orphan like me; here everyone knocks me about, and I am fearfully hungry; I can't tell you what misery it is, I am always crying. And the other day the master hit me on the head with a last, so that I fell down. My life is wretched, worse than any dog's ... I send greetings to Alyona, one-eyed Yegorka, and the coachman, and don't give my concertina to anyone. I remain, your grandson, Ivan Zhukov. Dear grandfather, do come."

Vanka folded the sheet of writing-paper twice, and put it into an envelope he had bought the day before for a kopeck. . . . After thinking a little, he dipped the pen and wrote the address:

To grandfather in the village.

Then he scratched his head, thought a little, and added: *Konstantin Makaritch.* Glad that he had not been prevented from writing, he put on his cap and, without putting on his little greatcoat, ran out into the street as he was in his shirt....

The shopmen at the butcher's, whom he had questioned the day before, told him that letters were put in post-boxes, and from the boxes were carried about all over the earth in mailcarts with drunken drivers and ringing bells. Vanka ran to the nearest post-box, and thrust the precious letter in the slit....

An hour later, lulled by sweet hopes, he was sound asleep.... He dreamed of the stove. On the stove was sitting his grandfather, swinging his bare legs, and reading the letter to the cooks....

By the stove was Eel, wagging his tail.

IN THE COACH-HOUSE

IT was between nine and ten o'clock in the evening. Stepan the coachman, Mihailo the house-porter, Alyoshka the coachman's grandson, who had come up from the village to stay with his grandfather, and Nikandr, an old man of seventy, who used to come into the yard every evening to sell salt herrings, were sitting round a lantern in the big coach-house, playing "kings." Through the wide-open door could be seen the whole yard, the big house, where the master's family lived, the gates, the cellars, and the porter's l odge. It was all shrouded in the darkness of night, and only the four windows of one of the lodges which was let were brightly lit up. The shadows of the coaches and sledges with their shafts tipped upwards stretched from the walls to the doors, quivering and cutting across the shadows cast by the lantern and the players. . . . On the other side of the thin partition that divided the coach-house from the stable were the horses. There was a scent of hay, and a disagreeable smell of salt herrings coming from old Nikandr.

The porter won and was king; he assumed an attitude such as was in his opinion befitting a king, and blew his nose loudly on a red-checked handkerchief.

"Now if I like I can chop off anybody's head," he said. Alyoshka, a boy of eight with a head of flaxen hair, left long uncut, who had only missed being king by two tricks, looked angrily and with envy at the porter. He pouted and frowned.

"I shall give you the trick, grandfather," he said, pondering over his cards; "I know you have got the queen of diamonds."

"Well, well, little silly, you have thought enough!"

Alyoshka timidly played the knave of diamonds. At that moment a ring was heard from the yard.

"Oh, hang you!" muttered the porter, getting up. "Go and open the gate, O king!"

When he came back a little later, Alyoshka was already a prince, the fish-hawker a soldier, and the coachman a peasant.

"It's a nasty business," said the porter, sitting down to the cards again. "I have just let the doctors out. They have not extracted it."

"How could they? Just think, they would have to pick open the brains. If there is a bullet in the head, of what use are doctors?"

"He is lying unconscious," the porter went on. "He is bound to die. Alyoshka, don't look at the cards, you little puppy, or I will pull your ears! Yes, I let the doctors out, and the father and mother in. . . They have only just arrived. Such crying and wailing, Lord preserve us! They say he is the only son. . . . It's a grief!"

All except Alyoshka, who was absorbed in the game, looked round at the brightly lighted windows of the lodge.

"I have orders to go to the police station tomorrow," said the porter. "There will be an inquiry . . . But what do I know about it? I saw nothing of it. He called me this morning, gave me a letter, and said: 'Put it in the letter-box for me.' And his eyes were red with crying. His wife and children were not at home. They had gone out for a walk. So when I had gone with the letter, he put a bullet into his forehead from a revolver. When I came back his cook was wailing for the whole yard to hear."

"It's a great sin," said the fish-hawker in a husky voice, and he shook his head, "a great sin!"

"From too much learning," said the porter, taking a trick; "his wits outstripped his wisdom. Sometimes he would sit writing papers all night. . . . Play, peasant! . . . But he was a nice gentleman. And so white skinned, black-haired and tall! . . . He was a good lodger."

"It seems the fair sex is at the bottom of it," said the coachman, slapping the nine of trumps on the king of diamonds. "It seems he was fond of another man's wife and disliked his own; it does happen."

"The king rebels," said the porter.

At that moment there was again a ring from the yard. The rebellious king spat with vexation and went out. Shadows like dancing couples flitted across the windows of the lodge. There was the sound of voices and hurried footsteps in the yard.

"I suppose the doctors have come again," said the coachman. "Our Mihailo is run off his legs. . . ."

A strange wailing voice rang out for a moment in the air. Alyoshka looked in alarm at his grandfather, the coachman; then at the windows, and said:

"He stroked me on the head at the gate yesterday, and said, 'What district do you come from, boy?' Grandfather, who was that howled just now?"

His grandfather trimmed the light in the lantern and made no answer.

"The man is lost," he said a little later, with a yawn. "He is lost, and his children are ruined, too. It's a disgrace for his children for the rest of their lives now."

The porter came back and sat down by the lantern.

"He is dead," he said. "They have sent to the almshouse for the old women to lay him out."

"The kingdom of heaven and eternal peace to him!" whispered the coachman, and he crossed himself.

Looking at him, Alyoshka crossed himself too.

"You can't pray for such as him," said the fish-hawker.

"Why not?"

"It's a sin."

"That's true," the porter assented. "Now his soul has gone straight to hell, to the devil. . . ."

"It's a sin," repeated the fish-hawker; "such as he have no funeral, no requiem, but are buried like carrion with no respect."

The old man put on his cap and got up.

"It was the same thing at our lady's," he said, pulling his cap on further. "We were serfs in those days; the younger son of our mistress, the General's lady, shot himself through the mouth with a pistol, from too much learning, too. It seems that by law such have to be buried outside the cemetery, without priests, without a requiem service; but to save disgrace our lady, you know, bribed the police and the doctors, and they gave her a paper to say her son had done it when delirious, not knowing what he was doing. You can do anything with money. So he had a funeral with priests and every honor, the music played, and he was buried in the church; for the deceased General had built that church with his own money, and all his family were buried there. Only this is what happened, friends. One month passed, and then another, and it was all right. In the third month they informed the General's lady that the watchmen had come from that same church. What did they want? They were brought to her, they fell at her feet. 'We can't go on serving, your excellency,' they said. 'Look out for other watchmen and graciously dismiss us.' 'What for?' 'No,' they said, 'we can't possibly; your son howls under the church all night.' "

Alyoshka shuddered, and pressed his face to the coachman's back so as not to see the windows.

"At first the General's lady would not listen," continued the old man. "'All this is your fancy, you simple folk have such notions,' she said. 'A dead man cannot howl.' Some time afterwards the watchmen came to her again, and with them the sacristan. So the sacristan, too, had heard him howling. The General's lady saw that it was a bad job; she locked herself in her bedroom with the watchmen. 'Here, my friends, here are twenty-five roubles for you, and for that go by night in secret, so that no one should hear or see you, dig up my unhappy son, and bury him,' she said, 'outside the cemetery.' And I suppose she stood them a glass . . . And the watchmen did so. The stone with the inscription on it is there to this day, but he himself, the General's son, is outside the cemetery. . . . O Lord, forgive us our transgressions!" sighed the fish-hawker. "There is only one day in the year when one may pray for such people: the Saturday before Trinity. . . . You mustn't give alms to beggars for their sake, it is a sin, but you may feed the birds for the rest of their souls. The General's lady used to go out to the crossroads every three days to feed the birds. Once at the cross-roads a black dog suddenly appeared; it ran up to the bread, and was such a . . . we all know what that dog was. The General's lady was like a half-crazy creature for five days afterwards, she neither ate nor drank. . . . All at once she fell on her knees in the garden, and prayed and prayed. . . . Well, good-by, friends, the blessing of God and the Heavenly Mother be with you. Let us go, Mihailo, you'll open the gate for me."

The fish-hawker and the porter went out. The coachman and Alyoshka went out too, so as not to be left in the coach-house.

"The man was living and is dead!" said the coachman, looking towards the windows where shadows were still flitting to and fro. "Only this morning he was walking about the yard, and now he is lying dead."

"The time will come and we shall die too," said the porter, walking away with the fish -hawker, and at once they both vanished from sight in the darkness.

The coachman, and Alyoshka after him, somewhat timidly went up to the lighted windows. A very pale lady with large tear stained eyes, and a fine-looking gray headed man were moving two card-tables into the middle of the room, probably with the intention of laying the dead man upon them, and on the green cloth of the table numbers could still be seen written in chalk. The cook who had run about the yard wailing in the morning was now standing on a chair, stretching up to try and cover the looking glass with a towel.

"Grandfather what are they doing?" asked Alyoshka in a whisper.

"They are just going to lay him on the tables," answered his grandfather. "Let us go, child, it is bedtime."

The coachman and Alyoshka went back to the coach-house. They said their prayers, and took off their boots. Stepan lay down in a corner on the floor, Alyoshka in a sledge. The doors of the coach house were shut, there was a horrible stench from the extinguished lantern. A little later Alyoshka sat up and looked about him; through the crack of the door he could still see a light from those lighted windows.

"Grandfather, I am frightened!" he said.

"Come, go to sleep, go to sleep! . . ."

"I tell you I am frightened!"

"What are you frightened of? What a baby!"

They were silent.

Alyoshka suddenly jumped out of the sledge and, loudly weeping, ran to his grandfather.

"What is it? What's the matter?" cried the coachman in a fright, getting up also.

"He's howling!"

"Who is howling?"

"I am frightened, grandfather, do you hear?"

The coachman listened.

"It's their crying," he said. "Come! there, little silly! They are sad, so they are crying."

"I want to go home, . . ." his grandson went on sobbing and trembling all over. "Grandfather, let us go back to the village, to mammy; come, grandfather dear, God will give you the heavenly kingdom for it. . . ."

"What a silly, ah! Come, be quiet, be quiet! Be quiet, I will light the lantern, . . . silly!"

The coachman fumbled for the matches and lighted the lantern. But the light did not comfort Alyoshka.

"Grandfather Stepan, let's go to the village!" he besought him, weeping. "I am frightened here; oh, oh, how frightened I am! And why did you bring me from the village, accursed man?"

"Who's an accursed man? You mustn't use such disrespectable words to your lawful grandfather. I shall whip you."

"Do whip me, grandfather, do; beat me like Sidor's goat, but only take me to mammy, for God's mercy! . . ."

"Come, come, grandson, come!" the coachman said kindly. "It's all right, don't be frightened. . . .I am frightened myself. . . . Say your prayers!"

The door creaked and the porter's head appeared. "Aren't you asleep, Stepan?" he asked. "I shan't get any sleep all night," he said, coming in. "I shall be opening and shutting the gates all night. . . . What are you crying for, Alyoshka?"

"He is frightened," the coachman answered for his grandson.

Again there was the sound of a wailing voice in the air. The porter said:

"They are crying. The mother can't believe her eyes. . . . It's dreadful how upset she is."

"And is the father there?"

"Yes. . . . The father is all right. He sits in the corner and says nothing. They have taken the children to relations. . . . Well, Stepan, shall we have a game of trumps?"

"Yes," the coachman agreed, scratching himself, "and you, Alyoshka, go to sleep. Almost big enough to be married, and blubbering, you rascal. Come, go along, grandson, go along. ..."

The presence of the porter reassured Alyoshka. He went, not very resolutely, towards the sledge and lay down. And while he was falling asleep he heard a half-whisper.

"I beat and cover," said his grandfather.

"I beat and cover," repeated the porter.

The bell rang in the yard, the door creaked and seemed also saying: "I beat and cover." When Alyoshka dreamed of the gentleman and, frightened by his eyes, jumped up and burst out crying, it was morning, his grandfather was snoring, and the coach-house no longer seemed terrible.

AT A COUNTRY HOUSE

PAVEL ILYITCH RASHEVITCH walked up and down, stepping softly on the floor covered with little Russian plaids, and casting a long shadow on the wall and ceiling while his guest, Meier, the deputy examining magistrate, sat on the sofa with one leg drawn up under him smoking and listening. The clock already pointed to eleven, and there were sounds of the table being laid in the room next to the study.

"Say what you like," Rashevitch was saying, "from the standpoint of fraternity, equality, and the rest of it, Mitka, the swineherd, is perhaps a man the same as Goethe and Frederick the Great; but take your stand on a scientific basis, have the courage to look facts in the face, and it will be obvious to you that blue blood is not a mere prejudice, that it is not a feminine invention. Blue blood, my dear fellow, has an historical justification, and to refuse to recognize it is, to my thinking, as strange as to refuse to recognize the antlers on a stag. One must reckon with facts! You are a law student and have confined your attention to the humane studies, and you can still flatter yourself with illusions of equality, fraternity, and so on; I am an incorrigible Darwinian, and for me words such as lineage, aristocracy, noble blood, are not empty sounds."

Rashevitch was roused and spoke with feeling. His eyes sparkled, his pince-nez would not stay on his nose, he kept nervously shrugging his shoulders and blinking, and at the word "Darwinian" he looked jauntily in the looking-glass and combed his grey beard with both hands. He was wearing a very short and shabby reefer jacket and narrow trousers; the rapidity of his movements, his jaunty air, and his abbreviated jacket all seemed out of keeping with him, and his big comely head, with long hair suggestive of a bishop or a veteran poet, seemed to have been fixed on to the body of a tall, lanky, affected youth. When he stood with his legs wide apart, his long shadow looked like a pair of scissors.

He was fond of talking, and he always fancied that he was saying something new and original. In the presence of Meier he was conscious of an unusual flow of spirits and rush of ideas. He found the examining magistrate sympathetic, and was stimulated by his youth, his health, his good manners, his dignity, and, above all, by his cordial attitude to himself and his family. Rashevitch was not a favourite with his acquaintances; as a rule they fought shy of him, and, as he knew, declared that he had driven his wife into her grave with his talking, and they called him, behind his back, a spiteful creature and a toad. Meier, a man new to the district and unprejudiced, visited him often and readily and had even been known to say that Rashevitch and his daughters were the only people in the district with whom he felt as much at home as with his own people. Rashevitch liked him too, because he was a young man who might be a good match for his elder daughter, Genya.

And now, enjoying his ideas and the sound of his own voice, and looking with pleasure at the plump but well-proportioned, neatly cropped, correct Meier, Rashevitch dreamed of how he would arrange his daughter's marriage with a good man, and then how all his worries over the estate would pass to his son-in-law. Hateful worries! The interest owing to the bank had not been paid for the last two quarters, and fines and arrears of all sorts had mounted up to more than two thousand.

"To my mind there can be no doubt," Rashevitch went on, growing more and more enthusiastic, "that if a Richard Coeur-de-Lion, or Frederick Barbarossa, for instance, is brave and noble those qualities will pass by heredity to his son, together with the convolutions and bumps of the brain, and if that courage and nobility of soul are preserved in the son by means of education and exercise, and if he marries a princess who is also noble and brave, those qualities will be transmitted to his grandson, and so on, until they become a generic characteristic and pass organically into the flesh and blood. Thanks to a strict sexual selection, to the fact that high-born families have instinctively guarded themselves against marriage with their inferiors, and young men of high rank have not married just anybody, lofty, spiritual qualities have been transmitted from generation to generation in their full purity, have been preserved, and as time goes on have, through exercise, become more exalted and lofty. For the fact that there is good in humanity we are indebted to nature, to the normal, natural, consistent order of things, which has throughout the ages scrupulously segregated blue blood from plebeian. Yes, my dear boy, no low lout, no cook's son has given us literature, science, art, law, conceptions of honour and duty. . . . For all these things mankind is indebted exclusively to the aristocracy, and from that point of view, the point of view of natural history, an inferior Sobakevitch by the very fact of his blue blood is superior and more useful than the very best merchant, even though the latter may have built fifteen museums. Say what you like! And when I refuse to shake hands with a low lout or a cook's son, or to let him sit down to table with me, by that very act I am safeguarding what is the best thing on earth, and am carrying out one of Mother Nature's finest designs for leading us up to perfection. . ."

Rashevitch stood still, combing his beard with both hands; his shadow, too, stood still on the wall, looking like a pair of scissors.

"Take Mother-Russia now," he went on, thrusting his hands in his pockets and standing first on his heels and then on his toes. "Who are her best people? Take our first-rate painters, writers, composers. . . . Who are they? They were all of aristocratic origin. Pushkin, Lermontov, Turgenev, Gontcharov, Tolstoy, they were not sexton's children."

"Gontcharov was a merchant," said Meier.

"Well, the exception only proves the rule. Besides, Gontcharov's genius is quite open to dispute. But let us drop names and turn to facts. What would you say, my good sir, for instance, to this eloquent fact: when one of the mob forces his way where he has not been permitted before, into society, into the world of learning, of literature, into the Zemstvo or the law courts, observe, Nature herself, first of all, champions the higher rights of humanity, and is the first to wage war on the rabble. As soon as the plebeian forces himself into a place he is not fit for he begins to ail, to go into consumption, to go out of his mind, and to degenerate, and nowhere do we find so many puny, neurotic wrecks, consumptives, and starvelings of all sorts as among these darlings. They die like flies in autumn. If it were not for this providential degeneration there would not have been a stone left standing of our civilization, the rabble would have demolished everything. Tell me, if you please, what has the inroad of the barbarians given us so far? What has the rabble brought with it?" Rashevitch assumed a mysterious, frightened expression, and went on: "Never has literature and learning been at such low ebb among us as now. The men of to-day, my good sir, have neither ideas nor ideals, and all their sayings and doings are permeated by one spirit—to get all they can and to strip someone to his last thread. All these men of to-day who give themselves out as honest and progressive people can be bought at a rouble a piece, and the distinguishing mark of the 'intellectual' of to-day is that you have to keep strict watch over your pocket when you talk to him, or else he will run off with your purse." Rashevitch winked and burst out laughing. "Upon my soul, he will! he said, in a thin, gleeful voice. "And morals! What of their morals?" Rashevitch looked round towards the door. "No one is surprised nowadays when a wife robs and leaves her husband. What's that, a trifle! Nowadays, my dear boy, a chit of a girl of twelve is scheming to get a lover, and all these amateur theatricals and literary evenings are only invented to make it easier to get a rich merchant to take a girl on as his mistress. . . . Mothers sell their daughters, and people make no bones about asking a husband at what price he sells his wife, and one can haggle over the bargain, you know, my dear. . . ."

Meier, who had been sitting motionless and silent all the time, suddenly got up from the sofa and looked at his watch.

"I beg your pardon, Pavel Ilyitch," he said, "it is time for me to be going."

But Pavel Ilyitch, who had not finished his remarks, put his arm round him and, forcibly reseating him on the sofa, vowed that he would not let him go without supper. And again Meier sat and listened, but he looked at Rashevitch with perplexity and uneasiness, as though he were only now beginning to understand him. Patches of red came into his face. And when at last a maidservant came in to tell them that the young ladies asked them to go to supper, he gave a sigh of relief and was the first to walk out of the study.

At the table in the next room were Rashevitch's daughters, Genya and Iraida, girls of four-and-twenty and two-and-twenty respectively, both very pale, with black eyes, and exactly the same height. Genya had her hair down, and Iraida had hers done up high on her head. Before eating anything they each drank a wineglassful of bitter liqueur, with an air as though they had drunk it by accident for the first time in their lives and both were overcome with confusion and burst out laughing.

"Don't be naughty, girls," said Rashevitch.

Genya and Iraida talked French with each other, and Russian with their father and their visitor. Interrupting one another, and mixing up French words with Russian, they began rapidly describing how just at this time in August, in previous years, they had set off to the hoarding school and what fun it had been. Now there was nowhere to go, and they had to stay at their home in the country, summer and winter without change. Such dreariness!

"Don't be naughty, girls," Rashevitch said again.

He wanted to be talking himself. If other people talked in his presence, he suffered from a feeling like jealousy.

"So that's how it is, my dear boy," he began, looking affectionately at Meier. "In the simplicity and goodness of our hearts, and from fear of being suspected of being behind the times, we fraternize with, excuse me, all sorts of riff-raff, we preach fraternity and equality with money-lenders and innkeepers; but if we would only think, we should see how criminal that good-nature is. We have brought things to such a pass, that the fate of civilization is hanging on a hair. My dear fellow, what our forefathers gained in the course of ages will be to-morrow, if not to-day, outraged and destroyed by these modern Huns. . . ."

After supper they all went into the drawing-room. Genya and Iraida lighted the candles on the piano, got out their music. . . . But their father still went on talking, and there was no telling when he would leave off. They looked with misery and vexation at their egoist-father, to whom the pleasure of chattering and displaying his intelligence was evidently more precious and important than his daughters' happiness. Meier, the only young man who ever came to their house, came—they knew—for the sake of their charming, feminine society, but the irrepressible old man had taken possession of him, and would not let him move a step away.

"Just as the knights of the west repelled the invasions of the Mongols, so we, before it is too late, ought to unite and strike together against our foe," Rashevitch went on in the tone of a preacher, holding up his right hand. "May I appear to the riff-raff not as Pavel Ilyitch, but as a mighty, menacing Richard Coeur-de-Lion. Let us give up sloppy sentimentality; enough of it! Let us all make a compact, that as soon as a plebeian comes near us we fling some careless phrase straight in his ugly face: 'Paws off! Go back to your kennel, you cur!' straight in his ugly face," Rashevitch went on gleefully, flicking his crooked finger in front of him. "In his ugly face!"

"I can't do that," Meier brought out, turning away.

"Why not?" Rashevitch answered briskly, anticipating a prolonged and interesting argument. "Why not?"

"Because I am of the artisan class myself!"

As he said this Meier turned crimson, and his neck seemed to swell, and tears actually gleamed in his eyes.

"My father was a simple workman," he said, in a rough, jerky voice, "but I see no harm in that."

Rashevitch was fearfully confused. Dumbfoundered, as though he had been caught in the act of a crime, he gazed helplessly at Meier, and did not know what to say. Genya and Iraida flushed crimson, and bent over their music; they were ashamed of their tactless father. A minute passed in silence, and there was a feeling of unbearable discomfort, when all at once with a sort of painful stiffness and inappropriateness, there sounded in the air the words:

"Yes, I am of the artisan class, and I am proud of it!"

Thereupon Meier, stumbling awkwardly among the furniture, took his leave, and walked rapidly into the hall, though his carriage was not yet at the door.

"You'll have a dark drive to-night," Rashevitch muttered, following him. "The moon does not rise till late to-night."

They stood together on the steps in the dark, and waited for the horses to be brought. It was cool.

"There's a falling star," said Meier, wrapping himself in his overcoat.

"There are a great many in August."

When the horses were at the door, Rashevitch gazed intently at the sky, and said with a sigh:

"A phenomenon worthy of the pen of Flammarion. . . ."

After seeing his visitor off, he walked up and down the garden, gesticulating in the darkness, reluctant to believe that such a queer, stupid misunderstanding had only just occurred. He was ashamed and vexed with himself. In the first place it had been extremely incautious and tactless on his part to raise the damnable subject of blue blood, without finding out beforehand what his visitor's position was. Something of the same sort had happened to him before; he had, on one occasion in a railway carriage, begun abusing the Germans, and it had afterwards appeared that all the persons he had been conversing with were German. In the second place he felt that Meier would never come and see him again. These intellectuals who have risen from the people are morbidly sensitive, obstinate and slow to forgive.

"It's bad, it's bad," muttered Rashevitch, spitting; he had a feeling of discomfort and loathing as though he had eaten soap. "Ah, it's bad!"

He could see from the garden, through the drawing-room window, Genya by the piano, very pale, and looking scared, with her hair down. She was talking very, very rapidly. . . . Iraida was walking up and down the room, lost in thought; hut now she, too, began talking rapidly with her face full of indignation. They were both talking at once. Rashevitch could not hear a word, but he guessed what they were talking about. Genya was probably complaining that her father drove away every decent person from the house with his talk, and to-day he had driven away from them their one acquaintance, perhaps a suitor, and now the poor young man would not have one place in the whole district where he could find rest for his soul. And judging by the despairing way in which she threw up her arms, Iraida was talking probably on the subject of their dreary existence, their wasted youth. . . .

When he reached his own room, Rashevitch sat down on his bed and began to undress. He felt oppressed, and he was still haunted by the same feeling as though he had eaten soap. He was ashamed. As he undressed he looked at his long, sinewy, elderly legs, and remembered that in the district they called him the "toad," and after every long conversation he always felt ashamed. Somehow or other, by some fatality, it always happened that he began mildly, amicably, with good intentions, calling himself an old student, an idealist, a Quixote, but without being himself aware of it, gradually passed into abuse and slander, and what was most surprising, with perfect sincerity criticized science, art and morals, though he had not read a book for the last twenty years, had been nowhere farther than their provincial town, and did not really know what was going on in the world. If he sat down to write anything, if it were only a letter of congratulation, there would somehow be abuse in the letter. And all this was strange, because in reality he was a man of feeling, given to tears, Could he be possessed by some devil which hated and slandered in him, apart from his own will?

"It's bad," he sighed, as he lay down under the quilt. "It's bad."

His daughters did not sleep either. There was a sound of laughter and screaming, as though someone was being pursued; it was Genya in hysterics. A little later Iraida was sobbing too. A maidservant ran barefoot up and down the passage several times....

"What a business! Good Lord! . . ." muttered Rashevitch, sighing and tossing from side to side. "It's bad."

He had a nightmare. He dreamt he was standing naked, as tall as a giraffe, in the middle of the room, and saying, as he flicked his finger before him:

"In his ugly face! his ugly face! his ugly face!"

He woke up in a fright, and first of all remembered that a misunderstanding had happened in the evening, and that Meier would certainly not come again. He remembered, too, that he had to pay the interest at the bank, to find husbands for his daughters, that one must have food and drink, and close at hand were illness, old age, unpleasantnesses, that soon it would be winter, and that there was no wood. . . .

•It was past nine o'clock in the morning. Rashevitch slowly dressed, drank his tea and ate two hunks of bread and butter. His daughters did not come down to breakfast; they did not want to meet him, and that wounded him. He lay down on his sofa in his study, then sat down to his table and began writing a letter to his daughters. His hand shook and his eyes smarted. He wrote that he was old, and no use to anyone and that nobody loved him, and he begged his daughters to forget him, and when he died to bury him in a plain, deal coffin without ceremony, or to send his body to Harkov to the dissecting theatre. He felt that every line he wrote reeked of malice and affectation, but he could not stop, and went on writing and writing.

"The toad!" he suddenly heard from the next room; it was the voice of his elder daughter, a voice with a hiss of indignation. "The toad!"

"The toad!" the younger one repeated like an echo. "The toad!"

A FATHER

"I ADMIT I have had a drop. . . . You must excuse me. I went into a beer shop on the way here, and as it was so hot had a couple of bottles. It's hot, my boy."

Old Musatov took a nondescript rag out of his pocket and wiped his shaven, battered face with it.

"I have come only for a minute, Borenka, my angel," he went on, not looking at his son, "about something very important. Excuse me, perhaps I am hindering you. Haven't you ten roubles, my dear, you could let me have till Tuesday? You see, I ought to have paid for my lodging yesterday, and money, you see! . . . None! Not to save my life!"

Young Musatov went out without a word, and began whispering the other side of the door with the landlady of the summer villa and his colleagues who had taken the villa with him. Three minutes later he came back, and without a word gave his father a ten-rouble note. The latter thrust it carelessly into his pocket without looking at it, and said:

"*Merci*. Well, how are you getting on? It's a long time since we met."

"Yes, a long time, not since Easter."

"Half a dozen times I have been meaning to come to you, but I've never had time. First one thing, then another. . . . It's simply awful! I am talking nonsense though. . . . All that's nonsense. Don't you believe me, Borenka. I said I would pay you back the ten roubles on Tuesday, don't believe that either. Don't believe a word I say. I have nothing to do at all, it's simply laziness, drunkenness, and I am ashamed to be seen in such clothes in the street. You must excuse me, Borenka. Here I have sent the girl to you three times for money and written you piteous letters. Thanks for the money, but don't believe the letters; I was telling fibs. I am ashamed to rob you, my angel; I know that you can scarcely make both ends meet yourself, and feed on locusts, but my impudence is too much for me. I am such a specimen of impudence — fit for a show! . . . You must excuse me, Borenka. I tell you the truth, because I can't see your angel face without emotion."

A minute passed in silence. The old man heaved a deep sigh and said:

"You might treat me to a glass of beer perhaps."

His son went out without a word, and again there was a sound of whispering the other side of the door. When a little later the beer was brought in, the old man seemed to revive at the sight of the bottles and abruptly changed his tone.

"I was at the races the other day, my boy," he began telling him, assuming a scared expression. "We were a party of three, and we pooled three roubles on Frisky. And, thanks to that Frisky, we got thirty-two roubles each for our rouble. I can't get on without the races, my boy. It's a gentlemanly diversion. My virago always gives me a dressing over the races, but I go. I love it, and that's all about it."

Boris, a fair-haired young man with a melancholy immobile face, was walking slowly up and down, listening in silence. When the old man stopped to clear his throat, he went up to him and said:

"I bought myself a pair of boots the other day, father, which turn out to be too tight for me. Won't you take them? I'll let you have them cheap."

"If you like," said the old man with a grimace, "only for the price you gave for them, without any cheapening."

"Very well, I'll let you have them on credit."

The son groped under the bed and produced the new boots. The father took off his clumsy, rusty, evidently second-hand boots and began trying on the new ones.

"A perfect fit," he said. "Right, let me keep them. And on Tuesday, when I get my pension, I'll send you the money for them. That's not true, though," he went on, suddenly falling into the same tearful tone again. "And it was a lie about the races, too, and a lie about the pension. And you are deceiving me, Borenka. . . . I feel your generous tactfulness. I see through you! Your boots were too small, because your heart is too big. Ah, Borenka, Borenka! I understand it all and feel it!"

"Have you moved into new lodgings?" his son interrupted, to change the conversation.

"Yes, my boy. I move every month. My virago can't stay long in the same place with her temper."

"I went to your lodgings, I meant to ask you to stay here with me. In your state of health it would do you good to be in the fresh air."

"No," said the old man, with a wave of his hand, "the woman wouldn't let me, and I shouldn't care to myself. A hundred times you have tried to drag me out of the pit, and I have tried myself, but nothing came of it. Give it up. I must stick in my filthy hole. This minute, here I am sitting, looking at your angel face, yet something is drawing me home to my hole. Such is my fate. You can't draw a dung-beetle to a rose. But it's time I was going, my boy. It's getting dark."

"Wait a minute then, I'll come with you. I have to go to town to-day myself."

Both put on their overcoats and went out. When a little while afterwards they were driving in a cab, it was already dark, and lights began to gleam in the windows.

"I've robbed you, Borenka!" the father muttered. "Poor children, poor children! It must be a dreadful trouble to have such a father! Borenka, my angel, I cannot lie when I see your face. You must excuse me. . . . What my depravity has come to, my God. Here I have just been robbing you, and put you to shame with my drunken state; I am robbing your brothers, too, and put them to shame, and you should have seen me yesterday! I won't conceal it, Borenka. Some neighbours, a wretched crew, came to see my virago; I got drunk, too, with them, and I blackguarded you poor children for all I was worth. I abused you, and complained that you had abandoned me. I wanted, you see, to touch the drunken hussies' hearts, and pose as an unhappy father. It's my way, you know, when I want to screen my vices I throw all the blame on my innocent children. I can't tell lies and hide things from you, Borenka. I came to see you as proud as a peacock, but when I saw your gentleness and kind heart, my tongue clave to the roof of my mouth, and it upset my conscience completely."

"Hush, father, let's talk of something else."

"Mother of God, what children I have," the old man went on, not heeding his son. "What wealth God has bestowed on me. Such children ought not to have had a black sheep like me for a father, but a real man with soul and feeling! I am not worthy of you!"

The old man took off his cap with a button at the top and crossed himself several times.

"Thanks be to Thee, O Lord!" he said with a sigh, looking from side to side as though seeking for an ikon. "Remarkable, exceptional children! I have three sons, and they are all like one. Sober, steady, hard-working, and what brains! Cabman, what brains! Grigory alone has brains enough for ten. He speaks French, he speaks German, and talks better than any of your lawyers – one is never tired of listening. My children, my children, I can't believe that you are mine! I can't believe it! You are a martyr, my Borenka, I am ruining you, and I shall go on ruining you. . . . You give to me endlessly, though you know your money is thrown away. The other day I sent you a pitiful letter, I described how ill I was, but you know I was lying, I wanted the money for rum. And you give to me because you are afraid to wound me by refusing. I know all that, and feel it. Grisha's a martyr, too. On Thursday I went to his office, drunk, filthy, ragged, reeking of vodka like a cellar . . . I went straight up, such a figure, I pestered him with nasty talk, while his colleagues and superiors and petitioners were standing round. I have disgraced him for life. And he wasn't the least confused, only turned a bit pale, but smiled and came up to me as though there were nothing the matter, even introduced me to his colleagues. Then he took me all the way home, and not a word of reproach. I rob him worse than you. Take your brother Sasha now, he's a martyr too! He married, as you know, a colonel's daughter of an aristocratic circle, and got a dowry with her. . . . You would think he would have nothing to do with me. No, brother, after his wedding he came with his young wife and paid me the first visit . . . in my hole. . . . Upon my soul!"

The old man gave a sob and then began laughing.

"And at that moment, as luck would have it, we were eating grated radish with kvass and frying fish, and there was a stink enough in the flat to make the devil sick. I was lying down – I'd had a drop – my virago bounced out at the young people with her face crimson, . . . It was a disgrace in fact. But Sasha rose superior to it all."

"Yes, our Sasha is a good fellow," said Boris.

"The most splendid fellow! You are all pure gold, you and Grisha and Sasha and Sonya. I worry you, torment you, disgrace you, rob you, and all my life I have not heard one word of reproach from you, you have never given me one cross look. It would be all very well if I had been a decent father to you – but as it is! You have had nothing from me but harm. I am a bad, dissipated man. . . . Now, thank God, I am quieter and I have no strength of will, but in old days when you were little I had determination, will. Whatever I said or did I always thought it was right. Sometimes I'd come home from the club at night, drunk and ill-humoured, and scold at your poor mother for spending money. The whole night I would be railing at her, and think it the right thing too; you would get up in the morning and go to school, while I'd still be venting my temper upon her. Heavens! I did torture her, poor martyr! When you came back from school and I was asleep you didn't dare to have dinner till I got up. At dinner again there would be a flare up. I daresay you remember. I wish no one such a father; God sent me to you for a trial. Yes, for a trial! Hold out, children, to the end! Honour thy father and thy days shall be long. Perhaps for your noble conduct God will grant you long life. Cabman, stop!"

The old man jumped out of the cab and ran into a tavern. Half an hour later he came back, cleared his throat in a drunken way, and sat down beside his son.

"Where's Sonya now?" he asked. "Still at boarding-school?"

"No, she left in May, and is living now with Sasha's mother-in-law."

"There!" said the old man in surprise. "She is a jolly good girl! So she is following her brother's example. . . . Ah, Borenka, she has no mother, no one to rejoice over her! I say, Borenka, does she . . . does she know how I am living? Eh?"

Boris made no answer. Five minutes passed in profound silence. The old man gave a sob, wiped his face with a rag and said:

"I love her, Borenka! She is my only daughter, you know, and in one's old age there is no comfort like a daughter. Could I see her, Borenka?"

"Of course, when you like."

"Really? And she won't mind?"

"Of course not, she has been trying to find you so as to see you."

"Upon my soul! What children! Cabman, eh? Arrange it, Borenka darling! She is a young lady now, *delicatesse, consommé,* and all the rest of it in a refined way, and I don't want to show myself to her in such an abject state. I'll tell you how we'll contrive to work it. For three days I will keep away from spirits, to get my filthy, drunken phiz into better order. Then I'll come to you, and you shall lend me for the time some suit of yours; I'll shave and have my hair cut, then you go and bring her to your flat. Will you?"

"Very well."

"Cabman, stop!"

The old man sprang out of the cab again and ran into a tavern. While Boris was driving with him to his lodging he jumped out twice again, while his son sat silent and waited patiently for him. When, after dismissing the cab, they made their way across a long, filthy yard to the "virago's" lodging, the old man put on an utterly shamefaced and guilty air, and began timidly clearing his throat and clicking with his lips.

"Borenka," he said in an ingratiating voice, "if my virago begins saying anything, don't take any notice . . . and behave to her, you know, affably. She is ignorant and impudent, but she's a good baggage. There is a good, warm heart beating in her bosom!"

The long yard ended, and Boris found himself in a dark entry. The swing door creaked, there was a smell of cooking and a smoking samovar. There was a sound of harsh voices. Passing through the passage into the kitchen Boris could see nothing but thick smoke, a line with washing on it, and the chimney of the samovar through a crack of which golden sparks were dropping.

"And here is my cell," said the old man, stooping down and going into a little room with a low-pitched ceiling, and an atmosphere unbearably stifling from the proximity of the kitchen.

Here three women were sitting at the table regaling themselves. Seeing the visitors, they exchanged glances and left off eating.

"Well, did you get it?" one of them, apparently the "virago" herself, asked abruptly.

"Yes, yes," muttered the old man. "Well, Boris, pray sit down. Everything is plain here, young man . . . we live in a simple way."

He bustled about in an aimless way. He felt ashamed before his son, and at the same time apparently he wanted to keep up before the women his dignity as cock of the walk, and as a forsaken, unhappy father.

"Yes, young man, we live simply with no nonsense," he went on muttering. "We are simple people, young man. . . . We are not like you, we don't want to keep up a show before people. No! . . . Shall we have a drink of vodka?"

One of the women (she was ashamed to drink before a stranger) heaved a sigh and said:

"Well, I'll have another drink on account of the mushrooms. . . . They are such mushrooms, they make you drink even if you don't want to. Ivan Gerasimitch, offer the young gentleman, perhaps he will have a drink!"

The last word she pronounced in a mincing drawl.

"Have a drink, young man!" said the father, not looking at his son. "We have no wine or liqueurs, my boy, we live in a plain way."

"He doesn't like our ways," sighed the "virago." "Never mind, never mind, he'll have a drink."

Not to offend his father by refusing, Boris took a wineglass and drank in silence. When they brought in the samovar, to satisfy the old man, he drank two cups of disgusting tea in silence, with a melancholy face. Without a word he listened to the virago dropping hints about there being in this world cruel, heartless children who abandon their parents.

"I know what you are thinking now!" said the old man, after drinking more and passing into his habitual state of drunken excitement. "You think I have let myself sink into the mire, that I am to be pitied, but to my thinking, this simple life is much more normal than your life, . . . I don't need anybody, and . . . and I don't intend to eat humble pie. . . . I can't endure a wretched boy's looking at me with compassion."

After tea he cleaned a herring and sprinkled it with onion, with such feeling, that tears of emotion stood in his eyes. He began talking again about the races and his winnings, about some Panama hat for which he had paid sixteen roubles the day before. He told lies with the same relish with which he ate herring and drank. His son sat on in silence for an hour, and began to say good-bye.

"I don't venture to keep you," the old man said, haughtily. "You must excuse me, young man, for not living as you would like!"

He ruffled up his feathers, snorted with dignity, and winked at the women.

"Good-bye, young man," he said, seeing his son into the entry. "*Attendez.*"

In the entry, where it was dark, he suddenly pressed his face against the young man's sleeve and gave a sob.

"I should like to have a look at Sonitchka," he whispered. "Arrange it, Borenka, my angel. I'll shave, I'll put on your suit . . . I'll put on a straight face . . . I'll hold my tongue while she is there. Yes, yes, I will hold my tongue! "

He looked round timidly towards the door, through which the women's voices were heard, checked his sobs, and said aloud:

"Good-bye, young man! *Attendez.*"

THE TROUSSEAU

I HAVE seen a great many houses in my time, little and big, new and old, built of stone and of wood, but of one house I have kept a very vivid memory. It was, properly speaking, rather a cottage than a house – a tiny cottage of one story, with three windows, looking extraordinarily like a little old hunchback woman with a cap on. Its white stucco walls, its tiled roof, and dilapidated chimney, were all drowned in a perfect sea of green. The cottage was lost to sight among the mulberry-trees, acacias, and poplars planted by the grandfathers and great-grandfathers of its present occupants. And yet it is a town house. Its wide courtyard stands in a row with other similar green courtyards, and forms part of a street. Nothing ever drives down that street, and very few persons are ever seen walking through it.

The shutters of the little house are always closed; its occupants do not care for sunlight – the light is no use to them. The windows are never opened, for they are not fond of fresh air. People who spend their lives in the midst of acacias, mulberries, and nettles have no passion for nature. It is only to the summer visitor that God has vouchsafed an eye for the beauties of nature. The rest of mankind remain steeped in profound ignorance of the existence of such beauties. People never prize what they have always had in abundance. "What we have, we do not treasure," and what's more we do not even love it.

The little house stands in an earthly paradise of green trees with happy birds nesting in them. But inside . . . alas . . . ! In summer, it is close and stifling within; in winter, hot as a Turkish bath, not one breath of air, and the dreariness! . . .

The first time I visited the little house was many years ago on business. I brought a message from the Colonel who was the owner of the house to his wife and daughter. That first visit I remember very distinctly. It would be impossible, indeed, to forget it.

Imagine a limp little woman of forty, gazing at you with alarm and astonishment while you walk from the passage into the parlour. You are a stranger, a visitor, "a young man"; that's enough to reduce her to a state of terror and bewilderment. Though you have no dagger, axe, or revolver in your hand, and though you smile affably, you are met with alarm.

"Whom have I the honour and pleasure of addressing?" the little lady asks in a trembling voice.

I introduced myself and explained why I had come. The alarm and amazement were at once succeeded by a shrill, joyful "Ach!" and she turned her eyes upwards to the ceiling. This "Ach!" was caught up like an echo and repeated from the hall to the parlour, from the parlour to the kitchen, and so on down to the cellar. Soon the whole house was resounding with "Ach!" in various voices.

Five minutes later I was sitting on a big, soft, warm lounge in the drawing-room listening to the "Ach!" echoing all down the street. There was a smell of moth powder, and of goatskin shoes, a pair of which lay on a chair beside me wrapped in a handkerchief. In the windows were geraniums, and muslin curtains, and on the curtains were torpid flies. On the wall hung the portrait of some bishop, painted in oils, with the glass broken at one corner, and next to the bishop a row of ancestors with lemon-coloured faces of a gipsy type. On the table lay a thimble, a reel of cotton, and a half-knitted stocking, and paper patterns and a black blouse, tacked together, were lying on the floor. In the next room two alarmed and fluttered old women were hurriedly picking up similar patterns and pieces of tailor's chalk from the floor.

"You must, please, excuse us; we are dreadfully untidy," said the little lady.

While she talked to me, she stole embarrassed glances towards the other room where the patterns were still being picked up. The door, too, seemed embarrassed, opening an inch or two and then shutting again.

"What's the matter?" said the little lady, addressing the door.

"Où est mon cravatte lequel mon père m'avait envoyé de Koursk?" asked a female voice at the door.

"Ah, est-ce que, Marie . . . que. . . Really, it's impossible. . . . *Nous avons donc chez nous un homme peu connu de nous.* Ask Lukerya."

"How well we speak French, though!" I read in the eyes of the little lady, who was flushing with pleasure.

Soon afterwards the door opened and I saw a tall, thin girl of nineteen, in a long muslin dress with a gilt belt from which, I remember, hung a mother-of-pearl fan. She came in, dropped a curtsy, and flushed crimson. Her long nose, which was slightly pitted with smallpox, turned red first, and then the flush passed up to her eyes and her forehead.

"My daughter," chanted the little lady, "and, Manetchka, this is a young gentleman who has come," etc.

I was introduced, and expressed my surprise at the number of paper patterns. Mother and daughter dropped their eyes.

"We had a fair here at Ascension," said the mother; "we always buy materials at the fair, and then it keeps us busy with sewing till the next year's fair comes around again. We never put things out to be made. My husband's pay is not very ample, and we are not able to permit ourselves luxuries. So we have to make up everything ourselves."

"But who will ever wear such a number of things? There are only two of you?"

"Oh . . . as though we were thinking of wearing them! They are not to be worn; they are for the trousseau!"

"Ah, *mamam,* what are you saying?" said the daughter, and she crimsoned again. "Our visitor might suppose it was true. I don't intend to be married. Never!"

She said this, but at the very word "married" her eyes glowed.

Tea, biscuits, butter, and jam were brought in, followed by raspberries and cream. At seven o'clock, we had supper, consisting of six courses, and while we were at supper I heard a loud yawn from the next room. I looked with surprise towards the door: it was a yawn that could only come from a man.

"That's my husband's brother, Yegor Semyonitch," the little lady explained, noticing my surprise. "He's been living with us for the last year. Please excuse him; he cannot come in to see you. He is such an unsociable person, he is shy with strangers. He is going into a monastery. He was unfairly treated in the service, and the disappointment has preyed on his mind."

After supper the little lady showed the vestment which Yegor Semyonitch was embroidering with his own hands as an offering for the Church. Manetchka threw off her shyness for a moment and showed me the tobacco-pouch she was embroidering for her father. When I pretended to be greatly struck by her work, she flushed crimson and whispered something in her mother's ear. Ther latter beamed all over, and invited me to go with her to the store-room. The latter beamed all over, and ivited me to go with her to the store-room. There I was shown five large trunks, and a number of smaller trunks and boxes.

'This is her trousseau," her mother whispered;"we made it all ourselves." After looking at these forbidding trunks I took leave of my hospitable hostesses They made me promise to come and see them again some day.

It happened that I was able to keep this promise. Seven years after my first visit, I was sent down to the little town to give expert evidence in a case that was being tried there.

As I entered the little house I heard the same "Ach!" echo through it. They recognised me at once. . . . Well they might! My first visit had been an event in their lives, and when events are few they are long remembered.

I walked into the drawing-room: the mother, who had grown stouter and was already getting grey, was creeping about on the floor, cutting out some blue material. The daughter was sitting on the sofa, embroidering.

There was the same smell of moth powder; there were the same patterns, the same portrait with the broken glass. But yet there was a change. Beside the portrait of the bishop hung a portrait of the Colonel, and the ladies were in mourning. The Colonel's death had occurred a week after his promotion to be a general.

Reminiscences began. . . . The widow shed tears.

"We have had a terrible loss," she said. "My husband, you know, is dead. We are alone in the world now, and have no one but ourselves to look to. Yegor Semyonitch is alive, but I have no good news to tell of him. They would not have him in the monastery on account of – of intoxicating beverages. And now in his disappointment he drinks more than ever. I am thinking of going to the Marshal of Nobility to lodge a complaint. Would you believe it, he has more than once broken open the trunks and . . . taken Manetchka's trousseau and given it to beggars. He has taken everything out of two of the trunks! If he goes on like this, my Manetchka will be left without a trousseau at all."

"What are you saying, *mamam?*" said Manetchka, embarrassed. "Our visitor might suppose . . . there's no knowing what he might suppose. . . . I shall never – never marry."

Manetchka cast her eyes up to the ceiling with a look of hope and aspiration, evidently not for a moment believing what she said.

A little bald-headed masculine figure in a brown coat and goloshes instead of boots darted like a mouse across the passage and disappeared. "Yegor Semyonitch, I suppose," I thought.

I looked at the mother and daughter together. They both looked much older and terribly changed. The mother's hair was silvered, but the daughter was so faded and withered that her mother might have been taken for her elder sister, not more than five years her senior.

"I have made up my mind to go to the Marshal," the mother said to me, forgetting she had told me this already. "I mean to make a complaint. Yegor Semyonitch lays his hands on everything we make, and offers it up for the sake of his soul. My Manetchka is left without a trousseau."

Manetchka flushed again, but this time she said nothing.

"We have to make them all over again. And God knows we are not so well off. We are all alone in the world now."

"We are alone in the world," repeated Manetchka.

A year ago fate brought me once more to the little house.

Walking into the drawing-room, I saw the old lady. Dressed all in black with heavy crape *pleureuses,* she was sitting on the sofa sewing. Beside her sat the little old man in the brown coat and the goloshes instead of boots. On seeing me, he jumped up and ran out of the room.

In response to my greeting, the old lady smiled and said:

"Je suis charmée de vous revoir, monsieur."

"What are you making?" I asked, a little later.

"It's a blouse. When it's finished I shall take it to the priest's to be put away, or else Yegor Semyonitch would carry it off. I store everything at the priest's now," she added in a whisper.

And looking at the portrait of her daughter which stood before her on the table, she sighed and said:

"We are all alone in the world."

And where was the daughter? Where was Manetchka? I did not ask. I did not dare to ask the old mother dressed in her new deep mourning. And while I was in the room, and when I got up to go, no Manetchka came out to greet me. I did not hear her voice, nor her soft, timid footstep. I understood, and my heart was heavy.

THE ALBUM

KRATEROV, the titular councillor, as thin and slender as the Admiralty spire, stepped forward and, addressing Zhmyhov, said:

"Your Excellency! Moved and touched to the bottom of our hearts by the way you have ruled us during long years, and by your fatherly care...." "During the course of more than ten years..." Zakusin prompted. "During the course of more than ten years, we, your subordinates, on this so memorable for us... er ... day, beg your Excellency to accept in token of our respect and profound gratitude this album with our portraits in it, and express our hope that for the duration of your distinguished life, that for long, long years to come, to your dying day you may not abandon us...."

"With your fatherly guidance in the path of justice and progress..." added Zakusin, wiping from his brow the perspiration that had suddenly appeared on it; he was evidently longing to speak, and in all probability had a speech ready. "And," he wound up, "may your standard fly for long, long years in the career of genius, industry, and social self-consciousness."

A tear trickled down the wrinkled left cheek of Zhmyhov.

"Gentlemen!" he said in a shaking voice, "I did not expect, I had no idea that you were going to celebrate my modest jubilee.... I am touched indeed ... very much so.... I shall not forget this moment to my dying day, and believe me... believe me, friends, that no one is so desirous of your welfare as I am. .. and if there has been anything... it was for your benefit."

Zhmyhov, the actual civil councillor, kissed the titular councillor Kraterov, who had not expected such an honour, and turned pale with delight. Then the chief made a gesture that signified that he could not speak for emotion, and shed tears as though an expensive album had not been presented to him, but on the contrary, taken from him.... Then when he had a little recovered and said a few more words full of feeling and given everyone his hand to shake, he went downstairs amid loud and joyful cheers, got into his carriage and drove off, followed by their blessings. As he sat in his carriage he was aware of a flood of joyous feelings such as he had never known before, and once more he shed tears.

At home new delights awaited him. There his family, his friends, and acquaintances had prepared him such an ovation that it seemed to him that he really had been of very great service to his country, and that if he had never existed his country would perhaps have been in a very bad way. The jubilee dinner was made up of toasts, speeches, and tears. In short, Zhmyhov had never expected that his merits would be so warmly appreciated.

"Gentlemen!" he said before the dessert, "two hours ago I was recompensed for all the sufferings a man has to undergo who is the servant, so to say, not of routine, not of the letter, but of duty! Through the whole duration of my service I have constantly adhered to the principle;— the public does not exist for us, but we for the public, and to-day I received the highest reward! My subordinates presented me with an album... see! I was touched."

Festive faces bent over the album and began examining it.

"It's a pretty album," said Zhmyhov's daughter Olya, "it must have cost fifty roubles, I do believe. Oh, it's charming! You must give me the album, papa, do you hear? I'll take care of it, it's so pretty."

After dinner Olya carried off the album to her room and shut it up in her table drawer. Next day she took the clerks out of it, flung them on the floor, and put her school friends in their place. The government uniforms made way for white pelerines. Kolya, his Excellency's little son, picked up the clerks and painted their clothes red. Those who had no moustaches he presented with green moustaches and added brown beards to the beardless. When there was nothing left to paint he cut the little men out of the card-board, pricked their eyes with a pin, and began playing soldiers with them. After cutting out the titular councillor Kraterov, he fixed him on a match-box and carried him in that state to his father's study.

"Papa, a monument, look!"

Zhmyhov burst out laughing, lurched forward, and, looking tenderly at the child, gave him a warm kiss on the cheek.

"There, you rogue, go and show mamma; let mamma look too."